That Year in Boston

That Year in Boston

G. D. Spilsbury

BERGAMOT

Printed in the United States

10 9 8 7 6 5 4 3 2 1

ISBN: 978-0-578-65251-1
ISBN (2014): 978-0-9899838-7-7

For Joseph Vaughan

ONE

Wind whipped Nick Turner in the face as he left his apartment and stepped into the darkening street. He was in a hurry to meet his daughter, Emily, for her birthday dinner. He had been scratching his head over a badly written manuscript for a client, keeping his eye on the clock, but in the end couldn't resist finishing a chapter even though it would make him late. Emily was usually punctual. He pulled his cell phone from his pocket and tapped her number as he half-ran along Cedar Street toward Boston Common, the quaint streetlamps coming on in a sudden flash. It was early October but felt like winter, though the region would still enjoy a few days of Indian summer before true winter set in.

Emily's voicemail picked up. Well, Nick thought, when you were outside you couldn't count on hearing the phone ring, and maybe she was still on the subway. But as he hustled along Beacon Hill's picturesque streets, he worried because whenever Emily didn't pick up, he thought she might be in trouble. She had been hospitalized earlier that year during an acute psychotic episode, her second, after which she had fallen into depression, which was typical of the manic cycle. Fortunately, this time hadn't been as severe, and she kept to a daily routine.

He left a message that he was running, literally running, ten minutes late. He had to cut through the Public Garden, whiz down Commonwealth Avenue, and then watch the side streets for the Lebanese café she had chosen for the occasion. Her live-in boyfriend, Eric, a rock-band drummer, wouldn't be joining them because he had a gig.

Nick put away his phone and skirted through rush-hour traffic at the insane intersection separating Boston Common from the Public Garden. He loved this swath of land—Boston's historic heart. Just as the Common had once served as pasture for the colonists' livestock, it now served local residents' dogs, which romped on the open slopes at each end of the day. Anything public, from a concert to a protest, happened on the Common. The Garden, in contrast, was a refined landscape with tree species labeled and signs posted to keep off the grass. A fairy-book iron bridge painted robins-egg blue crossed a dreamy lagoon, where in summertime the famous swan boats glided and real swans bathed. This was the strolling territory of minds like Henry James, and Nick always felt the Victorian heyday when he crossed through the Garden.

Soon, he thought, the city would set up the annual skating rink over Frog Pond in the Common, and lamplit nights would fill with the sound of blades scraping ice to the accompaniment of scratchy music and happy voices. It was a winter enticement. New Englanders grew up on skates. The vigorous sport helped them survive winters with heartiness. As a kid, Nick had skated on ice-cold school nights in Concord and skied in Vermont and New Hampshire. At Dartmouth skiing was part of the curriculum. Now he mostly walked, though he did put on skates once or twice a year to relive the invigoration of his youth. Skating was best with companions, and his current life was fairly solitary. He lived alone, had no romantic involvements, and didn't want any. Where would he find the time? His work—that is, financial survival—and Emily filled his day-to-day world. He readily met friends for dinners, movies, theater, or an occasional day or weekend trip, but a deeper relationship took a lot more than a few hours, a few conversations, each week. Lately he had been thinking a lot about his age and how his processing of life had changed with the mounting years. He was approaching sixty, a major milestone in life, but fortunately still two years away.

His phone vibrated near his hip, and he wrestled it from his pocket.

"Hello," he said, and after a pause repeated his greeting in a louder voice, for the person calling hadn't heard him.

"Hiiii," a woman sang out on a long note. "Is this Nick Turner?"

He said he was, in the pleasant, professional manner he always used when answering the phone, for most people who called him related to work. The woman on the other end unleashed a current of warmth and vivacity, a nervous kind, her voice airy, breathy, rhythmic.

"Oh, good, Nick, I'm so glad I reached you, and sorry about the late hour! My god, it was meetings all day and this is the first time I'm back at my desk facing the mounting piles, which will keep me here till at least ten o'clock, which my husband is not going to like. We moved here from New York specifically to get out of the rat race. But you don't need to know all that. Sorry, I'm so sorry!"

She was wound up from her long day, he thought, and she needed to vent. She hadn't even introduced herself.

"Don't worry," he said, knowing exactly how she felt, only she had a husband to purge to each night, while he had only his spiral notebook.

"I'm Florence Wright, editorial director at Churchill & Co. Oscar Wheeler gave me your name, and our board gave me his. How's that for networking? I'm calling because we're desperate for another hand around here—it's chaos. I'm fairly new myself and I've done everything in my power to reorganize things—forget that. I need help, experienced help, and Oscar said: call Nick. Am I catching you at a bad moment?"

"Not at all—I'm outside, in case you hear traffic, but tell me what you need."

"I need you, Nick, full-time, starting last month, ha-ha. But listen, is there even the slightest chance you could come to the office tomorrow to talk about a job with us?"

He was glad she couldn't see him laughing silently as he passed the bronze ducklings from McCloskey's children's book, which had become mascots in the Garden. At Eastertime people dressed the parading statues in spring bonnets and toddlers sat on them while their parents snapped photos. Sometimes secret night squads dressed them in Patriots or Bruins outfits. They did the same thing to the imperial George Washington statue at the Garden's Arlington Street entrance.

He was late and almost trotting, his voice bouncing as he replied, "That's fine, any time tomorrow is fine, I can walk over."

"I just knew you'd say yes! Oscar praised you to the heavens, so I know you're going to be our savior."

Was it flattery or charm? He didn't know, but her fluttery, almost ditzy voice compelled him. They agreed on 11 a.m. and wished each other a good night, with her adding dramatically, "That is, if you can call a good night sitting in an empty office building all by yourself. Maybe I'll just call it quits and go home like a normal person. But I hear the weather's gotten bad. Maybe

I'll just stay here—isn't that what the office couch is for? Tell me, Nick, you're from Boston—why does Boston have so much wind? I read in the *Phoenix* that Chicago can't compare to Boston when it comes to wind."

"It builds character," he said.

"The standard Boston line," she quipped back. "You people from Boston are in love with yourselves. You think Boston's the center of the universe."

"Plain living, high thinking."

"And the Cabots talk to God. We can argue about that later. Let's take care of business first. I look forward to meeting you tomorrow."

Five minutes later, breathless from jogging, Nick whooshed into the shelter of Café Beirut. He quickly spotted Emily at a corner table in the back, her dark head bent over a book, a glass of water in front of her. The wooded, bohemian décor with rustic Middle Eastern decorations on the walls suited her perfectly, and him as well. Their tastes had always been similar. Whenever he saw her, he felt a momentary twist of grief that she, not he, had been afflicted with bipolar disorder, that she, not he, struggled valiantly to hang on to her mind, her life. How many times had he read those brochures in doctors' offices listing the symptoms of depression and bipolar, hoping to find himself among the bulleted points to give cause for her illness? But his down times, even when prolonged, never fit the criteria.

He leaned in to give her a hug. "Happy birthday, sweetie! How're you? Sorry I'm late."

"You always said, never leave home without a book." She smiled, her mother's smile. Emily was a pretty woman with a delicate Madonna face, lustrous dark hair, and intelligent blue eyes behind black-framed glasses. Her natural and genuine smile belied any inner turmoil she might actually be feeling. Like many of her artsy peers, she dressed in vintage clothing—tonight, a fitted tweed jacket from the 1940s and a black skirt. She had a good figure and liked to walk and ride her bike. She closed her thick green book: *Medicinal Herbs*. She wanted to go to grad school in nutrition, a complete switch from her comparative literature degree in college. He too had studied comparative literature, and they had always enjoyed talking books together. She had been a frisky, happy child who loved dark tales involving fairylands and magic or distant, exotic worlds that filled her imagination.

He handed her a pink envelope from his backpack.

"Thanks, Dad." She put her thumb into the opening to raise the flap. "I really and truly appreciate it, and the dinner too."

She read the card and nodded fondly, her eyes acknowledging the check inside. "Thank you, you're always so generous."

"You're my daughter. I love you."

"I'm so lucky."

He hoped she meant it, for he and Charlotte had shattered her teenage life by getting a divorce. He suspected that now, at twenty-five, she fully understood that both of them were there for her. Oddly, Emily's illness, which had begun her junior year at Bowdoin, had brought Nick and Charlotte closer together again, for above all they shared the same devotion to their only child. Charlotte had remarried soon after their divorce and lived in their former Concord home. Nick had moved to the city, closer to his job at Trowbridge & Co., which he had left the year before, when the bankrupt publishing house had been sold to a media giant and moved to New York. Senior editors had lost their jobs, and he had been freelancing ever since, paying for his own exorbitant health insurance. Times were hard, and at his age it was not easy to find another job when younger editors could be hired for half his salary. It had been the same throughout history, people losing their jobs late in their careers, just when their faculties and productivity operated at peak performance.

A serious-faced young waiter took their order, the platter they usually shared—hummus, baba ghanoush, tabouli, grape leaves, and pita bread. Fresh-squeezed juice for Emily; Nick would stick with water. Neither of them drank alcohol, Nick because he had done enough drinking for a lifetime by age fifty, and Emily because she had made a vow not to drink for one year following her hospitalization back in January. He knew it would be next to impossible for a young person who liked drinking to accept the vast future—a lifetime—without the pleasure of spirits being part of it, especially when leading a singles lifestyle. Social life revolved around drinking, didn't he know? But if she ever hoped to maintain her health naturally, all potential triggers for mania would have to go. She still smoked pot, not to mention cigarettes. And Eric was no saint; in fact, Nick suspected he supported his music career by selling pot.

"How was class?" he asked. She was taking biology as a prerequisite for grad school.

"Fine. Today was lab. I like the T.A., Brad. He takes time to tell us more than what's in the book or the experiment."

"And I'm sure he has a special liking for you." Nick smiled.

"We get along. It's just mutual respect."

"I know, but I was thinking you're probably his best student."

"Well, it's not like going to Harvard."

He nodded. The course was at UMass, where students came from diverse backgrounds.

"I just wish I didn't have to take the GRE," she said. "I'm going to flunk it. Forget math, and I've never heard of half the vocabulary words in the practice book. But you would know them."

He shook his head with a laugh. "Not me, Emmy. Standardized tests were never my thing. Do you want a tutor?"

"No, it's too late. The test is in two weeks."

"Then don't sweat it. You're a strong candidate. Tell me about the herbs." He tapped her book.

"They're not for class. I want to learn more about alternative medicine. It relates to nutrition."

"Good. I'm sure there's valuable stuff in there." They both hoped that one day she might be able manage her illness through lifestyle, without meds. A growing contingent of psychologists believed this was possible, particularly if meditation was part of the lifestyle. Emily had taken a meditation class at Bowdoin after her first serious depression and found it helpful. Also in that period she had experienced terrifying out-of-mind-and-body states when she tried to sleep at night. She had described the details to Nick and how the phenomenon had led her to read books on the human organism's ability to transport to such realms, to see and feel such visions, including near death. "The mind's vast," she had told him, "too vast to ever comprehend, and it's hardly utilized in ordinary life."

The waiter delivered their food just as Nick was pulling Colm Tóibín's *The Master* from his backpack and sliding it over the table to Emily. "Thanks," he said to the waiter, who nodded and moved away.

"Did you like it?" Emily asked with an eager face.

"I loved it. It was deep."

They began helping themselves to the platter with large spoons. Globs of creamy hummus and baba ghanoush fell on their plates, followed by light, lemony tabouli.

"I loved the construction," Emily said. "How he developed certain characters from James's life, like Minnie and his brother, and then brought James to 3-D life through those relationships."

"That's what was so sad for me," Nick said. "Experiencing his interior life."

"Probably Tóibín's interior life."

"Probably—it was all about 'the writer.'"

"And did you notice how he used James's literary approach?"

"It was a masterpiece. I can't thank you enough for discovering it."

"I wanted to go through Tóibín's process—read what he read, the diaries, biographies, novels—and see how each chapter emerged from his own imagination."

"Me too, only I knew I didn't have time."

"Same," she said. "I want to spend my time helping people have healthier lives. Even though I smoke. But I plan to quit."

"You have to."

"You tell me that every time I see you." Then a combative gleam lit her eyes. "How old were you when you quit?"

"Twenty-seven."

"Then I have two more years. Ninety percent of bipolar people smoke."

"But 10 percent have your kind of willpower to quit."

She nodded with an annoyed roll of her eyes. "I hate these conversations, even though I started it. Obviously I want to quit smoking. I'm not dumb."

He laughed. "No question about that. I know you'll figure it out soon."

It had been obvious to Nick since her first year of college that she had brilliance. She had read and churned out term papers on world writers that offered new, compelling perspectives. Her professors had noticed her and encouraged her to think about an academic career. Then, during her junior year in Lisbon, depression had struck—her first episode—but it went away when she came home and senior year started. Then, as the fall term wore on, she began running on unusual energy, writing reams of poetry that had astounded her teachers and also Nick, for she sent him some of it. That was the year she devoured books on the brain, on mind-body experiences, and on mental disorders. She read biographies of creative geniuses like Beethoven and Van Gogh, who had struggled all their lives with manic depression. She was on a quest to learn all she could about what was happening to her own life, the solitary and at times agonizing path that was already hers. She wasn't sleeping at all; she couldn't sleep when her brain wouldn't stop putting out and taking in around the clock. By Christmas vacation, when she came home, she was jabbering insanely. The four-week break saved her, for the dull time at home away from school brought her down. She slept. She went back to school and continued to sleep. By March she had sunk into mute depression and had trouble getting out of bed. Somehow she completed her coursework and graduated. She had refused medical help, and while Nick and Charlotte tried to figure out how to help her, she once again stabilized, probably by getting a job in a Cambridge bookstore that forced a regular routine on her. But she was changed, quieter and watchful. She no longer bubbled over with exuberant dreams for her future. She never spoke of her future, and when Nick tried to brainstorm ideas she never followed up.

After a year in the bookshop she found a new job on Craigslist, being the office assistant to a man running a mail-order vitamin business. That had been a disaster with a traumatic ending in January, and now she was more or less stable again, with a plan for her long-term future. Her coursework kept her busy and she volunteered part-time in a senior center's nutrition program. But her mood was low-key, watchful, and analytic. She wasn't a participant.

When Nick read *The Master*, he couldn't help but wonder how a twenty-five-year-old could possibly read it the same way as someone his own age. He had lived the greater part of his life already and now saw everything objectively—in fact, he lived objectively, an unsettling thought. But it seemed Emily too, because of her mood disorder, lived objectively, and this was another deep pain for her to accept, for the young were entitled to live as young, with crazy dreams and expectations, wild and romantic love, the ego unleashed, and the "greater future" something distant and hazy, the purview of old folk. But he knew she already owned the wisdom of the old folk. She had underlined in pencil the same passage in *The Master* that had brought a physical ache to his own heart, and it had stunned him to think she already shared such reflections.

"You know, we loved the same passage," he said.

"Which one? I loved so many."

"The one you underlined about memory."

"Oh, yeah, that one was good." She opened the book straight to the page and read the paragraph aloud, with competent articulation: "Anderson was too young to know how memory and regret can mingle, how much sorrow can be held within, and how nothing seems to have any shape or meaning until it is well past and lost and, even then, how much, under the weight of pure determination, can be forgotten and left aside only to return in the night as piercing pain."

Her eyes came up, full of appreciation through her glasses.

Nick nodded. "Well stated."

She pushed the book back to him. "Keep it, Dad. You liked it."

"So did you."

"I'll get another copy. I see it remaindered everywhere. That's what happens to good books. Tell me your news."

"I don't have much. I'm still editing that horrible psychology book. I get so angry at it, at the author, but what's the point? No one's going to publish it—it's phony—so all I have to do is finish my job and say what's wrong with it as politely as I can."

"I have to see this. Can I?"

"Sure. I'll e-mail you the manuscript, but then please delete it when you're done. Oh! Some real news happened—on my way here, an editor from Churchill called and I'm going in tomorrow, an interview."

"That's great!"

He laughed. "She made it sound like I'm hired already. Oscar recommended me."

"Good old Oscar. I want to hear what happens. Will you call me?"

He nodded. She was always thoughtful, considerate of his world, his daily events, and he had no wish to make her his codependent in any way. He found it challenging to discern the fine line between positive family sharing and unhealthy codependency. For Emily it was easier; she was his daughter and needed parental help in many ways, which was natural and normal. But as her father, how free should he be in sharing his own life, his feelings and reflections? He didn't want to turn her into his daily confidante—that was the fine line.

After dinner they bent their heads against the wind and walked to the Copley T and then rode to Park Street together. With a hug they parted in the station, promising to meet again on the weekend for a movie, one of their mutual passions. With a final wave, Emily headed to the Red Line for Somerville and Nick hiked the stairs to the street.

The next morning when Nick set out for Churchill & Co., the wind had died down. Beacon Hill was quiet, or his side of it, the slope facing the two parks. The government end of the hill, presided over by the majestic statehouse with its gold Bulfinch dome, buzzed like a mini Washington, D.C., its two or three streets the territory of politicians. Lunch pubs in the quaint London tradition catered to this enclave, although streams of tourists also wandered through, looking curiously at yet another symbol of the city's monopoly on liberty. Boston reigned supreme in that category, with Paul Revere's home, the Old North Church, Faneuil Hall, and other relics of the Revolutionary and Federalist periods.

Everyone loved Beacon Hill, including Nick. It was old and venerable—Brahmin—with red-brick townhouses and sidewalks. Doors, shutters, and trim gleamed like black lacquer, and corner shops along the narrow, hilly streets gave the settlement a cozy and exclusive feel. Louisburg Square, near the middle of the hill, was the crowning jewel, with elegant townhouses facing a small private park. Cobblestone lanes circled the green's wrought-iron fence, and signs warned of residential privacy. Nick had no interest in elitism, though his *Mayflower* name, Turner, could be an asset when dealing with the city's extant aristocrats—not many of them left, or rather, their direct influence had become negligible. Nick's mother, Valerie Vieira, was Portuguese, from the whaling town of New Bedford. Hers had been a maligned immigrant community for several generations, including at the time of her marriage to Nick's patrician father, whose North Shore parents had protested—not only an immigrant but a Catholic! But then, with the advent of grandchildren—Nick and his older sister, Ann—everything had turned out all right. And Boston, by the end of the twentieth century, had become a global village and immigrants had an easier time. Nick's parents, now in their upper eighties, lived in a retirement home on Buzzard's Bay, near where the family had spent summer vacations.

Nick knew every corner of Beacon Hill and never tired of walking its streets and admiring its architecture, or at least the well-kept portion of it. A certain squalor marked the north side, which faced Cambridge Street and Mass General Hospital. Up until the 1960s, a lower-income neighborhood had surrounded Scollay Square, and when the area was razed for the new, eclectic buildings of Government Center, the seamier side of life lingered. Homeless people congregated in patches around the vast brick plaza or parked at other favorite spots along Cambridge Street, where fast-food joints and convenience stores proliferated. They slept under the small marquee of the library branch and felt at home on benches close to the hospital.

Beacon Hill's commercial strip, Charles Street, ran six blocks from the hospital's subway stop to the busy junction of the Common and Public Garden and drew crowds throughout the year, especially on weekends. Classic black storefronts with gold lettering on their signs exuded history and tradition. An old brick meetinghouse in the shape of a church now housed a café with outdoor seating. Other restaurants, a few of them good, catered to the constant influx of tourists. Boutiques, antique shops, hair salons, and two Starbucks—one at each end of the street—created a lively and exclusive realm detached from the rest of Boston.

The city's core was small and walkable, and Nick's breaks from his desk took him in all directions, including the riverfront, where a path followed the serpentine Charles River for miles, passing MIT's Great Dome and Harvard's elite steeples. These symbols of erudition and leading minds added to the city's spirit of eminence and indomitability. Bostonians were proud. They couldn't care less if the rest of the country pooh-poohed them for being provincial. The entire world could prefer dazzling New York, but they were content with their own city, for to them it was better, from its rowdy sports bars and beloved teams to its annual marathon and symbols of liberty and learning. Boston had the Cape and sailing, it had New Hampshire, Vermont, and Maine for nature, it had a rich colonial history of ships and trade with the Far East (that is, capitalism and wealth), not to mention leadership from Revolutionary times and preeminence in education and medicine.

Nick didn't buy into Boston's excessive pride, but it was the only place he wanted to live if he couldn't afford to be a world wanderer in the Graham Greene style. He liked the local flavor, the quick wisecracking of the people, and their tough but direct manner. He ended up on elitist Beacon Hill only because one of his high school friends had moved out and the timing and price had been right. He would have been happy in Inman or Union Square or another neighborhood in Cambridge, but the hill was now his home—ten years in the same one-bedroom apartment, and he loved it.

As he walked briskly down Cedar Street for his appointment at Churchill, he nervously double-checked his clothes. He had dressed appropriately to meet Florence Wright—casual but professional, a tie for the occasion and a leather jacket. He was in decent shape for his age, although that age showed instantly in his head of salt-and-pepper hair, once dark and glossy like Emily's. His black brows remained, the legacy of his Portuguese genes.

He glanced at his watch. He was on time. He knew exactly

how many minutes it would take to walk to Copley Square, where Churchill had its offices. He wore his backpack with his résumé and a few clips inside. And a book, in case he had to wait. He was reading *The Beast in the Jungle*, discussed in *The Master* as subtly revelatory of Henry James's repressed homosexuality. But Nick wasn't enjoying James's storytelling as much as he had enjoyed Tóibín's. The construction was too predictable, and for him had become tedious.

The early October day was bright, luscious, the sky over the Common and Garden a pure healing blue that he tried to drink in with his eyes and his breathing, for how quickly it would be lost and forgotten in the busyness of the day—his own typically spent holed up in front of his computer until he broke for exercise or a fast trip to Government Center for photocopying. He hated being laid off, but he loved working out of his home, the pace of his day and the sheer amount he could fit into it compared to his former office job with its constant interruptions and meetings. The unending solitude and incumbent reflections got to him sometimes, but not often, for he made it a point to get together with friends or walk over Longfellow Bridge to watch a movie at the Kendall Cinema. But he needed a job, a steady paycheck and benefits, and was more than willing to imprison himself in an office again for that financial relief. Churchill was an old and highly regarded press—he had always wanted to work there. Just thinking of the possibility made him pick up his pace.

The company occupied one story in a tall, Depression-era building off Copley Square, once the cultural heartland of the city, home to museums and several colleges, but now only McKim, Mead, and White's public library remained, and Trinity Church. At the lobby desk, the elderly receptionist in spectacles and gentlemanly attire seemed to know which office Nick was visiting by his appearance, as if editors and publishers were a breed with a dress code. "Churchill?" he asked.

"Yes," Nick said with a smile. "Fourth floor?"

"That's right," and he waved at the elevators. "Sign's on the glass door."

An attractive young woman—probably an aspiring editor—greeted Nick from the front desk as he came through the glass doors to the offices. He smiled back, experiencing déjà vu, for thirty years before, fresh out of the Peace Corps, he had entered the same foyer on an interview for a job he didn't get. Back then, in the early eighties, jobs still appeared in newspapers and applicants could meet people. Now everything was processed online and applicants never dealt directly with humans, just human resources, unless they made the interview cut. Having contacts inside had become all the more important for mid- to late-career people, since jobs were scarce and filled by connections and recruiters.

The young woman phoned Florence and then, with a polite smile, told Nick to follow her. They moved down a long corridor with doors opening to offices where Nick glimpsed young women hard at work behind computers, proofs and manuscripts on their shelves and countertops, even on their floors. Books covered walls and carpeting, and empty cartons stood by doors waiting for the night crew to pick up.

At Florence's large, elegantly furnished office, faintly redolent of lilies, Nick's escort said a few introductory words and departed. Florence, quite a pretty woman of about forty, instantly conveyed character and glamour. She wore a black dress, intensified by her sable brown hair that swept the sides of her face. She tossed the soft layers back every few minutes, or used a hand to fling them back with a ritualistic gesture. The long, ringed fingers, with nails polished a deep rose, were a prominent feature in her communication. They moved up and down expressively to emphasize her speech. With nervous body language, she paced two steps toward the sunny windows and then two steps back toward the inner wall. She twisted toward her desk as if she had forgotten something, but then jerked back to face him full-on with shiny brown eyes and a cover-girl smile, all the while keeping the flow of her conversation constant, her voice like a light breeze on the ocean.

"It's been chaos around here, but I won't go into the dirty details. Or maybe I should. My job has been vacant for three years—can you believe it? You can imagine the consequences when books have to be planned out years in advance and the industry is imploding. You were at Trowbridge, and I promise you Churchill is a different, Neanderthal animal. I wear several hats and so would you if you come on board. After the financial crisis, editors and production staff were laid off and the company tried to limp along using interns and recent college grads. The top brass finally realized that experience is necessary if we're going to survive in the digital age. They recruited me from New York last winter, and even though you Bostonians think you're the best and the smartest at everything, we New Yorkers know publishing. It's in our DNA. But whenever I try to implement standard publishing practices, I run up against the old guard and their wacko ways of doing things, and frankly, I'm sick of it. I can't turn things around, I can't produce positive results, if I have to be involved in every aspect of the work flow from acquisitions to finished product." Her lips turned down at the corners as she spoke, suggesting a person who had defended herself righteously against wrongs and injustices throughout childhood and beyond. But in the next instant, the same rather luscious lips broke upward in a radiant smile, showing large even teeth and a fresh, friendly face. He couldn't help but see her as a smart woman whose pretty looks had moved her up the career ladder in a man's domain, for publishing at the top was still male. Even so, he knew she also had to have talent to have made those leaps by forty.

"So that's it in a nutshell, Nick. When can you start as my managing editor cum everything else? I promise things will get better in the long run." The smile beamed again, expectantly, the arched dark brows raised above a set of Leonardo da Vinci eyes, or were they Virginia Woolf's in that famous profile from her teens? The sockets were splendid, the line over the eyeball's curve drawn by an artist.

"Oh me oh my!" she said, lightly striking her forehead and then graciously waving the same hand at the couch. "I haven't even asked you to sit down—please, forgive my rudeness. I'm simply slammed, but that's no excuse. And I want you on board as soon as possible."

"How about Monday?" he said, sitting down. "I have a project to finish up."

She sank into the upholstered chair facing him, curled her side against its back, and draped her right arm across the top. Her long legs crossed as if seeking repose. Now she was a John Singer Sargent portrait, her languorous pose impossible to ignore. "I guess I can wait a few more days," she said. "After all, I've waited nine months, nine months of lobbying for everything I want, which isn't much. I want normal practices, efficiency, but the bosses, they plan to expire with the company's anomalies. Seriously, they've been here since 1980, before the Internet. You'll meet them all on Monday—still wearing bow ties—and then you can tell me what you think." She got up, went to her desk to move some papers as if looking for something, but then turned back, gave him that stunning smile that could arrest the world.

He stood up. The interview was over. He had been hired. Impossible, too easy. He unzipped his backpack. "I brought some clips . . . my résumé."

"Oh, good, I'll enjoy reading them tonight. I have to admit that after Oscar recommended you, I Googled you and got your Brazil book from the library. I plan to read that too, though I imagine it'll be too sad to finish."

He tried to cover his surprise with a smile and a lame, "Oh, so much has changed—I was just out of college, inexperienced—"

"You were unafraid of writing what you saw. I couldn't handle looking at poverty like that—the children. I'm content to curl up in an armchair with Jorge Amado and *Gabriela . . . Cinnamon . . .*"

"*Gabriela, Clove and Cinnamon.*"

"Yes, and I wish I had more time to read, don't you? I used to read all the time and now I just read for work. I'm the de facto acquisitions editor, though Margie continues to bring in serious books for Sam."

"Are you writing anything?"

"No, I leave that to writers, like you. I'm what you call an old-fashioned editor—Max Perkins is my alter ego."

But Nick had Googled her too. "But you wrote a book."

Her eyes widened, but with pleasure. She looked like a purring cat. "You've seen it."

"Only last night, online."

"Isn't it amazing how we all Google each other to see what we can find out before we meet? I can't remember life before the Internet, and it's not even that old, or Google isn't. But thanks for checking me out. I confess to Googling myself now and then, just to see what others see about me, in case something pops up that's god-awful, though my life's been utterly, tragically ordinary. Mostly," she added with an "ugh" of distaste for her life.

Nick smiled, knowing that she didn't believe her own words, for she was the first woman to be editor in chief of Boston's oldest, snobbiest publishing house, certainly a position of stardom to her New York colleagues. "So then, no plans for another book?" he said.

"Nope. I love the one I wrote, I love all the women I met during my research—can you believe that movie with Juliette Binoche came out around the same time? What was it called? How could I forget?"

"*Elles.*"

"Yes, *Elles*, so much for minoring in French at Barnard. But what I wanted to say was, it shows how topics are timely, and it's all a race to see who gets there first. And making that book took an incredible amount of hair-tearing and heartbreaking labor. I have absolutely no desire to do another. What about you?"

He hesitated behind his relaxed smile. He was always writing—always. "No plans. I've wanted to write more, but . . ." his head shook slowly.

"I know, life took up all your time."

He nodded, noting how she put his life in the past tense. Well, more than fifteen years separated them. "I was a househusband in the late eighties." He smiled, remembering playgrounds with Emily. "I thought being at home would give me free time to write."

She was laughing silently, incredulously, shaking her head. "How could you be so naive? All you needed to do was remember your mother, what her life was like."

"True, but young parents think they're reinventing family life."

"I guess you're right. I've seen it in my brother and his wife, Jim and Nora, get that!" She laughed, eyeing him.

He smiled. "I get it." She meant the James Joyces, Jim and Nora.

"Well, Jimmy and Nora have adorable Claire de Lune, my one-year-old niece, and you'd think both of them had PhDs in the science of parenting. Everything's by the book, by scholarship and endnotes—that is, until the little one comes down with a fever and they're frantically rushing to the doctor's under an invisible police escort. Oh, Nick, she's so cute, a little *poupée*, I can't stop snuggling with her. Why did I leave New York? I just hope I didn't make a mistake by choosing not to become a parent myself. I hope being an aunt will be enough. What about you? You're a parent, do you ever regret it?"

He held his breath. What did she mean, or know? Was Emily's illness online? Or had Oscar told her something? Was she implying that his challenges as the parent of a manic-depressive child might make him regret having her?

"Would I do it all again, if I knew what I know today?" He smiled, face revealing nothing of the commotion within him.

"It was a stupid question. I already know the answer—yes. It's easy to see you're the kind of person who wanted children."

He nodded, certain images tumbling into his mind with pain and joy. Yes, he had loved all of it. The bad things had evaporated, the acrimony with Charlotte. Only the beautiful things, the one-of-a-kind life experiences the three of them had shared as a family, remained. Cracked like a mirror? Maybe, but still whole and wonderful, laced with bittersweet. But all of life was bittersweet when recollected, for time's passage was ultimately sad, culminating as it did, inescapably, in loss upon loss, slow decrepitude, and death. The older one got, the more life became memories, unfinished, never resolved and permanently archived. Music brought back such memories, and until the moment of death, humans would puzzle over the scraps of their lives and feel pain.

They both sighed at the same moment, as if thinking the same thing, and then laughed, also in unison. Rapport was there, Nick thought, a natural similarity in sensibilities, perception.

"Well, Nick, I should take you to HR and get your paperwork started. And call me Flo, everyone does. I've forgotten my real name is Florence, illustrious as it is. But not for the nurse. I was named for the city—I was born there."

She straightened, a tall, distinguished woman, though her three-inch-high heels played a role in her height. Even so, she was long-legged and wider at the hips than women liked to be, but she was well made, handsomely dressed, utterly feminine, faintly perfumed, delicate and forthright at once, and with her nervous, chattery monologues and expressive, captivating facial features, her allure had no bounds. He liked all of her and knew he would gladly work for her, be a right-hand editor at her side, but never in this lifetime, or ten lifetimes, come to know her. She was that kind of person, rare, delectable, only to be viewed. He sensed she did and didn't want to be that way; it was just the way she was, the way she had been born, to be Florence Wright, unshareable. And yet she had a husband, Nick thought. But, even a partner wouldn't be able to access the inside architecture and complicated glues creating a person like Florence.

Suddenly she gasped and again fanned her hand against her forehead. "How could I be so forgetful? It's just that I'm so happy you're on board and to me salary isn't a question. What do you want?"

Two beats passed as their eyes locked—hers the depths of brown, his ocean blue, complete nakedness in both. In her heels she was exactly his height and their eyes were on a par. Quietly he said the figure he had in mind, one that had nixed him from every job for which he had applied in the past year. Publishers could get competent thirty-year-olds for less than half that amount, mainly because young professionals lived communally, and when they married shared two incomes. But he was alone and couldn't manage on less, and besides—though no one cared—he was worth it. Her Leonardo eyes with round whites and wispy black lashes stared back for two more beats, perhaps even with a superior's resistance, and then her smile flashed over the broad white teeth. "Obviously, I would be ashamed to try to get you for less."

And that was how Nick's Tuesday in early October ended on a high note. An hour in HR, a quick lunch at home, and then the inspired hours that followed, reorganizing his freelance life of the past year to become an office worker again. He would miss his comfy domicile and his silence, but the dependable paycheck and other benefits far outweighed his freedom. He used to be able to say, "This is fine for now, but I'll keep my eye out for something better." As he approached his sixtieth year, it had become clear how rarely new opportunities came to seniors. And what opportunity was he hoping for, anyway? To write the books that filled his notebooks? To work part-time for a celebrity who needed a ghostwriter? Every editor in the world wanted such a life. And almost all of them died still wishing, their boxes of notes and manuscripts with them.

Two

From the time Nick turned on his computer at Churchill until the day finished, his mind worked under intense pressure. He managed a full load of books in the making, each one requiring daily communication with authors, designers, editors, marketers, and any number of other cogs in the wheel of Churchill's workflow. He did more than manage, for the company's small staff and unorthodox manner of publishing made it necessary for him to sometimes jump in and clean up a freelancer's sloppy work. Flo too occasionally ran her pencil over a book's front matter or cover copy. She had an ear for trendy language, and even if Nick gave her copy he had personally polished, Flo's pencil invariably improved it.

Susie Mumford, the hard-driving production editor, added to Nick's ad hoc roles in the office. At least once a week she stopped by to remind him that proofs or bluelines sat in the Abbott Room waiting for his sign-off. "Don't worry, you only have to eyeball them. And I can give you an extension to noon tomorrow." She always smiled to sweeten her pressure, and his eyes always fastened on the gash between her young, pert brows that Churchill's workload must have carved there. All the books had assigned editors, whether in-house or freelance, but Churchill's way of operating kept Nick involved in a hands-on way throughout the process. It was full immersion in a deadline-driven, market-frenzied business. Luckily he loved it. He also knew that an old and reputable company like Churchill would one day fall to a media giant like Random House, itself under Bertelsmann. But for now, under Flo's fresh direction, Churchill's leadership hoped to hang on to the company's independence. She had brought in Dave Howell, a best-selling mystery writer, and had focused on health, psychology, lifestyle, and gift or "merch" categories for the company's list. To the old-school chieftains, integrity had been shed for profit and survival, but as Flo pointed out, and Nick sadly agreed, "Integrity has morphed in meaning because taste has changed."

It was the talk of the age how no one read anymore, just texted. Newspapers had become obsolete; books had to be short and bulleted. Prose, especially good prose, took too much work to read for the tempo and attention span of current society. Of course highbrows and book-club aficionados still searched, almost desperately, for quality reads, and Churchill still produced them—the best novels they could afford to buy and socially relevant works by journalists, politicians, historians, and biographers. Select memoirs related to historic events or far-flung cultures still came to print through Churchill. The company's publisher Sam Noyes loved these subjects and Margie Rockwell acquired them for him. She also drummed up new ideas for their line of New England recreation guides that had served a faithful local community for more than one hundred years. But for income, and to bring the company out of deep debt, Flo had been brought in not only to direct books but also to work her New York network to acquire popular books in the areas of self-help, relationships, glamour, diet, entrepreneurship, sports, and social media—the vast Condé Nast market. Once, dropping off paperwork to her chair, Nick had noticed *People* magazine by her computer, and after his initial surprise realized she was searching for trends and new voices.

Those first weeks on the job, Nick saw little of Flo. She was rarely at her desk and he too was consumed by work. In the morning, when she passed by his open door on her way to her office, he never noticed her, and she didn't disturb his concentration with a greeting. Nor did she create the ripple of wind that other employees stirred up as they sped by on their pressing missions. Her high heels moved noiselessly over the carpet, and only afterward did he sniff the trace of pleasant perfume she had left behind. Sometimes he lifted his head to wonder how she managed to walk to work each day in her array of spike heels, for he knew where she lived on Marlborough Street, an expensive address about five blocks from the office. He varied his route to work and often passed her Victorian townhouse, now converted into condominiums, and he liked to imagine her world behind those tall, elegant windows on the first floor.

Nick saw Flo at meetings—once a week at the editorial gathering she headed, and afterward in her office for a brief update on their projects and goals. Flo was a mainstay at jacket shows, where her opinion mattered, though it was her style to forthrightly declare her preferences and then immediately back off with an uncertain and solicitous face directed at each of her colleagues in the room, whether designers, editors, or marketing heads. "Of course I defer to all of you," she invariably said with her gracious smile. "You're the experts. Lou, you're our sales genius. Tell me, what do you think?"

"The same thing as always," Lou Moser, head of sales, typically growled back. He was short and heavy with a tough, Manhattan style and had been recruited from Barnes and Noble. "Covers sell books. I like the design and the type, but I keep telling you, I hate pink. Never show me pink."

"It's a book about love. Hating pink's a personal preference. What about sales?" Flo argued benignly with an engaging smile.

"I'm talking about sales. I can't sell pink because it makes me sick. Try red. Isn't love red hot?"

"But love makes me think of pink."

"Fine, make it pink, it's girly. But I can't promise you Costco."

"Costco will love pink."

"I'm assigning the book to Rudy."

"Are you going to be mad at me if we do pink?"

"No Flo, I want you to be happy and if pink makes you happy, well then . . ."

She clapped her hands under her chin, face and eyes shining like a child's. Nick loved watching these Flo scenarios. So did everyone else.

It was early November, with Election Day pending and the entire country fixated on the Republican-Democratic divide. Nick didn't know any Republicans, but his democratic friends all expressed worry about Obama's chances for reelection. Nick felt that any incumbent held the advantage, and during the debates, after the first undistinguished performance, the president had shown his position of authority and direct access to agency statistics for the economy, whereas the Romney team had to fabricate theirs from secondary corridors. Nick didn't detest Mitt Romney the way his friends did, even though he didn't want Romney's views holding the reins, but he would panic if someone like Paul Ryan became vice president and then ruled the country one day. That would be the end of the ideal of the United States, as far as Nick was concerned. The man's ideas were insane. Romney came across as a man with solid values and an American work ethic, despite his fake smile and plasticity. His downfall was his neglect of citizens who mattered, citizens who did not come from the wealthy echelons the Republicans shamelessly favored. Nick felt sure that Romney's gaffe about 47 percent of American voters being worthless leeches on the government bankroll would cost him the election—most of those "humbugs" were middle-class citizens who paid taxes entitling them to medicare or unemployment benefits, while the richest people in the country avoided taxes by moving their wealth offshore. But the Republicans could not see the disparity; they could not comprehend that regular people paid their taxes and struggled to make ends meet while fabulously rich people legally avoided taxes and lived lifestyles that should be capped or fairly taxed. When the 2008 crash happened, many of the eateries and shops frequented or owned by the 47 percent went out of business, while the fine restaurants afforded by the wealthy continued to welcome patrons. The Democrats could not understand how the Republicans got such a distorted view of society, the financial world, and justice, and the Republicans couldn't understand the Democrats for the same reasons. Far worse, Nick didn't see how this polarized viewpoint could ever be bridged. The American dream—everyone had a fair chance at colossal success—just wasn't true. All kinds of legal and sneaky leverages increasingly aided the rich and powerful and lowered the prospects of every other economic group in the country.

Early on Election Day, as Nick got settled in front of his computer, Flo phoned him. "Hey, are you free? Can you come by for a minute? You'll never guess who's here."

She and Oscar Wheeler were seated on the couch in her

office when Nick entered a minute later. The men—old friends, once regular drinking buddies at the Harvard Club—shook hands and then hugged. Oscar had recently retired from the *Globe* and years before had hired Nick for his first job after the Peace Corps. Later, after his stint as a househusband, Nick had found his true calling as a book editor at Trowbridge, a job he would not have gotten without Oscar's connections and support. And it had been Oscar, who was eight years older, who had taken Nick's book on Rio de Janeiro's favela Rocinha to a friend at Scribner's. From the start, friendship had grown quickly between them, and Oscar had been Nick's best man when he married Charlotte. For years Oscar had come to their Thanksgiving and other holiday meals, but such occasions had ended with Nick's divorce and single life. Now they met once in a while for lunch or dinner, sometimes with Emily, since those two from the start had formed a special relationship. Oscar, a lifelong bachelor with several long-term girlfriends in his past, had been a self-appointed godfather to Emily, remembering her birthday and otherwise showering her with books. Now in his mid-sixties, he looked in far better shape than during his newspaper days, when he had been overweight, alcoholic, and a cigar smoker. Even before his retirement he had given up his vices on doctor's orders, but for months now he had been working out at the gym, and it showed. His rugged face and good-natured affability put people at ease and had been an asset during his long career, which had begun in Vietnam.

Oscar sat back down, but Flo remained standing near Nick. She was abuzz with ideas, and her light voice purred around them like a butterfly's wings enveloped in the soft cloud of her scent. "Wait till you see what Oscar has brought us. A best seller, a true story but also a thriller—a bloodcurdling, hair-raising tale. I didn't want to call you before your fan club here finished praising you to the high heavens, in case it went to your head, or embarrassed you. And I didn't know you wrote poetry, Nick. I want to read it."

Nick looked at Oscar, *What?*

"You were damn good at it, published, why be shy?" Oscar said amiably.

"So what's this *Clear and Present Danger* we're going to publish?" Nick said, sitting down at Flo's polished conference table. The manuscript, not too tall, was waiting there.

"Tell him about it," Flo said.

"Well, one of my old newspaper pals, John Baker—"

"You know him, Nick," Flo interrupted. "He covered all the drug-lord stories in the nineties."

Nick shook his head—he didn't know him. He hadn't paid that much attention to the drug-lord tales, though he had watched a few eye-opening films—*Medellín* and *City of God*. The drug wars in Rio's favelas happened after he left.

"Well," Oscar continued, "John called me about an American in Brazil named Chad Winters who survived a harrowing drug-war experience. John ghostwrote Winters's book." He pointed to the manuscript.

Again Flo cut in, her enthusiasm palpable. She couldn't wait for Oscar to tell the story. She had to tell it herself. "Winters, from Florida, inherited money and bought beachfront property on an island off Rio. He built a small resort—coral, exotic marine life, birds, a private beach. It took him and his Brazilian-American wife a few years to get it going—I mean, this was a partially protected island with no electricity or plumbing. But they took care of all that and eventually had bookings, including some odd regulars who helicoptered in every few weeks and holed themselves up in the guest lodge for the entire weekend. Chad and his wife served them meals, handled their transportation and logistics, and asked no questions. Later, according to the book, these guys turned out to be local officials involved in the drug trade. Over the several years they parked at Chad's, they helped build a hideout in the jungle and used it as a transit station for some kind of cocaine derivative. Winters found out about it, but before he could decide what to do, the drug lords attacked his resort—burned it to the ground—and he and his wife barely escaped on their speedboat. His ear was shot off in the escape, and one of the government guys was killed. Obviously the book uses a pen name—Ricky Harmon—don't you love it?" Flo's eyes were so wide that the whites circled all the way around the intense coals at their center. She picked up the manuscript and held it out to Nick. "We have his story! *Island Peril.*"

"Are you sure it's all true?" Nick asked, taking the book.

"John's reliable," Oscar said from the couch. "He met Winters soon after the episode and did some follow-up sleuthing, enough to think the story had merit. He offered to ghost it in a favorable deal."

"What happened to Winters?"

"He has a refreshment stand at Copacabana."

"Copacabana? That's ritzy. Isn't he afraid the bad guys will track him down and kill him if he publishes the book?"

"According to John, no one down there cares about Chad's story. Crime and corruption are a way of life."

"Then are you sure he wasn't a cog in the wheel? That would make more sense," Nick said.

"Don't be such a party pooper," Flo said, making a face at Nick.

"I'm just posing questions. We don't want a publishing scandal right when Churchill's struggling for its life."

"That's just the point, Nick," Flo said. "We need this book, and if we don't take it, Random House will!" She took the manuscript back and chucked it on the table, showing her impatience. "John Baker was a correspondent for the *New York Times*. He's written for the *Atlantic*, the *New Yorker* . . . he won a Pulitzer for Vietnam."

"I felt it should have been mine," Oscar said with a droll grin, lightening the mood. "We covered Nam together."

"I can't wait to read it," Nick said, reaching for the manuscript. He knew Flo would publish it even if he found it implausible. Fire was in her eyes, zeal—here was a book, ready to go, that could make money. She was there to find new authors, au courant material. *Island Peril* fit the bill.

The meeting concluded soon after, and the three editors stood up for farewells, Flo pressing down her fitted skirt of expensive black wool. Her fingers, nails painted charcoal gray that day, nervously checked the lower buttons of her ruffled black sweater, open just enough to show a deep rose top that matched the lipstick she had chosen for the day. And her gray eye shadow matched her nails, and somehow the color combination emphasized her lovely complexion. "I only wish it was closer to lunchtime so we could all get out of here and enjoy ourselves on Newbury Street," she said hurriedly, hustling them to the door. "Thank you so much, Oscar, for this book, which Nick and I will read right away. In fact, I won't get any sleep tonight, but then again, when do I ever get sleep? This place gives me too much anxiety, not to mention indigestion. Poor Garrett has to suffer through the night with me turning on the light every other hour, so I can jot down notes and munch Rolaids." But her smile was radiant, inviting them to like her in spite of her flaws. Nick had no problem with that. It was all too easy to stop and stare for two beats at her face, its expression, the skin smooth over the cheekbones, enhanced, he suspected, by the faintest veil of foundation. Her eye makeup was always different, and though he had never liked makeup on women, with Flo it was something to notice, like artwork the artist changed every day, obsessively. She was a fascination.

Moving down the hall, eventually out of earshot, Oscar said, "Well, Flo's a knockout."

"No joke," Nick replied. "And a better editor than either of us. Shall we get a coffee?"

He grabbed his jacket as they passed his office, and they rode the elevator down.

At the corner Starbucks they quickly caught up on weeks of news—the country's future happening that very day, Emily's grad school plans, Nick's parents' health, Oscar's retirement, and progress on the Vietnam novel that he had been writing for thirty years. Only when they had finished their coffees and stood up to leave did conversation return to Flo.

"That woman sticks in my mind," Oscar said, glancing at Nick.

Nick pushed first through the glass door to the cold November air. Copley Square's traffic was loud—Yellow Cabs, delivery vans, the usual stream of chattering tourists, even in winter. He didn't feel like talking about Flo or divulging that she attracted him. "Which way are you heading?" he said.

"Home. Green Line to Red Line. Come on, buddy, tell me some stories. We've all had office jobs. How can you avoid Florence Wright? She gets right in your face."

"Easy. I got old."

"Ha, so what does that make me? She smote me at first sight. And besides, women her age like father figures."

Nick laughed. "I'm not in your category yet." But probably her parents weren't that much older than he—and that was food for thought. "Anyway, she's married."

"That never stopped office affairs."

"Not in your case."

"I tell you, man, you're doomed—the vibes in that room almost choked me."

Nick shook his head. "I'm not tempted."

"How can that be true? I know you!"

Nick laughed again. "Okay, I was pretty wild in my day—but you were worse—and ultimately I survived my marriage without an affair. Even though I was dying for one."

Nick's thoughts tumbled with images from the past—himself in his thirties and early forties, falling in love with every talented woman he met, pursuing them in collegial, safe ways but never making a definitive move. Way back in his brain, where he was barely aware of cogitations, his marriage commitment put brakes on his impulses. Then he saw, as he always saw in his memory, Charlotte's pale, trembling face announcing that she wanted a divorce, that she was in love with Bill, another teacher at her school. It had never occurred to Nick during all his tortured fantasies of other women that Charlotte would act on hers. Nor had he ever seriously considered not spending the rest of his life with her.

They crossed the street when the light changed to green.

"What do you say we organize a dinner date with Emily?" Oscar said as they reached the curb.

"Good idea. In fact, why don't you come with us tonight? *The Third Man*'s playing at the Brattle. We're getting some pho first."

"Pho? Right up my alley. We can kill time till Obama's safe in the White House."

"That's the hope. I'll e-mail you the details."

Back in the office, Nick found *Island Peril* on his desk with a hot pink Post-it from Flo, whose penmanship was crabbed. A few times during his short tenure at Churchill he had gone to her office to ask what her notes said. This one he could read, four words: A copy for you. He sat down and before checking the latest e-mails, flipped through the manuscript to skim the content. The prose was dramatic and captivating. It described an entrepreneur's ambitious risk-taking and love of ocean life. Each sentence built toward the violent conflagration and shoot-out in the middle of the night. The author, Chad Winters, a.k.a. Ricky Harmon, theorized that the drug cartel had had a falling-out with one of the government officials and so murdered him. At the same time, the island had become the cartel's distribution center, and Chad's resort was now in the way. So the thugs drove him off the island the same night they killed the official, with a missed shot blowing off Chad's ear. Nick still found it hard to believe that Chad Winters had no involvement with the cartel—if only to lend his boat when helicopter service wasn't available or to handle a few shipments to the favela dealers himself. He would urge Flo to slow down and let the legal department check out the story.

He put the manuscript on a shelf for the morning and looked at his e-mails, the usual long lineup of requests for urgent action from editors, designers, packagers, agents, and authors. Susie wrote that the tenth edition of the *Massachusetts Guide Book* had been laid out by Janice, a seasoned in-house designer, who was screaming about text oversets and a host of style inconsistencies. Had Nick remembered to give the freelance editor the word counts? At any rate, he needed to talk to Janice A.S.A.P.

Generally Nick tried to avoid communication with Janice, for she was crabby, short-fused, and spent a lot of time huddled over her phone making private-life arrangements. She invariably came to work late and couldn't be counted on for important meetings.

Her petite figure was as taut as an army trainer's. She liked to chop firewood, she had once told Nick in the kitchen as she opened a can of tuna fish for lunch. "I like the hard work, and it sends a message to my husband and son watching from the window that life has regular chores." He could see the axe coming down and the grimace on her face.

Nick had heard through the grapevine that Janice had survived the 2008 layoffs because of her friendship with the senior vice president's wife. And she was good at spotting design mistakes in their illustrated books, which Churchill had a tradition of hanging up on the walls of the Abbott Room for interdepartmental review. On Nick's first illustrated project, Janice had shrieked at him. "You have a blank page at the end! We never have blank pages at Churchill! You should have noticed!"

You should have too, he said to himself, if you had started the design on time. He watched her march back to her office, griping loudly like a madwoman about Churchill's impeccable standards and its intolerance for amateurs. How could he be anything but amused by such a show? That was Janice.

The handful of staff editors and designers were in their mid-to-late thirties and stuck together. Liza Metcalf was the only editor Nick's age and it was said she had survived the cuts because she was a trust-fund baby content with the salary she had started out with decades before. She quietly reviewed proposals and manuscripts and helped the authors they signed on. More scholarly topics went her way. Churchill had no rigid roles—editors' skills got employed in various ways.

In late afternoon, having eaten lunch over his work while periodically checking CNN's election coverage, Nick heard his Google calendar beep, and a message popped up reminding him that he had a dummy show in ten minutes for the Wycliffe Gallery's fine art photography book on trees. He glanced at his watch. There was just enough time to print the fifteen chapters of Naomi Spizer's Holocaust manuscript that had just come in. It could be one of the last survivor memoirs to emerge, given the nearly seventy years since the end of the Second World War. Nick needed to look over the manuscript and then assign it to an editor.

Ten minutes later he grabbed a pad and headed to the dummy show, where the top brass came in to give nods of approval for the final proof of illustrated books. It was a mere formality, a vestige of past ways. The executives, all of whom were in their early seventies, would circle the room for a few minutes, complimenting the pages on the walls and congratulating the team for its excellent work. Occasionally they sat down to share the proceedings, another archaic practice ingrained in Churchill's DNA. The book's editor usually presented the project with the designer weighing in. In the case of *Trees*, Flo had overseen the project, for the company had been short-staffed and ailing when she first arrived.

When Nick entered the conference room that afternoon, the heads were already there and greeted him warmly. They were Sam Noyes, publisher, Tom Greenleaf, senior vice president, and Calvin Pratt, finance director. Nick noted that only Tom wore a bow tie; the other two had open collars, in keeping with the looser dress code now prevalent everywhere. Younger deputies from their offices, some whose names Nick didn't even know yet, stood against the walls with arms folded over their chests to listen to the proceedings. Lou Moser, head of sales, and Ruth Belknap from sponsored projects were also on hand, in addition to the book's designer and project manager, in this case Fran Turchi and Nick. Lory Gardner—the in-house jacket designer—had created the cover.

Flo entered the room last. Nick, and probably everyone else, inhaled her. She was like a star actress an eager audience has been waiting a lifetime to see in person. She moved across the room, her stage, with a proud, assured step, shoulders and pelvis tipped slightly forward in the fashion-model style, smile brilliant, head flicking her loose sable hair over her shoulders as she called out the friendliest hellos, as if blowing kisses to one and all. How easily her pulsing persona could melt even the hardest hearts, Nick thought, glancing around at the sober faces of the company leaders, stiff, blue-blooded Yanks. Their features had softened to childlike pleasure under Flo's glowing force.

"I'm just delighted to present to you our latest photography book, this one copublished with the Wycliffe Gallery in New York, which all of you know about so I don't have to explain, except to say, of all the galleries in the world devoted to photography, the Wycliffe is my own personal favorite—and not because I'm a New Yorker. The truth is, I don't know of any other venue that can come close to competing with its stature and also its connection to the very best photographers on the planet, from Australia to London to South Africa and, of course, New York. So we at Churchill can be proud to offer this new book on trees, I should say mind-blowing images of trees, to anyone who loves gazing at beauty, loves appreciating the miracle of trees in every season, including winter, when the branches become delicate, fragile webs." She stopped to gaze at a spread showing snow-covered trees. Her voice purred on. "The book makes you long for winter to come just so you can stare at bare trees against a blue sky, or shimmering under a coat of ice, even though we all know that beautiful ice like that kills a tree if it doesn't melt fast enough, but, oh my god, the sight of trees coated in wet, glittering ice sends shivers down my spine. It's a vision to die for."

She resumed her stroll of the room, left hand waving at the pictures. "As you can see, Fran has pulled off yet another design feat with this book—congratulations, Fran! She's managed to make every picture receive its due honor on the page. And Lory has come up with a jacket that's definitely going to bowl over juries in all the contests we're going to enter this book in. And Nick kindly pitched in and fixed up Michael Green's incredibly bad text so that it now reads like poetry. Which is appropriate coming from our resident poet, in case you didn't know that about Nick." Her eyes and smile flicked mischievously at him while she continued without a pause. "Thanks to our amazing and hardworking team for producing yet another Churchill smash hit. We hope everyone loves the book as much as we do—it's destined to be the new standard-bearer in our photography category. And for all publishers who hope to compete. Best of all, Wycliffe is paying most of the bill. We have Ruth and her unparalleled negotiating powers to thank for that."

The gray heads of the top executives nodded. They reiterated thanks. Everyone murmured praise for the book. Nick wondered whether the room's attention was arrested by the photographs on the walls or by Flo's graceful movements, which seemed choreographed to her eloquence. She now waited expectantly, her ageless smile traveling from face to face.

"Nick, what do you think?" she said almost gaily.

"I love it. It's a winner." Even if no one buys photography books, he added to himself. But of course the Wycliffe Gallery would be selling *Trees* in its shop and online, and it was a small print run of 7,000, for which the gallery was covering all costs and Churchill had only to design and distribute in order to earn its hefty share of sales. "Great title," he added.

"Yes," Flo said, moving her eyes to study the jacket. "*Trees* just about says it all."

Everyone chuckled, and then Moser said as if stamping the glossy jacket, "I'm fine with it."

"Good job, everyone," Sam agreed as he got up to leave. "I look forward to Wycliffe's response when they get the bound book."

"They're going to drool," Flo said to his retreating back, and as soon as the important personages and their cortege had filed out, she collapsed in a chair, dropping her stage mask. In her rare down times, she liked to rehash a project's past hurdles. It was a way to hang out, hang loose with the regulars. "Of course all those fussy people at Wycliffe have sabotaged the design a dozen times till we were back at the beginning," she said, slouched in her chair. "And talk to Lory about how they controlled the jacket. I'll be so happy to say goodbye to that persnickety Michael Green—what a squeaky, passive-aggressive twerp." She gave a nasty little grin, mimicking his face. "All right, Donna, do you want to run through the specs?"

"I do," the attractive but rather stern head of manufacturing said, focusing her attention on her notes. "It'll be quick because I don't think anything has changed after Michael's last interference. And I agree with you, he's pretty much an ass—we had to deal with him a few years ago on their architecture project."

"Glad I wasn't around for that," Flo said cheerlessly.

Donna then read off all the book's printing specifications, to which the designer nodded agreement. Nick was anxious to get back to his desk to finish up loose ends before his early departure to meet Emily on election night. Flo, though, was content to linger at the table revisiting the ups and downs of the book as if past decisions could still be reconsidered. How could they print a book called *Trees*? How blah was that for a title? It needed another word or two to give it the emotional impact trees conveyed. Like *Simply Trees*, or *Trees of Life*—anything but *Trees* all by itself. But she guessed it was too late to revisit the issue. And she still didn't like the final jacket image, nor the title below the image instead of on top, the way Lory had first designed it. Plus why did the Wycliffe Gallery have to insist on its ugly logo marring a work of art? Why was its name more important than an image of a tree? Talk about hypocrisy—celebrating trees as the symbol of unadulterated nature but then covering the symbol with man's greed for recognition and profit. "I guess I'll just have to live with a jacket that's not my first choice," she said glumly.

"It's decent," Nick said, getting up and patting her shoulder as he passed her chair, unable to sit still another minute. He hated meetings but understood that for Flo and a few others, the aftermath of a show offered the chance for a brief time-out to talk shop until a more interesting topic came up, such as vacation destinations or a tip on a good restaurant in Boston. Such subjects would kindle Flo's conversation, her need to express herself passionately and dramatically, leaving little room for others to participate.

"Thanks, Nick," she said softly, with appreciation.

He then applied his extra reserves of energy to get out of the office by five. As was his habit, he looked at every sheet or pile of paper on every tabletop and memorized its status for the following day, placing the most important project right on top of his keyboard. His to-do list on a theme pad sat to the right. Flo kept a notebook, one with Botticelli's *Primavera* wrapping the cover, and all details from past meetings and phone conversations could be found there, though she hated to search through them and sometimes phoned him to see if he had the information handy. She also stuck hot-pink and neon-green Post-its around the border of her large computer screen. That system would drive him crazy, those little flags wagging at him every day as he tried to focus on the screen. But everyone had a personal way of keeping organized. Even Susie Mumford, rigidly neat in her appearance and responsible for upkeep of their complex workflow and databases, had her own invisible methods, for her office was cluttered with several years' worth of books and old proofs, and her giant computer screen looked like a solid brick wall of file folders. How could she ever find the folder she needed?

Nick was pulling on his jacket and heading into the hall when Flo came by wearing an elegant black coat belted at the waist.

"You're off too?" she said.

"Election night—I'm meeting Emily, my daughter."

"Good. I'm meeting Garrett and some friends. I'm not really psyched for a night in front of a fifty-inch TV with nothing to do but pour more drinks."

"Yeah, I try to avoid election parties."

"You're smart. I wish I was."

He laughed. "I can't keep up with you, Flo."

She nestled into her coat collar as if it were luxurious mink. "Thanks—coming from you, that means a lot. Here, I wanted to give you this. I just found it on my shelf."

She handed him Don Trevor's *Dance Till Dawn*, a best-selling novel set in 1920s Paris. Trevor, a first-time author, had become a multimillionaire overnight.

"Thanks, I've been meaning to read it. It got rave reviews."

"I adore Paris," she said, smiling. "I like to think if I'd been born in Paris, that would be my name. Wouldn't that be incredible— Paris Wright?" She laughed and then sobered with a sudden scowl. "Do you know what I just found out? Back in 2005 Trevor's agent came to Churchill, and Sam Noyes said, Sorry, no, not our DNA. Christ, Lionsgate is making the movie!"

"Wait till Lionsgate hears about Paris Wright's *Island Peril*."

She laughed. "Now don't diss that book till you read it."

"I took a quick peek, and obviously legal should check it out."

"Oh, fiddlesticks, it's just not your kind of book."

"Maybe not, but I can see that it's compellingly written, it has mass market appeal, and I agree Churchill can't remain 'exclusive Churchill' and survive."

"Exactly my point. Our backlist isn't enough. It's yellowing. We need authors. New, on-the-rise celebrities. But I'll talk to legal. And, I'm glad you're on my team. Have fun with Emily tonight and let's pray Obama wins. *À demain.*"

"*Até amanhã.*"

She smiled. "*Je ne parle pas portugais.*"

"*Pas de problème.*"

"That's sneaky of you, French too." She glided off down the hall like a runway model. He should have followed, but instead he turned back to his office and ridiculously fiddled with his piles of paper to avoid riding the elevator with her and perhaps walking her home. Why? She was nice, she was friendly—*she was a magnet.* And if she weren't married, could he really pretend he didn't have time in his life to go after her?

He took the stairs down, headlong, his feet matching the tempo of his thoughts. No, his resistance was more complex than a matter of having time. He had found out with Kathy, his only relationship since Charlotte, that his life had Emily attached to it, and Emily's needs came first, ahead of his own and ahead of his lover's. And then there was something else. He had found with Kathy that it wasn't possible to fall in love twice, not really. It was the first, youthful love and almost innocent bonding, filled with dreams, including dreams of family, that had depth and meaning. It happened only once in a person's life. Anything after that was something else— caring, loyal companionship at best. After Kathy he knew he didn't want a caring companionship more than he wanted to be alone with memories of his past family life.

Running a bit late, Nick pushed through the glass door of the Harvard Coop. It was like entering a cathedral devoted to books, the central nave high with balconies forming a U, their walls coated with the spines of books. The main aisle displayed everything new in paperback and hardcover on table after table and on adjacent racks, like rows of portable library stacks. Other spaces, small like chapels, specialized in topics such as music and poetry. Books were incredibly precious, so why were erudition and curiosity in the throes of death, being replaced by some lower species the latest generation wanted—tweets, texts, bytes? Nick didn't want to be a dinosaur; he wanted to keep up with trends and follow the path of civilization. But he also lamented the declining interest in books and serious authors, although the display tables in the Coop offered reassurance. The plentiful clientele, bent with absorption over the offerings, still sought and devoured ideas, learning, beauty, and creativity, not to mention words, sentences, and the art of the written word.

He found Emily and Oscar at a table toward the back. Oscar had already been there for a while and carried a half-dozen books under one arm. He and Emily were poring over the back cover of a book in Emily's hands. After greetings she quickly told Nick that it was the latest scoop on the hot topic of grains and the brain, the main tenet being that gluten eroded brainpower. "It got a good review."

"Let's get it," Oscar said, taking it from her and adding it to his pile.

"Hey, let me," Emily protested, reaching for the book, but Oscar laughed and turned away, blocking her efforts.

"Emmy, I haven't given you a book in ages. I have to keep up our little tradition."

"Except it's one-sided," she said.

"No, you gave me that David Mitchell book."

"Did you read it?"

"If it weren't so long, I'd read it again. Have you read it, Nick?"

"No, not yet, but I will. I'll order it used from Amazon."

"Better to support our nearly extinct indie bookstores," Oscar said.

"Barnes and Noble runs the Coop."

"You're kidding," Oscar said. "When did that happen?"

They checked out and walked a block to the Vietnamese pho shop, where they had plenty of time to chat before the movie and at the same time keep tabs on the election results pattering away repetitiously on the TV screen above the bar. The candidates were running neck-and-neck, causing a state of unease for both the Republicans and the Democrats.

Oscar distracted them with the story of his escape from Saigon in the last minutes before the Viet Cong seized the city. "It was unreal. Mobs on the streets, chaos. Everyone was terrified and frantic to get out. Me too. And the helicopters chopping away only intensified the panic. I still see the faces. It was the biggest wartime evacuation in history. And a lot got left behind."

"I can't believe you were there. Is that what your novel's about?" Emily said.

He nodded. "And more, if I ever finish it. Maybe you'll finish it for me some day."

"You mean Dad. I'm focusing on health."

"No, your dad's a romantic, too soft for war writing. I need a Graham Greene clone. But maybe Greene already wrote the book and I should give up my efforts."

"Don't," Emily encouraged him. "Every story's different. Your Vietnam was a different era from Greene's."

"True. Maybe you'll inspire me."

They talked a bit more about Vietnam and then about McNamara and his *Fog of War* apology, which didn't win him any admirers but garnered at least some grumbling respect that he had come out with both the truth and important historical lessons. Not that lawmakers ever paid attention to history, Nick thought. The wars, lies, and massacres continued; in fact, they seemed to have become pandemic.

It was 9:30 when they got out of the movie, which had been a captivating diversion, perfectly plotted, perfectly acted, and perfectly shot, at least from Nick's point of view. He immediately checked his phone for the election results, which by then he felt sure would be definitive. But they weren't. Not only were the candidates still running neck-and-neck, but Romney was in the lead by several percentage points. "Damn, it's not clear yet," he told the others. "Pennsylvania, Ohio, and Florida are still undecided."

"Home to the TV," Oscar said perkily. "Want to come? Plenty of couches chez moi."

He lived right up the street in a nineteenth-century mansion he had inherited.

"Thanks, but I want to get home and settle into my bed with the radio," Nick replied.

"Em? I can drive you home later."

"Thanks, another time. We should watch some DVDs, to catch you up."

"Gladly. This was fun. Best time I've had all year."

Agreeing to meet again soon for another film, they all hugged goodbye and then headed off in separate directions—Oscar down

Brattle Street, Emily up Mass Ave., and Nick to the Harvard Square subway. Eager to get back to the election, he sped down the stairwell. He could hear the rumble of the underground trains and didn't want to miss the one heading back to Boston. His thoughts hammered relentlessly. For the first time in the two-year campaign, he considered the possibility of a Republican administration, and it stunned him, completely voided his life. He couldn't face the reality of it; he didn't know how he could still be an American if the Republicans took office again. Getting through the Bush years—eight long years—had been hard enough; the idea of returning to them after a mere four-year hiatus stripped him of all meaning. Obama had hardly nicked the surface of reforms needed to repair the incredible financial mess the Republicans had created, not to mention the messes in domestic and foreign policies. Obama needed more time, more support; the past four years, he had hardly been able to get legislation through. The mere dribbles in initiatives would stop abruptly if Romney were elected. Another four years were needed to make any kind of noticeable change—if that was even possible. Another Democrat in 2016—he hoped Hillary—could continue the nascent recalibration of fair rights to the majority of Americans.

At home, Nick washed up fast and got into bed with the radio already turned on next to him. For what seemed like hours the newscasters repeated the same information, but finally a breakthrough came, and that was Ohio. It wasn't official yet, but with Ohio going to Obama and the new tally in electoral votes, there was no way, no possible way, Romney could make up the difference, not with Florida, not with Pennsylvania. Nick dozed off feeling incredible relief, but he still wanted the official word. Around midnight he woke up again and all the buzz was about Obama—he was president, though Florida's final count had yet to come in. Soon after, Romney conceded, and Nick experienced deep gratitude to his fellow citizens out there in the vast and diverse country. Together they had delivered a message to their government that they were still part of a nation where the people, the regular people, and their quality of life mattered. There would never be equality anywhere on earth, but for now, America had been spared further steps toward a capitalist oligarchy with an oppressed underclass. Congress was yet a battle to be waged.

Three

Nick got on the road late morning Thanksgiving Day to drive south to Marion, where his parents had retired. The weather was good: a blue sky with cottony clouds placed like decoration and decent sunshine producing warmth. The radio was entertaining him with classical music, and he enjoyed the occasional hour's drive for his thoughts to wander wherever they pleased, which never happened in his apartment or at Churchill, two work zones. The traffic wasn't bad—most people had traveled the day before. The period between Thanksgiving and Christmas was intense as everyone prepared for two megaholidays a few weeks apart. Although work continued during this time, far less got accomplished as vacation schedules varied and most people's thoughts were focused on preparations for their family get-togethers and the requisite shopping, planning, cooking, and travel. The holidays themselves were one thing, but the days before and after also involved activities, including heavy partying on New Year's Eve.

For years Nick and Charlotte had hosted the greater family and any stray friends for Thanksgiving, but that tradition had ended with their divorce. The past two years, Nick had driven to Marion for the holiday meal at his parents' retirement home. He had offered to take them out for a lobster dinner instead—his own first choice—but they preferred to eat the traditional turkey, cranberries, and pumpkin pie. Ann, Nick's older sister by four years, lived in Augusta, Maine, and did her own family gatherings. This year, however, she too was coming to Marion, for her grown children had other plans with their spouses.

Ann was also divorced. Most people were, Nick thought as he drove the empty road. He imagined humans weren't coded to be in relationships more than fifteen or twenty years, and longer-lasting relationships weren't always healthy; that is, the partners chose to live in a negative atmosphere rather than separate. Sure, a few marriages worked through the accumulated rot and disgust of long-term commitment; some even achieved, miraculously, mutual respect, overall harmony, but he doubted such successes made up even one percent of enduring couples. It wasn't that he had a vociferously pessimistic view of partnership, just an objective one. He hadn't liked the way his father had bullied his mother, but how had he himself treated Charlotte? And how had she treated him? Who was immune from maltreating another human being living for years in close proximity, in intimacy? The only antidote to inevitable moments of bad behavior was awareness of it and the ability to apologize and be fair. He and Charlotte, overall, for all their lashings-out, had shared that value, which made it possible, eventually, when all their anger had subsided, to communicate again with respect. Weirdly, he had even begun to speculate with the passage of years what it would be like to be a family again—he and Charlotte reunited. He couldn't hold the idea long, for obstacles quickly tumbled into the prospect—their basic clash of temperaments, for instance, something young, ambitious lovers could never fathom. Still, he and

Charlotte had shared at the beginning friendship, love, values, and dreams, ingredients for a durable bond. Their Peace Corps experience in Brazil was another meaningful tie in their formation as a couple. But their energies and life pursuits had been far apart, and became noticeable only after Emily was born, when time management became such a premium.

His phone rang, and glancing at the screen he moved to the slow lane to answer Emily's call.

"Hey, Dad, I have bad news. Mom's throwing up with a fever, so Thanksgiving's canceled."

"You're kidding. All that food—what about her guests?"

"It was just us this year, and Bill's kids. Mom said to ask if I could join you and take some of the food to Grandma's."

"By all means come, but I don't know about the food. I'll have to ask Grandma. This is her thing. Doesn't the turkey have to roast?"

"It's done. Eric and I can bring it, or a big chunk."

Oh, Eric too . . . Why wasn't he having Thanksgiving with his own family? He was so annoying. "Okay, hon, I'll call you right back."

Nick's carefree highway drive suddenly became a flurry of logistics, and he decided to pull over into the breakdown lane for his calls. His mother picked up on the first ring and sounded worried.

"Is everything all right?" she asked.

"Everything's fine. I'm on my way."

"That's good, Nicky. Ann's here already and it's so good to see her. *It's Nick*," she called out to the others. "*He's on his way.* Do you realize it's been almost a year since I saw Ann?" she continued. "Maine is as far away as California, or that's the way it seems. It amazes me how we're all so cohesively American, when we're a bunch of states with separate governments and laws, not to mention cultures—think of Texas, North Dakota, L.A., Vegas. Our distances are so vast in every way, even in tiny New England."

"It's true," Nick said, feeling his mother's animation. She loved family gatherings. She loved having her children nearby. "I'm glad Ann's there, and I'll see you in about an hour."

"An hour! Please, don't be late for the dinner—it starts promptly at twelve-thirty."

"Don't worry, there's plenty of time. And listen, I just had a call from Emily. Charlotte woke up with the flu and had to cancel her dinner, so Emily and Eric are driving down to eat with us. I hope that'll be all right."

"Splendid! Though I hope the dining room doesn't freak out with the extra numbers. I'll go down there right now and explain."

"That's the other thing—if you like, Emily can bring the dinner and we can eat it in your apartment."

"No, no, I don't want to do that. We're all reserved. It'll be fun in the dining room, like a party, don't you think?"

"That's fine. I just thought I'd ask. No problem."

"But I'm thrilled Emily's coming!"

"Eric too."

"Yes, I heard that, though I wish to God they hadn't gotten back together again."

"Yeah, but that's what lovers do—it's easier than being alone."

"True. Well, I'll have a chance to talk to Emily myself and pass on some good advice."

After they hung up, Nick delivered the update to Emily and got back on the road again, turning up the volume on the radio for the mesmerizing sweetness of music he vaguely recognized but could not identify by name or composer. The mezzo-soprano's voice undulated tenderly, seamlessly, with the strains of love, or maybe the dear memory of it. Whatever it was, it held Nick in its thrall and reminded him of Flo.

＊

From the main country road leading to the western beaches of Buzzards Bay, Nick turned into Ballard Hill Farm's long, curving drive. The acres of late fall landscape looked natural, but the dry, chilled beauty had been carefully enhanced by a professional land-scaper with special plantings and nonnative trees such as magno-lias, cherries, dogwood, and Japanese maple, everything dormant. Graceful paths traced through exotic grasses, lavender, and shrubs to well-spaced gazebos nestled behind screens of wintering roses, inviting rest, reading, or conversation. Nature's variety and peace reigned throughout the undulating property that surrounded the shingled sprawl at the top of a gentle slope. It was a great place, in Nick's opinion. At a certain age, living independently became arduous, and eventually impossible—it was a fact of life. Choices for the elderly were limited, and settling into a place like Ballard Hill Farm was a premium option few could afford. But his parents had planned for it, saved for it. The drawback with Ballard was that the majority of residents came from the Boston Brahmin class, and many of them put on airs, including a pseudo-British accent. Nick had met Virginians of the same status who put on the same airs and accents—the southern version of upper-classmanship. Over the centuries, the contrived inflections had become a way to show others the speaker's proud ancestry. "I'm of first American stock, better than you." In every society on earth humans created a class system, Nick thought. It was part of their biological programming.

Everything inside the palatial complex ran formally, honor-ably, and with utmost courtesy. Nick could wave with a smile as he passed the front desk, knowing that was enough identification for any new employee to realize he was legitimate and didn't need to be questioned. The employees did not have pre-Revolutionary last names, and of course a handful of residents had Irish, Italian, and Jewish last names, but only a handful. Each demographic in the Boston area had its preferred retirement community, and the outliers at Ballard had some reason for being there besides their social grouping. Nick's Portuguese mother passed undetected behind the Turner name until she made friends who asked about her heritage. With her effervescence and outgoing personality, by the time the Brahmin women learned she was Portuguese and from working-class New Bedford, they had already accepted her. Valerie had always been popular. She had grown up on the water, and after her marriage had spent the summers with Nick and Ann on the other side of Buzzards Bay in the Turner grandparents' big, shingled house. Sheldon had joined them on weekends. Returning to the water for their final years had always been Nick's parents' goal. Most people from eastern Massachusetts were inseparable from the water with its salted sea breezes. They sighed in contentment with the feel and smell of brine, sand, fish, and tar surrounding them. Something was missing if they couldn't hear the muffled symphony of waves, seagulls, buoys, rocking docks, and distant foghorns. White sails on whitecaps, Winslow Homer lighthouses on points of land, harbors filled with wharves and masts that clacked—all of this was embedded in the Massachusetts organism.

Faux antiques and large vases of flowers gave elegance and comfort to the retirement home's common spaces. The Turners' apartment was the equivalent of a city block away, down several carpeted corridors made cheerful by artwork on both walls, some by Cape Cod artists and one hallway dedicated to Ballard's own seniors, many of these latter watercolors and oils astonishingly good. Probably after long careers in banking, law, medicine, or homemaking, some residents had returned to their youthful talent for drawing. The art studio was on the lower level, along with the gym, pool, and other facilities—all with picture windows and sliding doors to the inviting outdoors, including the beach a mile away.

Nick rang the apartment doorbell and it opened before his hand dropped from the button.

"Nick!" his white-haired mother cried out with pleasure, reaching up for a hug. She was petite, like Emily, and to Nick still pretty when she smiled. "They called from the desk to say you were here. How's that for surveillance? Gosh, you look good—just like my dad!"

She always said that, though the "dad" Nick remembered from childhood had been old, wizened, short, and stout. It was true, he had some of his grandfather's traits—head, hair, eyebrows, permanent suntan, and seaman's compact strength. But his own father's blue eyes, patrician features, and greater height had contributed to his appearance.

Ann and his father, Sheldon, came to the little foyer for greetings and hugs, Ann 100 percent the Anglo female from Sheldon's side of the family—hair now silver and cut plainly in a pageboy, sweater and slacks from Talbot's, and her aging, refined features left unadorned and honest, not even the pretense of lipstick. Valerie, with roots in a European culture, was the opposite, loving clothes and makeup. She wore her snow-white hair in a professional chignon that accentuated her once sculpted, almost always smiling face. She had never played sports, and under her loose boutique clothing her body had become pure flesh. Ann, in contrast, played tennis year-round and her figure was strong and erect. She was a county social worker, and her character seemed well suited to that profession. One minute in her company told you she was a good listener, down to earth, and empathetic. Her kind face invited confidence.

Their little entourage moved to the traditionally furnished living room, led by Sheldon who limped with a cane, his hip replacement of years before no longer of benefit. He was tall, almost a head taller than Nick, his angular physique stooped with age, but not badly, and he still had his hair, white like Valerie's.

"Now, if only Emily could get here on time, then I could stop worrying about the clock," Valerie said. "The dining room had no problem adding two more to our table—they changed us to a round table, which I like much better than the squares; they're so festive in feeling. I hope Eric remembers to bring a jacket—you know the rules."

"That nihilist is not going to bring a jacket, Valerie, don't be dumb."

Sheldon's usual cut made everyone stiffen as always, and Nick piped up, also out of habit. "Dad, it's not acceptable to call Mom or anyone dumb."

"That's dumb too."

In the old days a battle between father and son would have ensued, but for some time now Nick had been able to state his point and remain silent after that, closing his eyes to his father's provocative rebuttals. Well, sometimes he still bit back.

"I guess he can borrow one from the dining room if need be," Valerie said.

"Ann, how are you?" Nick said, seating himself next to his sister on the couch.

"Great, same as always—work, life, kids. Well, the kids are doing their own lives now. It happens later these days—Janey's thirty-five—but at least it still happens. How about you? Happy about Obama?"

"Totally. Safe for another four years. And hopefully with change at last."

"Don't kid yourself," Sheldon said. "The man's a weakling—he's not going to accomplish anything. He let the little taxpayers bail out the banks while the fat cheaters kept their wealth and loopholes."

"Did you vote?"

"Of course I did, against the Republicans."

"Nick, I got *Lisbon Story* from Netflix so we can watch it when we're too full to move from the couch," Valerie said, joining them with the DVD in her hand.

"Great. I love that movie."

"That's why I got it."

Ann hadn't heard of it, so Nick told her about its Lisbon setting and mesmerizing music by the ensemble called Madredeus. Sheldon listened from his armchair, his cane across his knees. He had always been on the outskirts of the family, Nick thought, brooding restlessly, irritably, and looking for a way to enter into their pleasant circle but finding a line he couldn't cross, one he himself had created with his irascible, insulting, and occasionally violent behavior, the latter brought on by drinking sprees. Drinking in general unleashed male rage, Nick thought, and remembered how he and Ann had hidden as children, or escaped through a window or back door whenever they heard Sheldon go on a rampage. But Ann had never been the target of Sheldon's wrath, only Nick and Valerie. And Valerie had been too petite to stop his vicious outbursts, particularly when he struck, shoved, or kicked Nick out of his way, but her love and personal responsibility for her children had been a positive influence in their lives. Nick and Charlotte had argued and shouted, but Nick had been so acutely sensitive to insults and innuendos shot from his father's mouth that he had never uttered such words himself—he had shouted only logic, or what he saw as logical defenses against her tirades. Charlotte had demanded so much, and relentlessly—everything her way. She had become a gendarme, a commando, never the fun, exuberant, and idea-filled young woman he had loved and bound his life to. She got serious, ultra-serious, and exacting, and completely involved in Emily's upbringing and in the labyrinth of school and community activities, with nothing left over for him or their relationship besides faultfinding. He and Charlotte drifted apart about the time Emily started kindergarten. By then Charlotte was teaching in the progressive private school she had carefully chosen for Emily, and Nick, the former househusband, got a job at Trowbridge. He loved the publishing scene, teeming with female editors—it was sexually electric. He thrived on his freedom at the city bars and clubs after work with colleagues. The years sped by, and suddenly love was gone and Charlotte had a new man.

As always, Valerie had put out Nick's favela book on the coffee table, its faded cover showing ragged children. No one ever mentioned the book if Sheldon was in the room, to avoid hearing him criticize its lack of scientific guidelines. All of Nick's information, passed off as truth, was purely subjective and thus not credible, he invariably groused. It didn't matter that the *Globe*'s review, now brown with age and tucked inside the front cover, had commended it. To Sheldon, Nick just wasn't as good as other writers, and should know it, from his father.

"Are you keeping up your squash?" Valerie asked.

"Haven't played it in years," Nick said.

"Oh, yes, I forgot," she said.

He had almost lost his right eye, his own fault for not wearing goggles, but no need to recall that oversight in front of Sheldon.

"It's a stupid sport anyway," Sheldon barked from his chair.

"You should have played more tennis. It takes more skill. How I miss it. Are you still playing, Annie?"

She nodded. "I have a new partner and we're pretty evenly matched, so I really hope it lasts."

"I gave up on that book you lent me," Valerie said to Nick, pressing her lips with a mixture of dislike and regret. "I got so bored."

Nick smiled. "Oh, well, it was worth a try."

"What was it?" Ann asked. She was another avid reader.

"One of Nick's highbrow imports," Sheldon said.

"Don't be silly, Shelly," Valerie said conversationally. "There's nothing wrong with reading Nobel Prize winners. Wasn't Saul Bellow one of your favorites?" She turned back to Nick. "I wasn't getting all the subtext—I know that because I looked it up on Wikipedia. After the first half, all Ricardo did all day was read the newspaper and comment on it inside his head. *Basta!* I said. Who cares about this news? I'm sorry, Nick, I know he's a great Portuguese writer and maybe there's something else by him I could try."

"Can I borrow it?" Ann said.

"Of course. It's right on the shelf—I'll get it."

"Mom's right, it does slow down in the second half, but the premise is incredible—I won't explain—you have to experience it for yourself."

"Why couldn't he just continue with his first half of the story instead of getting mired in newspapers?"

"He had a political agenda, and besides, Ricardo has to fade away so that the story threads in the beginning also fade away. Why don't you try *Blindness*? It's a page-turner."

"Hmm, the title sounds heavy. But I'll see if the library has it."

"How's your new job, Nick?" Ann asked.

"I love it. It's totally crazy but all about books."

"The subject is always books," Sheldon sighed.

"I'm so glad," Ann continued. "You're really lucky, given the economy and the book industry's struggles."

"And my age. I just hope I can last there another decade. I need the pension."

"Thank god for my state job," Ann said as Valerie handed her Saramago's book about Ricardo Reis. "Thanks, Mom. Do you want it back?"

"No, thank you, good riddance. No offense, Nick."

"With inflation, even your state benefits are not going to be enough if you live as long as we have," Sheldon said. "We manage to squeak by on our retirement funds, but it won't be the same for either of you, I guarantee it. And unfortunately, our assets aren't going to help you much."

"Let's not talk about money, Shel," Valerie said. "The kids already know everything about our estate."

But finances were the one subject Sheldon liked to talk about. His career had been with the oldest financial investment firm in Boston. His uncle, a partner there, had gotten him an entry-level job, from which he had risen through the ranks. Sheldon hadn't finished college; he had flunked out of Amherst because of his wild ways. The financial job had been intended as a stopgap until the profligate got steady enough to finish his degree. But he had never gone back, though he had taken business courses during his fifty-year tenure at the bank, probably the equivalent of an MBA. The way he ridiculed Nick about his Dartmouth education— "What a party school," "Fluff," "Literature is for women"—suggested his own insecurity, and probable shame about not graduating himself from another heavy-party school, where, oddly enough, he had been thoroughly involved in theater—not exactly a macho major. If anyone asked, Sheldon always said he was an Amherst man. He never criticized Ann's Mount Holyoke education, nor her degree in dance. His gripe was with his son, though Nick had never done anything to warrant the ire. Some bad baggage involving fathers and sons had simply been passed down the generations, and fortunately it stopped with Nick, not only because he had had a daughter and not a son, but also because he had no poison whatsoever inside him for others.

Why had Valerie fallen in love with Sheldon? Nick had asked himself that question many times. And he could guess the answer. It was apparent in the earliest family photo album. His father had been tall, handsome, a jock, and from a wealthy Brahmin family, though the wealth had not lasted. When smitten with Valerie one summer on the beach, Sheldon had undoubtedly shown his charm, not the chip on his shoulder, or the chip hadn't even been there yet. She had fallen for his bravado and confidence in his own superiority and heritage. Instant physical chemistry had hooked them. Nick, in contrast, had fallen in love with Charlotte's character and personality first as they worked together in the Rocinha cultural center. Friendship and love for who she was had stimulated chemistry. Nothing, Nick thought, especially love, was ever the same in life. It was random, serendipitous, and case by case. He suspected that his father early on had become jaded by his imprisonment in a banking business that stifled his natural creativity and zest, which he had not been able to harness in time for a career in theater.

The intercom phone rang to announce the arrival of Emily and Eric. A moment later, they breezed through the front door, Emily first, her face alight with her mother's sweet smile. Eric, long dark hair curling into his untrimmed beard, followed like a shadow, clearly a misfit in the sedate, antique-filled apartment.

Everyone looked straight through Emily to her shaggy companion and his rotting sneakers. His hemless jeans showed frayed holes in the thighs, and his black Metallica T-shirt was emblazoned with the words *Metal Up Your Ass*, with a graphic showing a toilet bowl with a sword sticking up out of it. Nick closed his eyes. Why was Eric wearing such a shirt on Thanksgiving Day? If asked, he would feign nonchalance, pure innocence: "Oh, I wasn't thinking. This was on the top of the pile." But the truth was, he was still going through his adolescent rebellious stage at age twenty-five. In contrast, Emily's vintage wool skirt that came almost to her ankles, laced black boots, and gray blouse with pleated front would pass muster in the dining room. In fact, Nick smiled to himself, she looked as Victorian as her namesake from Amherst. And she had appeal.

Valerie had to finish her thrilled hugs and kisses with her granddaughter before any other greetings could take place. Then she turned to Eric and said as she gave him a perfunctory hug, "Sorry, buddy, but the dining room won't admit you in that getup."

"I tried to get him to change," Emily said.

"What's wrong with my clothes?" Eric said. "This is how people in my profession dress and no one tells us we have to change."

"Where do you come from?" Sheldon growled.

Eric's hackles went up, but his voice kept calm. "I live with Emily in Somerville."

"I mean your family, your father, where did you grow up? The Bronx?"

"Granddad—" Emily warned.

"His dad teaches at Harvard Law School, Shel," Valerie said drily. "He's lived in Cambridge his whole life."

"Except when I went to Brown," Eric said. "Which only lasted two years."

Sheldon's eyebrows shot up—a college dropout like himself. "Is this how your family dresses on Thanksgiving Day?"

"What is this, an interrogation all because I like to dress like myself? I happen to have band practice right after this."

"He's a drummer," Valerie said.

"Oh, percussion," Sheldon said drearily and turned away to limp back to his comfortable armchair.

"Sheldon, Eric's going to need some duds," Valerie said.

Grumbles could be heard in response as Sheldon settled into the soft upholstery.

"Dad, I can help Eric borrow a few things, okay? Old stuff you don't use anymore." Ann said—Ann the therapist, who mediated troubled families for her daily bread.

"For chrissake, he's going to need shoes, goddammit, and I know he's got an incurable fungus from walking around 24/7 in those hideous things he's wearing. What an idiot."

"Granddad just talks like that," Emily said to Eric, who was staring openmouthed at Sheldon.

"Yeah, you warned me, but . . ." This was Eric's first face-to-face interaction with Sheldon. A grin suddenly broke over the renegade's face, and he sang to Emily the old Marvin Gaye and Tammi Terrell lyric, "'Ain't nothing like the real thing, baby.'"

Nick saw Ann smile. She always had a heart for the underdog.

"Hey," Eric said with sudden inspiration, "maybe I'll get a new song out of this little holiday, the Ballard Ballad."

And Sheldon would be the protagonist, a star at last, Nick said to himself.

"Eric, follow me," Ann said. "We can fix you up a bit for the dining room."

"As long as it's not too extreme," Eric said.

They were gone after that, and for a fair amount of time, though their voices could be heard from the bedroom, Eric's deep and glib and Ann's also deep but measured. It was a compatible exchange, whatever they were actually saying—probably the pros and cons of a solid versus a striped shirt, and which pants would match. Then the shoes. A few smirks could be heard from Eric, and made Nick think the young freewheeler had rejected Sheldon's wingtips from the fifties and his shiny penny loafers from the sixties. After that, their voices vanished into the bathroom for grooming around the face. Eric's long locks were only a few stages from becoming dreads.

Meanwhile, Valerie took the opportunity to have a fast one-on-one conversation with Emily. Nick went to the adjacent kitchenette for a glass of water, then washed the breakfast dishes in the sink to keep out of the living room a bit longer. His mother sounded satisfied to hear Emily's repeated confirmations that she was doing well, and no, her depression was much better, her mind was focused on getting into grad school and starting a new life. Yes, things were good with Eric too. He was okay—in fact, she loved him, at least right now. His clothes and beard didn't bother her—most of her guy friends dressed like that—and besides, what was important was their friendship. They could talk.

"Well, being able to talk is important," Valerie said.

"But Emmy, it's obvious he's far beneath you," Sheldon cut in loudly, no doubt hoping Eric would hear. "He's f-word dirty!"

"Granddad, be quiet! He can hear you! When I was a total mess last year, Eric took care of me. And when he went through a bad spell the year before, I took care of him. We remember that."

"That's definitely the wrong reason to be in a relationship," Sheldon objected.

"What do you mean? Love is about caring and helping, besides other things. It deepens bonds. Besides, you don't know anything about . . . about . . . what happened to me last year."

Sheldon backed off, and Nick conveniently came back into the room with a tray of ice water for everyone. No way he wanted Emmy telling his parents the details of last year's crisis.

"I'm sorry, Emmy," the old man rumbled and pointed his cane at her. "I just don't want to die tomorrow thinking you ended up with a hippie drummer dropout who goes to Thanksgiving dinner, as a guest, wearing an obscene T-shirt. And tattoos. He has to be out of his mind."

On cue the "hippie" emerged from the bedroom with his stylist. Silence greeted him, for he actually looked pretty good.

"Wow, I want to marry you, dude," Emily said.

"Done, I say yes," Eric said.

Everyone else froze at the thought.

Eric looked down at his pressed attire. "I have to admit, I feel kinda strange, but in a way it's fun to wear a costume and assume a different identity—like Halloween."

"Your beard looks good, and your hair, but I'm not sure about those Topsiders," Emily said with a smile.

"Unfortunately they were the only choice I was willing to accept." Eric grinned. "No offense, Sheldon."

"Those are my favorite shoes—souvenirs from sailing days on the Cape. I wish you had picked something else."

Ann had trimmed his beard and sideburns to a rakish shape along his jaw, and his dark tangle of hair had been brushed back into a neat ponytail.

"You'll do," Valerie pronounced. "Yes, indeed."

"And I'd appreciate it if you didn't spill on my clothes," Sheldon groused. "Better yet, take them to the dry cleaners after the meal and return them later."

"He's joking. Get used to it," Valerie said, smiling at Eric. Now that he looked halfway decent, she found she could talk to him.

"Don't contradict me, Valerie. I'm not joking in the least," Sheldon said.

"When I was a girl, I played the guitar and sang," Valerie told Eric. "Forties music, though I love all the folk music that came later—Dylan, Baez, Leonard Cohen—"

"I can't stand Leonard Cohen—he drones," Sheldon cut her off. "Isn't he dead yet?"

"I'll show you a picture of me," Valerie said, going to the bookshelf and taking down the oldest family album. "Here, that's me with the guitar."

"That's you? You're kidding!" Eric said incredulously. "Wow! I don't recognize you. I mean, it's natural to grow old, you look fine old, but back then you were a knockout."

"Don't you think Emmy looks like me?"

He stared down at the picture again. "Not really, but this is just a picture. I can't see your face in action. Who're all these guys you're playing for?"

"GIs. When they came home on leave, we entertained them at the local USO."

"What's that?"

"Shoot, I forget what it stands for," she said.

"What's wrong with your memory? United Service Organization," Sheldon said. He had served in the navy.

"It meant so much to the men—and to me too," Valerie went on happily. "I was singing 'We'll Meet Again' in this picture," and her eyes drifted off to her memory of the occasion, and she hummed the tune. Then the lyrics came and she opened her sparkling eyes to sing to Eric, "'We'll meet again, don't know where, don't know when, but I know we'll meet again, some sunny day.'"

"Cool."

Nick looked at his father, expecting a cutting remark, but the old man's lips held back and his eyes looked inward. Perhaps he was remembering Valerie singing and smiling at him personally, maybe on the beach under romantic moonlight. Who wouldn't have loved Valerie? Nick thought, tears welling up in his eyes. Why couldn't his father have simply loved her all those years—their lifetimes—instead of giving her a hard time? What a waste. Nick knew Sheldon loved and valued Valerie, making the waste even greater. But he doubted his mother felt the same way—too much had killed that love. Nor did Nick love his father. Familial duty was all that was left, but it was good enough, he thought. Love had to come from a parent first and not the other way around, if love was to flourish, for children naturally loved their parents, even confused, angry parents, although one day many of these children—and Nick included himself among them—gave up trying to love in order to save themselves. Ann loved Sheldon, for Sheldon loved her. The old adage was around for a reason: what you gave, you got back. In all families, Nick thought, love and relationships were in a state of constant flux or crisis. Ultimately, despite Sheldon's behavior, the family had functioned productively.

That night driving home, Nick couldn't turn off his thoughts of Eric and Emily and how he himself had not defended Eric against Sheldon's slurs. He should have, at least halfheartedly. Hearing Emily with emotion in her voice as she declared to Sheldon that he didn't know anything about what had happened to her the year before, and that Eric's support had helped her, impressed Nick with his own failure to accept and appreciate Eric. Emily's story was one that couldn't be told. Only a few people knew what had precipitated her psychosis and hospitalization, and Eric was one, and he had not abandoned her. Nick needed to see other sides of Eric besides his immaturity, physical appearance, lack of responsibility, probable dope-dealing, and college-dropout status. Funny how Sheldon had heard that detail but had not harped on it.

And how nice, all in all, the Thanksgiving dinner had been at the round table in the dining room, with Sheldon happy to eat turkey, cranberries, and squash and thus less focused on sniping at others. And Valerie had regaled them with all kinds of tall tales about the early Portuguese explorers and navigators who had opened trade routes to India and Africa and even tested out the Americas before Columbus. Nick had no idea how much of her information was true or family lore. She told Eric how the wave of Portuguese immigration in the 1800s had brought her family to New Bedford. They were Azoreans—fishermen, shipbuilders— and New Bedford's whaling industry had been a draw. Unfortunately, the language had been lost because her grandparents had wanted to blend in, especially because the WASP establishment ridiculed them as a colored race. Luckily all that horrible prejudice was over, she had said with her usual optimism, and Nick had learned Portuguese and lived in Brazil, and Emily had studied in Lisbon, full immersion. Now it was even fashionable to boast about their heritage. They had come full circle. Didn't Eric think it was amazing?

Eric had asked a few questions and then confessed he hadn't known anything about Emily's family history until that moment.

"Then what do you two talk about? You live together, don't you?" Sheldon barked. "What are your roots?"

"Germany. We're Jewish, Holocaust survivors from Berlin, or my grandparents were."

Sheldon had mumbled something apologetic, like "I'm sorry to hear that, and I'm glad your family's safe in America."

"Actually, they all died in the camps except for my grand-parents."

Uncomfortable with the conversation that he had started, Sheldon had waved his fork. "The Turners came on the *Mayflower*. You've heard of that, I suppose?"

"You mean the *Mayflower* or the Turners?" Eric had answered, causing the others to laugh. Even Shelly had smiled.

Yes, there was lots to process from the long day in Marion. Well, he had the whole holiday weekend ahead and no further plans, though probably he should make some. He wondered what Flo had done that day—had she gone to New York and feasted with a large contingent of her family? What was her family like? How did she interact with them? Did they have black sheep and martyrs? He had her book on college prostitutes; she had given him a signed copy just before the office closed for the holiday weekend. He would start reading it that night, find out about the world she had explored for several years of her life; he would enter her space, and through her subjects learn about her. Because of Emily, the subject of women and ownership of their bodies touched his life deeply. Being given the book by Flo gave them a strange and ironic connection, which he'd understand better once he read the book. His foot pressed down on the gas pedal in his eagerness to get home to the book.

FOUR

Boston got through the December and New Year's holidays. Nick attended the usual festive parties, enjoyed meals with Emily, and spent New Year's Eve at the Harvard Club with Oscar drinking club sodas with lime. Now the heart of winter lay ahead—January and February. Days were dark by six, and temperatures could be counted on to park in the twenties. To Nick, Boston's unrelenting cold seemed reflected in the biting personalities and harsh accent of the Bay Staters. They were a tenacious breed. And they ice-skated just as fiercely, as if to strike back at the cold and win an invisible battle. Winter was part of their blood and productivity.

Nick liked the winter, the gray landscape barren of green, the trees fanning their brittle branches against clotted, snow-threatening skies. His senses came alive, stimulated by the cold. After work, in the dark, the city's skyscraping lights dazzled with a diamond brilliance that invited the spirit to soar. Winter energized, and there was plenty to enjoy about it, especially the first big snowfall when it came. Or those periodic, liquid blue skies under hard sunshine that demanded gratitude.

Early January sped by with the work routine revving up to its familiar breakneck pace. Each morning Nick took one of his regular routes to the office, now wearing his parka, hat, and gloves. He was feeling settled with the Churchill routine, accustomed to the grueling Monday-through-Friday workflow. By the end of the those five days, he was ready for the weekend, all of his projects funneled into the semblance of order on his desk and shelves—a process that had taken him the entire week to accomplish. Then Monday rolled around again and bombed his systematization. E-mails from the weekend were a yard long and created new, urgent matters to tend to, or undid all the work he had accomplished the week before. This happened frequently when the acquisitions editor Margie Rockwell, who worked much of the time from her home in Maine and rarely during business hours, decided to dig into one of her projects just after Nick, tired of waiting to hear from her, had gone ahead with decisions for it. Margie supposedly commuted but usually called in to say something had come up that would keep her at home, such as relatives descending on her for lunch on a weekday, or a problem with a family member, or a house repair. She was notorious for upending projects after their deadline, but because she was a valued acquisitions editor, she had not been fired. Slowly Nick heard the same complaints about her from his colleagues: changes after deadlines, no foresight, can't plan, always forgetting to do something she intended. Forgetful, period. He knew every workplace had its bad colleague who sabotaged projects, possibly pathologically, and at Churchill it was Margie. He also observed that she blamed her shortcomings on others.

Despite the Margie factor, and Churchill's idiosyncratic process for making books, he loved his job; he loved the constant, intense production process that brought colleagues to his door asking for this or that. He loved the urgent dynamism of the place, everyone ratcheted up to his or her capacity in the business of publishing books. It was a deadline-driven business, a world of launches, jacket shows, and meetings, and felt like chaos but highly stimulating and exciting chaos.

Island Peril had moved ahead before Thanksgiving, cutting standard steps, such as proper legal review, all because of Flo's arm-waving assurances. "The book has a Pulitzer Prize–winning author, for cripes sake!" she bleated.

Editorial work had begun even before Chad and John signed contracts. Nick had assigned the book to Liza Metcalf because of her erudition. He had wanted to test the book out on a critical reader and wasn't surprised when her spare figure and graying ponytail came to his office door within twenty-four hours, manuscript in hand, to say, "Nick, do you really believe this story?"

"I think it's embellished, to say the least."

"It might seem fine to an average reader," she said, "but anyone who thinks is going to question the facts. It doesn't add up."

"Please tell Flo that."

"I will."

But Flo was in a hurry, eager to show her superiors, and the world, that she could produce a blockbuster on a crash schedule. "I have instincts about this book, Nick, and they're good—or the book's good."

"The writing's really good. Why don't we send it back to Chad and John and ask for a novel?"

She shook her head. "True stories get devoured by everyone— men, women, Oprah, filmmakers."

They had plunged ahead, with Flo asking Fran to make the layout a priority. Fran had finished the design in two days—again, all before Thanksgiving. Susie Mumford had handled the workflow from there, dealing with an outside copyeditor and proofreader who were willing to work during the holidays. Now, the second week in January, the book was at the printer's. Press releases sat ready for the advance copies that would be sent to reviewers and booksellers. Never had Churchill produced a book so fast. That was the power of Flo's influence.

As another frantic day at Churchill concluded, Nick gladly pulled his backpack over his parka sleeves to head home. Quiet time in his comfy domicile awaited him—and dinner. He liked unwinding in the kitchen and putting together an appetizing meal from fresh produce. Nuts and fruit for dessert. Occasionally, for a treat, he bought pizza on the way home and enjoyed the indulgence in bread and melted cheese.

Flo was standing at the elevators in an elegant, belted black parka with a fur-trimmed hood. She wore boots and wine-colored leather gloves. They rode down together and stepped out of the building into the frosty evening with the smell of snow in the air. Copley Square twinkled like an old-fashioned Boston scene painted by Childe Hassam.

"I'll walk you home," Nick said. "If you're going home."

"I am. For once I don't have to meet someone after work, meaning keep on working. But it's not on your way, is it?"

"Sure. I take the Marlborough route half the time. It's my favorite street."

"Mine too. Cozier. Now that I have you for a minute, I should ask you about the history of Back Bay."

"It's a landfill."

"Duh. That's the first thing they tell you when you shop for a condo. Hey, why don't we go for a drink? We never get a chance to relax and say hello to each other in the office. You must know some good places around here."

He looked around, hating all the rowdy pubs on Boylston Street. "How about Dunne's?"

"Dunne's? Garrett and I end up there every time the fridge is empty, which is most of the time."

"Then—"

"No, Dunne's is perfect, Jake's my pal. Do you know Jake? The bartender?"

Nick shook his head. "I haven't been there in years."

She told him what she knew about Dunne's as they walked to the bar, briskly, the cold propelling them and her boot heels keeping time. They talked about other Boston restaurants, which they agreed couldn't compete with New York's variety and plentitude. But still, good food was to be found. "It's funny, isn't it," Flo said, chatting pleasantly, "in New York you'd find a thousand Dunne's, maybe ten thousand, but in Boston there's one Dunne's. And one Union Oyster House. One of everything."

"And twenty-thousand Dunkin' Donuts."

"I was just about to add that. What is it with Dunkin' Donuts?"

"Tradition, habit, decent coffee."

"Not a habit I'm likely to develop."

"No, I can't picture you standing in line at Dunkin' Donuts."

She laughed, so did he, and he had to hold back from throwing his arm around her. He felt a surge of happiness—walking in cold weather with someone you were powerfully attracted to was one of winter's delights. The cold air stimulated everything and easily led to welcome hugs not just to keep warm but also to let out exuberance.

"Helloooo." Flo smiled at him. "Knock, knock . . . did you hear what I just said?"

"Oh, sorry—"

"What were you thinking?" She held him with her amused, expectant eyes, as if she already knew and actually believed he would tell her. He laughed. Oh, yeah, she had an idea all right.

The tavern saved him. "Here we are," he said, opening the varnished wood door for her and following her in.

The long bar gleamed and the clientele seated there was not the boisterous crowd along Boylston Street. A lot of gray heads sipped drinks and ate standard bar food.

Flo greeted Jake, the balding, heavyset bartender, like an old friend, and he in turn, a classic straight-faced proprietor, smiled tightly and waved his arm for them to be seated wherever they liked. Booths lined the walls and small wooden tables, the kind used by Van Gogh's card players, filled the center.

"Does this look good, Nick?" Flo asked, moving toward one of the booths.

"Perfect. Here, I'll take your coat."

He hung their coats on pegs and then slid into the booth opposite her. The table was hard and nicked, the varnished benches the same. Jake came over to take their order.

"Jake, this is Nick Turner, our new and bestest editor at Churchill. Can you believe this is the first time since he came on board that we've had a moment to get a drink after work?"

"This breaks the ice then," Jake said with a crooked smile, "no pun intended. What can I get you, Nick? You're chardonnay, right, sweetheart?"

"Make it a scotch on the rocks tonight, since we're breaking the ice."

Nick ordered the same, wondering if he would drink it or just sniff it and pretend to drink. He had been unable in that moment to be himself and order soda water. Or maybe he was actually being himself by ordering the scotch, for every moment existed in its own peculiar right, and this was a rare moment with Flo that involved spirits.

They talked about New York. She had grown up on the Upper East Side, but modestly, she stressed. Her father was a literary attorney and her mother a wannabe writer. "Oh, I shouldn't diss her like that," Flo said. "She had, or still has, talent and published some stories when she was young, but she gave it all up for Jim and me. Are you still writing?"

"No, just my notebook—my journal."

"That's good. I used to keep a journal too, but now . . . when do you find time?"

"I have time. I live alone."

"I guess that does give you a few hours to yourself."

The drinks arrived and Flo in her solicitous way detained Jake for a moment to ask him how long the tavern had been in Back Bay.

"You got me," he shrugged, his solid black eyebrow in a permanent frown. "But anything you want to know about the Bruins I can tell you." The flat-screen TV at the far corner of the bar was tuned in softly to the evening's game.

"What's the score?" Nick asked.

"Nothing yet, they just started. I'll let you know when we score." He sallied back to the bar.

Nick leaned forward. "I read somewhere that Beacon Street was once a long mill dam that didn't work out. It also blocked the regular tidal flushing so that sewage and trash that got dumped there stayed there and eventually caused a health problem with rats and mosquitoes. Besides stinking. So they filled the flats and built Back Bay."

"From sewage to beauty," Flo said, brown eyes shimmering

in the table's candlelight. She leaned toward him conspiratorially, hands fanning on the table. "I have a secret to confess—I don't miss New York, or maybe just the sizzle of its nightlife, all that entertainment. I mean, Boston's pretty tame, wouldn't you say? But then, it's got something else. Something indelible. Character. And I'm hooked."

The scotch was flowing in Nick's veins and tingling his lips. "I'm glad." He smiled. "That means you'll stay."

"I want to."

"Which reminds me, I've never had a chance to talk to you about your book, besides saying I read it," he said.

"And I'm grateful you read it."

"It was deep. I learned so much about that kind of prostitution. Things I never considered before. Like how much the enjoyment of luxury plays into it, and how some of these women actually enjoy their gigs."

"People like sex. I learned so much myself. And I wanted to contribute something."

"You did. I kept wondering what made you tackle the topic. It's painful. The stories are sad. It must have been depressing to write about."

Her head moved slowly from side to side, her lips parted and her eyes drifting down, as if she had no easy answer to his question. In the shadows, the romantic shadows, her soft brown hair fell over the sides of her face. Those lovely contours in soft focus now wore a veil. Nick suddenly thought that perhaps she had firsthand experience in the world she had so intrepidly interviewed and exposed, and that had led to the book. Or maybe a close friend. He quickly shifted the conversation.

"At any rate, the book's great—the stories cover the whole spectrum and with such compassion." He didn't add how the book also connected poignantly to his own life through Emily, and how many times tears had stung his eyes reading the young women's stories of selling their bodies.

"Tell me about Brazil," she said, her smile and eyes inviting him to divulge his inner life, as if she really cared.

"I haven't been back since a vacation in '93."

"Your favelas were just as sad as my prostitutes."

"The world changes—those same favelas are little cities now, even tourist destinations."

"Incredible. Though I'm not sure they'd be my tourist destination."

"Or mine. Where would you go tomorrow if you could go anywhere?" he asked.

"It's not a question of where I would like to go, but where I'm actually going. Garrett and I are taking a very long weekend in Dominica."

"The Antilles?"

"How did you know? I never heard of it before. We're taking an eco-tour. Garrett's into that kind of thing. Organic food, sustainable everything, save the planet. I don't know why he married me. I never think about my carbon footprint. Anyway, Dominica's supposed to be the most beautiful of all the islands—pure nature. Rainforest, wildlife, endless views. I'm ready for that kind of repose. It's been a tough year at Churchill, and we had to forfeit our summer vacation, though we did take a week in the Berkshires. Nick, I fight that old guard every day—I haven't come close to making all the changes I planned."

"You've done a lot. Everyone sees it."

"Thank you. No such encouragement from above, though we get along."

"I think they love you."

"If only."

He smiled, but he wasn't going to press the point by saying, Everybody loves you; you've seduced us all. And by the way, is your come-on natural or intentional? Are you real or fake? That's what no one can figure out. In my case, I feel you're real, or I want to believe you are.

He saw her smiling so warmly at him that he couldn't help but trust her. And if she looked deeply enough into his eyes, she would see that he loved her.

The charged moment was broken when Nick's cell phone rang and he automatically pulled it from his pocket to note the caller. Eric. The name made him pause, for Eric never called him, and the night before, when he and Emily had met in Cambridge for dinner, he had noted her signs of mania—agitation, rapid speech, and the sensation of omnipotence. At one point she had leaned forward to whisper that she could hear conversations from across the room and some of the people there were spies. She was pretty sure they had been at the senior center that afternoon and had followed her to the restaurant and now wore disguises so she wouldn't suspect. "Do you think they're spies, Dad?" she had then asked with a sudden vulnerable plea in her eyes, begging him to confirm her beliefs, as if in spite of her inflated confidence she still doubted herself, having lived through two previous manic episodes.

"No, honey, they aren't. What's going on? Are you sleeping?"

"No, I've been up for three and half days and I can't shut down. I want to, but I can't."

"Then you need to call Dr. Coolidge. Don't let this escalate out of control. Can you do that?"

"I will."

"Let's call him now, leave him a message."

"Okay," she said dully, getting out her phone and putting it on the table. "We had a wild weekend. One of my college friends was in town and we hung out the whole time. Eric's band played guitars and we sang and talked. It was one of the best weekends of my life."

But they hadn't slept much, and they had consumed pot and alcohol every day from noon on.

"You can't do that," Nick said.

"I know, but I did."

He didn't want to lecture her, especially when he had been young and lived the same way in his twenties. But he had to speak out, for with her brain chemistry she simply couldn't do those things—they spelled disaster. He said as much and she drew a tight mask over her face. That was the flip side of mania—going silent against all the enemies out there. He was now her enemy.

"Honey, you have to go home and somehow find a way to sleep. And sleep all day tomorrow if you can. You're running high and you've got to come down before it's too late. Try to remember last year."

"I do remember, but I'm not like that. I'm fine right now, I feel great."

"Yeah, but it's a fine line, and you're on it. Do you have any medication for sleeping?"

She nodded.

"Will you go home and take it? Can you force yourself not to party tonight? Why don't you stay at my place? Eric's lifestyle has to be avoided right now."

"Don't blame Eric—I'm the one who chose to drink and stay up."

"And look what's happened the first time you've had alcohol in a year. Do you see how dangerous it is for you?

"I do, Dad, obviously. But . . ." She glanced warily at him. "Maybe I'm right and you're wrong. Some people are born with special gifts, special powers. Maybe those people really are from the FBI."

He had driven her home, not trusting her to make her own way without detours that postponed sleep. He had made sure she left a message for Dr. Coolidge to call her and kept reiterating her need for sleep, her need for courage to avoid partying. He had pressed his invitation to come to his place for a few days of rest, but she had insisted on going home. He waited till she entered the house, a triple-decker with an apartment on each floor. She and Eric had the first floor, and he could see their silhouettes through the living room sheers as if a deliberate cue to him from her that all was in control. What control? he thought with frustration as he drove off a little too fast.

He took the call from Eric. "Sorry, Flo, it's my daughter's boyfriend. Maybe something's come up."

"By all means," Flo said generously, and settled back in the booth with her drink, her shimmering brown-black eyes watching him and expressing various emotions as he talked to Eric.

"Hi, Nick. Uhhh, I'm concerned about Emily."

"What happened? Where is she?"

"Uhhh, the truth is, she's flipped and I can't talk her down. I've been with her all day, though she's run off a few times. She's babbling and hyper, disconnected from reality—a lot like last year. I'm worried she might run into the street or something—have an accident."

Nick's heart was beating hard. "Where is she now?"

"That's the thing, she just took off again, and she's lost her phone."

"You mean she's walking your neighborhood?"

"Actually I think she might show up at your place, because I told her she needed to talk to you."

"Okay, thanks, and will you please keep your ringer turned on and answer when I call you?"

"Definitely." But Nick knew that Eric, Emily, and their generation rarely answered their phones. They preferred texting, and when they didn't want to communicate with a parent or friend, they didn't. It could be hard to reach them. And now the line, the only line, to Emily had just ended, and before Nick had thought to say, Call me if you hear from her.

"What happened, Nick?"

He sighed. There was nowhere to begin, but he needed to leave the bar sooner than planned. "Ahhh," he said with another sigh.

"Don't worry, you don't have to tell me," Flo said.

"It isn't that—I have no secrets. It's just a long story, too long. But the short of it is, Emily's bipolar and has flipped. She's out on the street somewhere and I have to find her."

"Why don't you call her?"

"She lost her phone—it goes hand in hand with mania, losing things. She's been stable for a year. I thought we were in an okay place, though last night I started to worry."

"Go—this is important."

They had just about finished their drinks anyway. "Come on, I'll walk you home, it's on my way," he said, getting up and pulling on his parka. He helped her into her coat and left money on the table. They waved to Jake that something had come up and then hastened out the door into the ice-cold night, always like a blast to the face.

How strange it was, Nick thought as they moved briskly down Marlborough Street to her brownstone, that on their first casual get-together outside the office everything had shifted to the deepest personal level, something Flo was treating naturally, as if she were one of his closest friends serendipitously involved in his crisis.

"Let me know what happens," she said when they reached her building, her hand lightly pressing his sleeve. "I hope everything turns out all right. And don't worry about work tomorrow. Do whatever you need to do. Emily comes first."

It was a long Thursday night for Nick, permeated with the surreal ambiance that Emily's psychosis evoked. He wasn't part of the ordinary world surrounding him, the chattering people on the street, the cars driving to destinations, the traffic lights changing from red to green—all was moving along the way it always moved along, only that night Nick was someplace else. It felt like a vast and complicated danger zone inside his head, where the seconds ticked away and his thoughts kept pace to solve the immediate and urgent problems dependent on him. Where was Emily, how was Emily? If they helped her quickly enough this time, the aftermath—the depression—might not be as severe as in the past. He left messages with her doctor and with Charlotte, and for more than an hour drove various routes between his home and hers, his eyes searching the night streets. Then he checked in with Eric, who had nothing to report. She was still at large.

"Why don't you walk around Harvard Square?" Nick said, torn between wanting Eric to contribute to the hunt and at the same time to hold the fort in case Emily returned home. "Eric, would she go to a close friend's?"

"I don't know. I thought of Dan's, but I don't have his number. I can walk over there—it's ten minutes away."

Dan was her closest friend from Bowdoin.

"Call me either way, and don't forget. I'm in Davis Square. I'm going to look around."

Eric agreed, and Nick parked his car. He bought a cup of coffee that his adrenaline didn't need and began patrolling the cold streets around the square, looking into the café windows to see if Emily was among the young people talking or studying.

Eric called. She was there, at Dan's.

"Great! What's the address? I'll be right over," Nick said, hustling back to his car and dropping his half-drunk coffee into a trashcan. Like a cop in hot pursuit of a delinquent, he swerved away from the curb and soared around the one-way streets to reach Powder House Boulevard. But when he swung in the short driveway next to a pale blue Victorian house with white trim, only Eric was waiting, his face wary. Nick knew the laid-back young man feared getting blamed, not only for Emily's latest escape but also for her psychotic episode.

"Where is she?" Nick said, getting out of the car.

"I'm sorry, Nick, I couldn't make her stay. She said she was going for a smoke on the porch—"

"Why didn't you go with her?" He wanted to punch the guy out.

"I did, but she took off."

"Why didn't you chase her down?"

"I did, buddy, but someone in Emily's state is faster than a cheetah and I'm not joking."

Nick clamped down on the unfair words he wanted to hurl at Eric and got back into his car. He took a few deep breaths and unrolled the window. "Come on, I'll drive you home. Maybe she went back there."

They drove through the grid of quiet streets surrounding Davis Square, the old frame Victorians with lights in their windows creating a charming scene that was totally lost on Nick that night as his eyes strained to spot Emily. She wasn't at the apartment, and

Nick drove back to Boston feeling defeated and anxious. The year before when Emily lost her mind she had left him a furious voicemail: "If you don't call me back in the next five minutes, I'm going to jump out this window!"

And that had been the start of finding out about her other life in the city's escort world. She was going to jump out the window because some pimp had trapped her in a Miami hotel room. Darrel Reed had a website cataloging his girls, Nick later discovered, after lots of digging on Google. Emily, thank God, had never gotten that far in his business. She had answered his Craigslist ad for an office assistant. For twenty hours a week at his home office in Brookline she brought his various databases up to date. He ran a mail-order business for discount vitamins and herbal supplements and told Emily he was a retired pharmacist. He was not bad-looking for a man in his early sixties, and since he was a charming sociopath, Emily liked and trusted him. Later, Nick could find no trace of his professional license or degree. He was a fraud and had moved out of state right after Emily's acute psychiatric crisis, probably fearing that Nick would send the cops after him and file a lawsuit. In fact Nick had contacted a private investigator who did an initial search but reported back that Darrel's history was so complex that it would take months and money to uncover. So Nick dropped the case.

Emily had not begun as an escort and had no idea about Darrel's hidden business, but the year in his office had slowly brought her into his subculture with prostitutes her own age, many of them in college. As her mania ascended that autumn, she lost her judgment. By then, she was familiar with Darrel's "other world" and had started to join the other girls at his extravagant parties, where Darrel's friends and clients fawned over her like a prized pet. They gave her rolled-up tips without asking for much in return—just nuzzlings and strokings of her curves. And she needed money—for rent, for food, for her pot and booze with Eric. Nick hadn't known she needed money; she had told him that working for Darrel covered her expenses. Flo's book had said it all: Need led to selling the body, gifts and a luxurious lifestyle became a hunger, and sex and foreplay were tantalizing, especially when free-flowing alcohol and other drugs loosened inhibitions.

Then, in the heat of mania's vanity and grandiosity, Emily had accepted her first invitation to dine at the home of a well-off restaurant owner, who then drugged her drink and raped her when she was barely conscious. She had rope marks on her wrists the next day, without which she would not have recalled anything of the incident. She had told all this to Nick later, while still manic but safe inside McLean Hospital. He suspected most or all of it was true, though manic people often distorted the truth unintentionally.

The rape had haunted her and made her uncertain about Darrel, though she did not tell him about it. His charm and mentoring of her in the vitamin business somehow won out, and she continued on in his world for another two weeks before her mania exploded into madness. Unbeknown to Nick and Charlotte, Darrel and Emily flew to Miami for a supposed natural health trade show, but shortly after arriving at their resort hotel he abandoned her for some kind of emergency business in the Keys. For three days Emily stayed awake, smoked pot, drank alcohol, and moved like a zombie through the resort's strange, excessive, transgendered escort world, and eventually slept with a bisexual drag queen. When Darrel returned to the hotel, Emily began screaming at him for bringing her to this warped cosmos, for using her to attract newbies to his cheap business. At this point Nick had actually heard her screaming, for she had called him from the hotel room. "Darrel's a liar, a liar! I need to get home. Now!" He didn't know how much was real or made up, but he did know Darrel was in the room and Emily was in terrible trouble. At one point Darrel took the phone from her, and in a pseudo-educated, professorial voice—one of his self-inventions—he said to Nick, "This is Dr. Reed, a friend of your daughter's, and unfortunately she appears to be in a psychotic state. She needs to go to the emergency room." Emily grabbed back the phone and reiterated violently that Darrel was a liar and a sociopath.

Nick assured her that he was coming to get her immediately, but it would take a day, for there wouldn't be flights till the morning. "It's important to stay on the phone with us," he told her. "I want you to talk to your mother while I arrange my flight and get packed. Then we'll talk again. We'll stay on the phone. Will you answer if Mom calls?"

Emily said yes, quietly, as if relieved, as if suddenly back in control. "And you're coming now to get me?"

"I'm leaving on the first flight available. Just stay calm."

After they hung up, he called Charlotte with the news, stressing the urgency of keeping Emily on the line. She said she would call her right away. Then Nick had raced around to book a flight and hotel room. He packed his bag. He called Emily, but she didn't pick up. He called Charlotte, but she didn't answer. He hoped that meant the two of them were talking. Sometime during this interlude Emily left him her threatening message, which he didn't notice until after he had arrived in Florida: "If you don't call me back in the next five minutes, I'm going to jump out this window!" It was the hotel window, and her dramatic response to Darrel's intent to "5150" her, which meant calling the cops and committing her to a seventy-two-hour lockdown. Nick knew that in her state of mind, impulses ruled and she was fully capable of throwing herself out the window, partly to hurt the world and partly to prove her bravado. But hotel security and the police had wrestled her down, handcuffed her, and tied her to a stretcher, which left the hotel for a waiting ambulance that drove her to one of the saddest cages for mental patients that Nick had ever seen. She was incarcerated there the mandatory time, while Nick went through difficult red tape to get her discharged. When finally they drove through the gates of red-brick McLean, it was like arriving at an Ivy League college. And the gentle admissions process and everything that followed in the ward for the next ten days was based on respect and the highest professional integrity.

And here they were again, just about a year later, facing a new crisis and probably another stay at the hospital that still carried the ghostly aura of its past luminaries, among them James Taylor and Sylvia Plath.

Nick's thoughts ran fast through his head as he drove across Longfellow Bridge to home, scrutinizing the sidewalks for Emily. When they went to the movies they often walked over the bridge at night, and once she had stopped to look down at the black, choppy waters. "How do people like Virginia Woolf stuff their pockets with stones and drown?" She had shuddered and moved on. "I couldn't die that way." He wanted to trust their pact that she would call him if she ever got that close to suicide, but he knew that a person in the throes of insanity would never remember a pact.

"How odd," he murmured to himself, coming off the bridge and heading for the garage where he had a space. Manic depression might actually have saved Emily from joining Darrel's fleet. He understood how once you were involved in a subculture like that—

a community of people you actually liked—your entire life could move in a bad direction. It was like *Boogie Nights*. If that cute young man hadn't wanted to make a quick fiver by showing his dick, he might not have ended up in the underworld of porn. Were some people more vulnerable to going astray than others, or was money such a heinous motivator?

To his amazement, Emily was sitting on his stoop when he came along the cold night street from the garage. Her cheetah legs had brought her there. She looked like a derelict, disheveled, eyes ultra-watchful, face unsmiling, even hostile. But if she was feeling hostile to him, why was she there? He sat down next to her, put his arm around her.

"How are you?"

She stared straight ahead, didn't answer. An unlit cigarette dangled from her right hand. He knew words coming from him entered her ears but with all kinds of potential distortions, and her responses would be automatic, not real responses, for her mind at that moment was whirling at breakneck speed, like an LP playing at 78 rpm. It left her no opening to process rationally and respond. And besides, everyone was an enemy, out to trick her.

"Let's go inside."

"No."

He was so afraid of pushing the button that would make her leap up and run away that he sat there, racking his brain about what to do. He needed to get her to the hospital, but the mention of that word or any word related to helping her would set her off.

"We can make some tea, relax on the couch. Watch a movie."

"I like it here."

Her brief glances at him showed a frozen face, steely, impenetrable eyes. He couldn't find the human in her, and that was the danger. Mass General was a few blocks away, but he wanted to get her to McLean, where they had her records and where she could stay until well again.

"Emmy, we need to help you."

"How? You're the devil. Everyone's the devil."

Before he could think of an appropriate response, she got up, thin as a rail and deerlike. "Let's walk," she said, setting off down the hill toward the river. The river—how he feared it.

He went right after her, his mind racing for solutions. He hoped that at Charles Street he would see a cop car and ask for help, but it was a freezing night and the usual nightlife was dead. He needed the police, or an ambulance; reining Emily in was beyond his power. But he also knew that the tactics of the police would set her off. She would kick and scream, fight for her freedom, and then they would face another kind of arrest—for assault—and courtroom ordeals once she got out of McLean. He had to get her himself, through peaceful means.

He was running to keep up with her. She was on the bridge, flailing her arms and yelling at the world for all its stupidities and atrocities. When she got to the other side, with him calling futilely after her, he knew it was hopeless. She was disappearing into the night, and her mind was gone. No good could come of it unless she landed in a place to rest, a safe haven. Panting, he came to a slow stop and watched her rapidly recede down Main Street. He did not call 911, and he knew Charlotte would denounce him the next day for that failure. But he'd ride that tide. Much as he had just lost Emily, something else had happened—he had placed faith in the kernel of sanity that still dwelled somewhere in her recesses. He placed faith in her ability to survive the night out there on the frozen streets. She would go home to Eric or she would go somewhere familiar, because she knew it was best to be safe; she knew her father was counting on her good sense.

He didn't sleep that night, though he dozed a few times, checking his cell phone whenever he woke up to see if he'd missed a text from Eric. Charlotte was now in the loop and would wait for more news from Nick; Dr. Coolidge had called back and would be ready for them at McLean. They just needed Emily and the right combination of factors to arrive at the hospital door.

Nick was showered, dressed, and ready to go out on the streets again when Oscar phoned him at seven.

"Emily's here."

"I'll be right over. Thank you, Oscar, thank you so much." He rushed out of his apartment while still talking on the phone. "What happened?"

"She came in my back door while I was asleep."

"Your back door was unlocked?"

"Let's not get into that. It was providence. She was sitting on the couch when I came downstairs a few minutes ago. Here, say hello to your dad."

After a shuffling noise, Emily's flat, monosyllabic voice grunted, "Hey."

"I'm so glad you're there, Emmy, I'm on my way to pick you up."

"Fine."

Oscar's voice came back on, quietly. "She's been through the wars, it looks like. But she's calm, not talking. I'm honored she came here and I can help."

"Just don't let her go."

Nick was just ahead of peak rush hour and made it over to Oscar's house in about ten minutes, calling Charlotte with the update as he drove. She would meet them at the hospital. At

Oscar's, the pick up was brisk. The old friends did not linger to chat; Oscar was fully aware of the severity of the crisis, though his pleasant demeanor in his plaid flannel pajamas made the brief encounter seem perfectly ordinary. With Emily finally in the passenger seat of his car, Nick sped as fast as he dared over the old, potholed streets to Belmont. Whenever he entered the gates to the noble, hilly McLean campus, he thought of Frederick Law Olmsted spending the last years of his life there. He had been a creative personage, a genius few Americans had ever heard of, though his and his firm's landscapes—Central Park, Boston's Emerald Necklace—could be found in most states.

"I'm not going here," Emily said hotly.

"Em, you need help, it's the only way. You have to sleep, you have to get well."

"I refuse. You can't make me go in there against my will. You're the devil. You're putting me in prison!"

He drove fast to the main building, no longer breathing. His eyes watched her hands in case she reached for the door handle to leap out. He parked at the entrance. A young man carrying files—presumably an employee—was crossing the drive just at that moment. Nick rolled down his window and the young man came over looking warily at them. Nick met his eyes directly, knowing that his own were beseeching. With a catch in his throat he said three words: "I need help."

Everything remained calm, though the tension coming from Emily's body was palpable. She might do anything; she was a captive lioness ready to spring, and the young man peering into the window noted it. "Hi there," he said to Emily as if everything were normal.

She glared at him. He was one of the devils not to be trusted.

Nick quietly introduced her. "This is Emily."

"How're you doing in there, Emily?"

Her eyes sizzled in reply.

"Will you come inside with me?" he asked.

She shook her head.

"Everyone's your friend here—you don't have to worry. We're here to lend a hand. Why don't I help you inside?"

Clenching her body and hands, Emily stared down and calculated her chances of bolting, or so Nick imagined. Then, with a wrench of anger, she threw in the towel and opened the car door to comply. Nick couldn't believe it. Was she doing this for him or for herself? Or to save face with the young man her own age?

Inside the admissions area it was another story, for after her records were located on the computer, she would not cooperate about going to a short-term unit. She kept pacing the corridor and shrugging off any gentle hands that touched her arms in hopes of guiding her to the door. "Get off of me. Leave me alone. I'm not supposed to be here. There's nothing wrong with me."

Nick remained anxious in the background, letting the staff handle the situation. His heart ached for his daughter, what she was going through, and because he was helpless to change the situation. But they were in a place of help, and this alone soothed his nerves and pain.

Inevitably, the forces moved in to handle Emily against her will. Three young men in street clothes, probably residents, arrived on the scene, and although their body language appeared calm and nonthreatening, their objective was clear: capture the prey. At the right moment all three of them put firm hands on Emily, and while she struggled rather politely and cried out in fear, they moved her toward the door to the evaluation unit, where they would surely subdue her. Emily became terrified, knowing exactly what lay ahead. Nick wanted to turn off his ears but another side of him wanted to listen with all his might to be completely part of her hell.

"Wait! Stop!" she cried desperately. "What're you doing? Please, please, I didn't do anything wrong! Darrel! Help me, Darrel! Stop!"

Nick would never forget, not for a moment, the sound of his innocent daughter's voice pleading with the unknown, evil perpetrators pulling her away to a fatal injection: "Please, I didn't do anything wrong!"

FIVE

A blizzard hit Boston in early February. Blizzards had been the delight of Nick's childhood and adolescence. The phenomenon of blinding snow whirling ferociously over the landscape elicited a thrill of adventure. When would it end? How much had accumulated so far? How many feet would they get? The day after a blizzard was always more excitement—the city and suburbs digging out, cleaning up, people working like ants and talking jollily to each other about it. These days big dump trucks hauled snow away from important locations instead of plowing it into high drifts that lasted until the spring thaw. And with advanced technology, everyone knew days in advance that the storm was coming straight at them, so they prepared, putting their shovels and boots by the door, parking their cars so they could get out easily, and stocking up on food, batteries, and whatever else they wanted handy for the twenty-four hours or more when they'd be stuck inside watching the white world from windows—DVDs, alcohol, companionship. In the old days school closings had been announced while Nick and his sister waited by the radio, dressed just in case. Now cancellations often happened the day before, when the path of a dangerous storm could be so accurately predicted.

The blizzard struck on time and Boston got about two feet. Early Saturday morning, before the snow had stopped, Nick put on his cross-country skis and headed out across the silent white town. He knew this would be his only chance in a lifetime to ski the usually busy streets, cross the magical Narnia of the Public Garden, and glide along Commonwealth Ave. in its nineteenth-century winter beauty, reminiscent of a time when only horse and carriage moved along its two aristocratic halves, divided down the middle by a mile-long greenway, now pure, downy white. Yes, plows with their blinking yellow lights were out, but Nick was far ahead of their work and let his spirit mix with the silent winter wonderland, which he had to himself.

On his return trip down Marlborough Street, Nick thought of the revolving seasons and how humans could easily count how many they might see in their lifetime. He had possibly thirty more snow seasons to witness followed by spring's joyous renewal, celebrated in Boston with the famous marathon. He loved the exhilaration that built up to that day and the open, free spirit of the marathon itself that seemed to personify Boston. As he passed Flo's house, he imagined being out in the marathon's scene with her, her breezy company at his side. He now harbored a fully flourishing love for her that made him clench inside whenever he interacted with her, for he felt like a guilty voyeur on her life, especially when he wrote about her in his notebook. Slowly he skied past her silent, stately home, the gated walkway under two feet of untouched snow, the border shrubs buried. She was stuck in New York, where she had gone for much of the week to meet with agents in her unending quest for books that would bring a profit. She had e-mailed the office about her delay, though it hadn't mattered, since the city would be operational again by Monday. He wondered if Garrett was with her in New York or still sleeping behind those tall first-floor windows. He wondered what they were like together. Garrett didn't have a nine-to-five but according to Flo pursued entrepreneurial prospects. He had sold a popular organic eatery when they moved to Boston. It had begun as a food truck in midtown. Flo kept his photograph on her desk; it showed a sandy-haired, good-looking guy with an artiste's slight beard.

Nick skied on, his thoughts turning to Emily and how she would have enjoyed the early morning outing had she lived close by. They had pursued such outdoor adventures during her elementary school years; after that she had hung out with her friends. They had been in touch by phone just before the storm and agreed to meet up the following week for a movie. They could invite Oscar too, she had suggested. "And Eric—he's also welcome," Nick had replied, for Eric never joined them on their outings. But no, Eric had band practice every night that week for an upcoming gig in Northampton.

Making weekly dates with Emily comforted Nick in his worries about her mood. Since her two-week hospitalization in January, she had been back home, attending an outpatient program and continuing with her part-time job at the senior center, but she was not herself, if a self for her could be defined. She was still running on high energy, her mood now agitated and grouchy, but the psychosis was gone. She hadn't yet recovered her listening powers or moderate enjoyment of conversation. She acted uncomfortable inside her own skin, and if sitting in a café, shifted and squirmed as if to get out of it. They had set a date for Tuesday. "I'll e-mail Oscar. He's my adopted godfather," Emily said, and Nick could hear her smile through the phone. He was glad she felt close to a loyal and stable family friend, but at the same time he hesitated. "Just be careful," he said automatically.

"What?" she answered, knowing exactly what he had meant.

"You're smart, you're pretty, and he's a guy. An old geezer."

"Dad, that is so gross."

"Glad to hear it."

She laughed with disgust and repeated, "Gross. Goodbye."

"Goodbye," he said good-naturedly, but he was glad he had put out his little warning. Men generally were predators.

Skiing back to Beacon Hill, he remembered his visits to Emily in the hospital and his sadness for the patients in her ward, the gifted minds needing help, and at such a young age, with all of life ahead of them. They hadn't gotten too far beyond childhood before their brain chemistry derailed them. Nick had listened to Emily talk to another young woman about the theories of contemporary thinkers he had never heard of—perhaps Internet personalities. He couldn't follow their high-speed banter, but the two of them understood each other perfectly and argued out competing views that involved astonishing knowledge. They were like two egotistical academics feigning respect in their cutthroat intent to win the intellectual contest. He had watched and listened in utter fascination and bafflement. Was it possible, he wondered, that "insane" people had open throughways to their unconscious minds, or to a fathomless brain realm that normal people couldn't access, which allowed psychotic brains to communicate with perfect sense to each other? He suspected Emily would say, Yes, that's what I've been trying to tell you.

By Monday the city was back to normal, except for snowbanks on smaller streets such as Charles. Shops dug out passageways to the sidewalks, but only every twenty feet, so that people had to walk in the streets to get to the openings. Rain came and slush gathered at intersections, making it necessary for pedestrians to leap over the deep puddles or go out of their way to find a dugout to the street.

At the office, the excitement of the weekend's snow filled the hallways, staff sharing their stories as if they had just returned from a hurricane at sea. Then there was the return of Flo, after what felt like a long absence, for the office needed her fluttery voice and trail of perfume in the atmosphere for inspiration; they needed the flower she was to add spice to their day.

She phoned Nick as soon as she settled in, though the first thing she told him was how impossible it was to get settled in with all the paperwork and e-mails that had bombarded her desk in just six days. Some of the staff who lived close by in Back Bay had stopped by the office over the weekend and left projects on her chair. "Don't New Englanders ever accept the bad news that they got a snow day?" she said through the phone, though he could almost hear her real voice from down the hall. She was always holding him accountable for Boston's weird behavior. It was a form of affectionate teasing, and her teasing won her devotees.

"Could you come here in about ten minutes? I know I missed checking in on the *Beautiful Food* book and Fran's showing us her samples this afternoon, but I need to talk to you about the intro. It's way too long. No one will read it. We have to get it down to three hundred words max, and punch it up. And marketing needs the author's questionnaire. Could you please ping Walter to send it in today? Or get hold of the editor. And where's the Boston architecture book at? Shit, I'm so snowed under, and I didn't say that to be funny. Garrett didn't even shovel our walk. I told him he's a wimp—in Boston, you do that kind of work yourself, you don't wait for the supe."

Nick loved listening to her rhythmic laments, uttered so lightly they were delicious, something she herself delighted in. There was no question that Flo gave pleasure to herself.

"It depends on your building," he said. "Our manager takes care of the shoveling."

"Well, don't tell Garrett that. He could use more physical activity. Unfortunately neither of us likes the gym. We're utter sloths."

"I doubt that. And don't worry about Fran's samples, we can use the current intro as a placeholder."

"As long as it cuts off at three hundred words. You're going to lose a page."

"I'll alert Fran. We'll add to the appendix."

"Good. I can check that off. Tell me where we stand with the *Best of Boston*? I'm seeing Susie's threatening e-mails about the schedule."

"Yeah, I'm on it, and Liza's doing her best, but Trevor owes us replacement text and captions. I've talked to Susie about the schedule."

"Thank you. I don't know what I'd do if you weren't taking care of all these details. I'll see you in a few."

Moments later he sat in one of the chairs facing her desk, while she swiveled from her big computer screen to her polished desktop and the *Beautiful Food, Beautiful You* manuscript that was making her so agitated. Her pencil made edits on the page, then erased, then scribbled again. She had bad penmanship, but the little flourishes with Gs and Hs made him think she took certain satisfaction in her illegibility, the way doctors did with their prescriptions, only her satisfaction was of an artistic sort.

"You see," she said while working, "we have to take a trendier tone, even if Walter hates it. What's another word for 'plant-based diet'—he uses it every paragraph and it's going to turn off meat-eaters, which translates into a sales bust. We have to get people eating vegetables without telling them they have to eat vegetables."

Nick smiled and nodded. "I'll think of something."

"Good, because I'm too nervous. And we don't have time to send it back to the editor. I shouldn't have gone away so many days—look at me."

"You're not that nervous."

"Compared to you I am. You're always so calm. And your eyes are so blue, they're actually azure. I never met anyone with azure eyes before, even though I've read about them in romantic novels. You couldn't have gotten those eyes from your Portuguese mother."

Still smiling, he shook his head. "Nope, they're a Turner gene."

Her voice was neutral. "I've always longed for blue eyes. No one's ever happy with what they've got." She started writing again, and when she seemed absorbed in the puzzle of wordsmithing he wondered if he should continue sitting there. He stirred as if ready to depart, and she instantly responded without looking up.

"Wait, don't go yet. Isn't it silly, I just need someone to hold my hand." Then she straightened and pushed the intro to him. "Here, take it, please fix it, you know what I want. Maybe there's time for Fran to reflow it before the show."

"I don't dare ask her."

Flo sighed. "What else do we have to go over? Do you know what marketing did the minute I left for New York? They changed the title of *Mellow Moments*!"

"I really tried to save it at the meeting."

"That was so sneaky of them—it was Moser. He's getting back at me for the pink love book. And I hate what he came up with." She made a disgusted face as she uttered, "*Heart and Mind*. And for fuck's sake, the subtitle's even worse—*Pocket Affirmations*. Would you buy a book that said *Pocket Affirmations*?"

"There's a big audience for it."

She scoffed. "My subtitle was elegant," and then she purred it, as if on the opera stage: "*Heal and Inspire the Heart*. My whole title had a lovely cadence that they've turned into something banal. Hallmark cards."

"That's one of their target markets."

She simmered down with a glum expression, "So what's the point of putting so much effort and imagination into a title in the first place?"

"Most of your titles stick."

"Really? I think it's just the opposite."

The rest of that morning Nick's phone rang and the little screen showed *Florence Wright*. He immediately took care of her requests: e-mail Molly in the legal office about Naomi Spizer's contract—did she sign? And please ask the intern if we have all the permissions for the quotes in *Heart and Mind*, and could you download the book's revised P&L to see what we have budgeted for printing? The calls kept coming: she needed this document, that form, a phone number for an author, the pub date for a spring '14 book, and the latest layouts for the architecture book—did Gil provide the high-res photos yet? And dammit, she still thought the first order of chapters was better; was there time to revisit that question? Could he please track down Justin to run to CVS for some antacids?

Nick barely touched his own work but felt satisfied about being there for Flo, or maybe he was just happy she was back. I'm like her dog, he thought, and the idea of it made him laugh with a mixture of amusement and disgust. But he *was* like her dog; he was devoted.

He set out for Liza's office, but she was already on her way to see him, papers in hand. They stood in the hallway to talk over *Best of*

Boston's problems. Liza, a New England stoic who reminded Nick of his sister Ann, was surprisingly close to tears. Her thin, once girlish face trembled with emotion as she let out her list of grievances: "Production's hounding me, and it's not my fault if Trevor owes me new text and missing captions. And Gil's late with a dozen images, which is making Janice throw fits at me. She has an anger management problem and you or Flo need to talk to her about it. She just blew up at me and said incredibly insulting things. And Nick, you owe me the appendix."

"I'll get it to you this afternoon—the contractor's late."

"And Flo's been calling every other minute assigning me new projects."

"What? Your plate's full."

"Will you please tell her that?"

Nick assured her yes, and he knew just how she felt. He had experienced the same overwhelming emotions himself, many times. Such was publishing life.

"You need a hug," he said spontaneously, giving her a strong, supportive hug that crunched her papers.

She nodded as he let go. "Thanks—that helps."

At that same moment he caught sight of Flo down the hall, her head tilted with curious eyes fastened on them—on the hug. As if remembering something, she disappeared back into her office.

"Don't worry, Nick, I'm just letting off steam. I can handle it. Janice's venom shook me up, that's all. She's gotten a lot worse this year," Liza said.

"Everything'll be better tomorrow. Today's Monday."

"True. Mondays are the worst." She turned to go. "Remember that appendix."

"I'm going to call the researcher right now."

"You can't. We have the *Beautiful Food* show in the Alcott Room."

"You're right. But I'll have it to you today."

Relevant staff filtered into the style shows on the late side, but the acquiring editor, the project editor, and the designer arrived on time to greet the marketing reps and photo editor. Once in a while Sam showed up if he was interested in the book being presented. In the case of *Beautiful Food*, Flo was key because the editor was a contractor and not present. Fran had hung two possibilities for the interior template and was prepared to present them. She had chosen the vegetable chapter for her sample, and the colorful pages looked trendy and inviting. The text blocks offered peppy messages about eating for health and sustainability. Everyone in the office, including Nick, mixed the book up with *Best of Boston*, since both were about food and in process at the same time. Most books got nicknamed, sometimes by their initials, sometimes by a short form of their title like *Beautiful Food*.

Nick loved the moment when Flo joined the group, whether as presenter or audience. That day she wore one of her dark wool jumpers, black tights, and pumps in a Mary Jane style. A ten-foot-long violet, gray, and pink scarf wrapped her neck and in her nervous manner she played with it, winding and unwinding its strands from her neck and flipping them over her shoulder with a toss of her hair. Her lips were red and her eyelids the gray-violet of her scarf.

"Beautiful," Nick said under his breath, startling himself, but with all the conversations going on in the room it was obvious that no one had heard. He thought of how the past few weeks, since the holidays, that word had automatically issued from him whenever he saw her, and its spoken softness was like a flower petal's texture, which was perfect since her name meant "blossom."

All eyes trained on her expectantly, but she deferred to Fran. "It's your design, tell us about it."

Fran took them through her two design options quickly. She might have had more to say, but Flo stepped over to the hanging samples and waved her arm at them.

"I have a particular love for this book," she said, beaming at her audience. The book had been her brainchild, Nick thought, developed speedily with a New York chef she knew who enjoyed local celebrity with his own TV show. "What do the rest of you think of Fran's designs? The layout in number one really catches my attention. My eyes naturally ogle the vegetables, all those pretty green leaves and colorful, appetizing shapes, even though I'm a carnivore, which I guess I'll have to hide in the future, since chewing meat has become as taboo as smoking. Luckily I never got into that other vice, but filet mignon, a resounding yes. You can't take that red, raw meat away from me, or anyone else. That's why, as you see over here, the author—Walter—has included a small chapter, only three modest spreads, on meat. Our token concession. After all meat's the fastest way to get protein—and fat, unfortunately. The bottom line is, the book won't sell unless we have a meat chapter. So what do you all think? Do we have a winner on the way?" Her smile gleamed once more, her impromptu speech over.

Voices sent out compliments. Janice in her squeaky voice pointed out a few inconsistencies in Fran's two designs and the need to find better photos for some of the foods. "Who would eat spinach if it looked like that?"

Moser, head of marketing, boomed, "I'm fine with it," and strode out.

Flo rolled her lavender-shadowed eyes at Nick. It's a go!

He felt like her special partner in the game, in the office. Well, in a way he was, psychically.

"Flo, what about the island book?" one of the PR people piped up. "Where are we with that?"

"On press. I wish to god all our books could sail through the process like *Island Peril*. We might even see advance copies this week. Susie, could someone check on that?"

When the meeting ended, Nick sped back to his office and scribbled some lines of poetry on a piece of scratch paper that he then pushed into the depths of his backpack. The words would keep till the evening, when he was alone at home. All he needed was those few lines to set off the torrent within him—the feelings, moments, and intangible qualities Flo inspired in him that normal words could never convey but poetry might. It was a joy to be full of poetry again, as in his younger years. But he had more to write than adulation for Flo. He also wanted to explore his own weird state of containing his passion inside his skin. He wanted to see and watch Flo with pure love, but not touch her or even connect in friendship with her, not because of Garrett, but because he felt too old. Was it really possible that all he cared about was experiencing her essence? He longed to find logic in the power of a voice's timbre, or the movements of a face from happy to petulant, or the peculiarities of a body and a woman's obsession with it. How he started in surprise in those rare moments when Flo laughed naturally instead of flashing her *Glamour* magazine smile. The natural face lasted three seconds before she recalled it in a kind of embarrassment for letting go, but the natural face engraved itself in his mind—the two tiny dents above her cheekbones. She was born to laugh, enjoy fun, carefree days—that's what her free laugh with the darling dimples showed the world—but her life as an editor was just the opposite. And her mature acumen demanded outlet, power. She would never be comfortable with a carefree life. Still, he treasured glimpsing those childlike dimples and the unmasked Flo. He wanted to paint her, a new painting every day, for each day she was a new blossom. And poems were his paintings.

He worked intensely the rest of the afternoon and handed Liza the *Best of Boston* appendix on his way out the door. It was six o'clock and he wanted to hang on to his inspiration. The muse was back. Love was always the muse. He walked fast over the icy streets and sidewalks toward home, loving the darkening sky and cold air on his face, loving Boston in winter with its inviting lights, and loving all the esoteric history in its air and the seaside so close.

With eagerness Nick turned the key in his apartment lock and entered. He put down his backpack and pulled necessities from it right away—glasses and the piece of paper with the pulsing lines scribbled on it. He kicked off his shoes and went to the bedroom to change into sweatpants and a long-sleeved tee. He cracked the bedroom window; the heat was always too much and controlled by the building. He went back to the living room, so comfortable for work with a couch, armchairs, reading lamps, and a dining room table by the windows facing the tree-lined street. There was no question of dinner; not only was he in a hurry to sit down with his notebook, but eating a meal would dull his brain after a strenuous day at the office. He made tea and put nuts and apples on the coffee table. Then he settled on the couch with his notebook and copied the lines from the scratch paper onto the next blank page. What he wrote after that was for himself and with complete abandon. His output reminded him of joggers who run for 100 yards and then walk, and then run again. He wrote segments of poetry and then passages of prose, the prose mere memories of images that had engraved themselves on his mind, such as Flo at the end of the hall—he often saw her there—and how her tallish figure in heels hunched at the shoulders, so that he could imagine her two ways, bent and droopy in future senior years and as a young girl long ago, shoulders tensed with self-conscious vulnerability. It made him marvel that perhaps, down deep, she was insecure, uncertain, and wavering in her self-esteem.

He wrote for a couple of hours, paying homage to his vision of Flo, her beauty that reminded him of a fresh, fragrant bouquet. She might fade and wrinkle with age, but what made her bloom, what made her a blossom, would always remain—her mind and personality. He wrote about aging, and how as looks faded so did the hungry pursuit of admirers, though never all the way. Flo was still on the youthful side of that divide. Her hormones and brain signals still operated on the egocentric pathways created for attraction. And Nick was on the other side—his hormones and brain waves no longer drove him to attract, or not in the overpowering way of his younger years. He was relatively content to watch life and live his own interests, ponder his experiences. In a way, people his age had lived their lives already, even if they had many productive years ahead. They had finished living what life was all about: being born, growing up, dreaming and building a future, finding a lover and partner, and raising a family. A lot happened after that, but mainly to do with work and personal fulfillment; the passion for building, getting somewhere, attracting admiration—all of that lay in the past. Ironically, in senior years—now one-third of a person's lifetime—life became "in the past." But Flo was younger and still longed to be admired. Like most people, she still wanted proof of her sex appeal. She was too beautiful and spent too much time on her appearance not to be seeking recognition. She was nearing the end of her peak, and he was already winding down, and part of the wall between them was the vast passage of his life that she had never known, and could never know. Did it matter? Did love have to embody all of another person's history? Maybe not. Then there was Emily, and until his death he would be watching out for her, ensuring her safety and health as best he could, or so he believed. How could he find any space in his life for a deep relationship? All of these things Nick wrote down, beginning in the fiery exuberance of love and finishing in the quiet acceptance of objectivity.

The next day at the office was a carryover from the day before, with everyone picking up where they had left off in the myriad projects demanding instant processing to the next step. Rarely did the staff chat. Work was all-consuming and on such a fast track that everyone focused stressfully on his or her own agenda. Lunching together was also rare, because that short break in the middle of the day was a welcome time-out for one's own peace of mind. And often lunchtime didn't even provide that, though food eaten at the computer still offered partial solace. Maybe the types who went into book publishing just liked to be alone much of the time.

In midafternoon Nick ran into Flo on his way to the men's room. He felt like a vandal caught in the act, having written so much about her the night before, but he smiled naturally and tried not to notice her clothes—every day something of unusual design and appeal. How curious that clothes served as a decorative attraction that a person might not possess without them. Where did she find such artifacts? She wore a black ribbed skirt, cream top, and black cardigan embroidered with black thread and discreet beads in a floral pattern across the chest. Generally her winter wardrobe came to the throat, a classic Chanel look, with a flash of her brighter top showing above her ladylike cardigan. She liked jewelry and rarely repeated what she wore in that department, which meant she had drawers full of it. Anyone who didn't know her but only saw her every day might think her sole passion was women's fashion.

"Nick, I was just going to stop by—I still need the latest set of layouts for the architecture book. I still want to switch the chapters, even if it means dealing with Janice. But designers do not decide where text goes." She smiled in a friendly way quite close to him, so that for the first time he saw she was lightly freckled, a skin of patterned brown, delicate and lovely. She wasn't wearing her usual makeup, except for eye shadow, and the freckles made her younger.

"I'll find them, unless you want an electronic copy."

"Both, if you don't mind, thanks!"

They parted ways and in the men's room the first thing Nick saw was his reflection in the mirror: old! He had been looking at her youthful face and then confronted his own. The contrast was shocking, and there was nothing he could do about it except laugh ruefully. The once handsome face in the mirror—his—lived in a world of silent reflections and probably would for the remainder of his life. With age, communicating, confiding, sharing all the tumbling thoughts inside—a lot of which had to do with a person's past and memories, not to mention physical decline—could find no outlet. The accumulated material was too colossal and emotional to transmit and thus remained archived inside, increasing the aging person's solitude, which in turn led to eccentricities on the outside. He hoped he didn't have many of those yet, but they would come soon enough.

Feeling an exhaustion he rarely admitted—all because of his face in the mirror—he decided to go out for coffee, just to get some air, as if its refreshment could erase the lines around his eyes. He went back to his office for his parka and found Flo seated in his chair looking at his computer screen, her hand on his mouse.

"Hi, you can have your chair back—I thought I'd just wait for those architecture layouts and see if I saw the electronic file sitting on your screen, but I don't."

Momentary panic about what might be visible on his screen quickly subsided, for he kept no personal things on the office computer. Still he felt an invasion of his privacy with her eyes ransacking his screen. At the same time, he felt heat rising on the back of his neck and into his face because of his secret thoughts about her, his love for her. She was in his office, in his chair. He had her close by, available. And he was on his way out for coffee. His hands reaching for his parka were nervous. Somehow this unimportant errand, which he could forfeit, had taken over his mind. He patted his leg for his wallet.

"Why won't anything slow down around here?" she asked. "I want to be in the world of that Eagles' song 'Taking It Easy'—know what I mean, Nick?"

"Yes, I do." *It's a girl, my lord, in a flatbed Ford, slowin' down to take a look at me.*

"Ha." She smiled a bit sadly, as if reading his mind but coming back with her own preference: "'We may lose and we may win, though we will never be here again.' I love all their songs. Did you know 'Witchy Woman' was about Zelda Fitzgerald?"

He didn't have time to answer no, for as usual she prattled on almost to herself. "But for you it's probably Satie, am I right, Nick?"

"Oh yes, and painful opera arias."

"I knew it. Puccini. And Neapolitan songs—heart-rending."

"I can't resist them."

"Me neither."

"And then there's Clapton," he said. "'Do you want to see me crawl across the floor to you?' That's my favorite."

"I don't know Clapton."

"I'll send you the link." They were talking in subtext, flirting, he loved it.

"And send me some Brazilian music, your favorite."

"Caetano Veloso." His voice, lyrics, and musical sound were as sensual and seductive as Flo. "You'll love him." And you'll think of me when you play him, the way I think of you.

At that moment Liza came in. "Nick, Flo, I'm glad I caught both of you at the same time. There's a new snag with *Best of Boston*."

"I swear, publishing books is harder work than giving birth," Flo said. "That book has been a pain from start to finish. What's wrong now? What's Trevor nitpicking about this time? Do you realize how lucky he is to be chosen for this book? How lucky no one in this über-smart city thought of publishing a book on the best yet?"

"That's because they're all so smart they don't need the book, they have it on the Web," Nick said. "Boston was first."

"Before San Francisco's *Best*?" Liza queried.

"I was just making that up," Nick said, "since Flo has an attitude about us. Do you two want coffee? I'm going for coffee."

"No thanks," Flo lamented, rolling her eyes up to him, the dark kernels beseeching. "What I want is a hug. Please give me a hug, Liza."

Liza obliged her with a hug over the shoulders as Flo still sat in Nick's chair, her expression droopy.

"I'll zap you the architecture files as soon as I get back, and I'll deliver the hard copy once I track it down." Nick smiled and left. In fact, he hurried out and heard his inner voice hammering away as he fled to the elevator: "What was that all about? What was that hug? And why the hell are you leaving? This was your chance to sit down and chat with her. The hug. She wanted a hug from you. No, not possible. Yes, she saw you hug Liza yesterday, and she wanted a hug too. Why did you leave? Because . . . For god's sake, *because why?* Because I only want a hug in my mind. I only want to love Flo in my mind. Coward!"

The next day Nick went to work fully prepared to be more open with Flo, to let any overtures play out. But at the first opportunity to take paperwork to her office, he found her in a state of retreat, withdrawn behind a pale mask of almost Kabuki makeup with the eyebrows a slate gray. It gave her a cool, distant look, and he could imagine her that morning spending more than her usual time staring dismally at herself in front of the mirror and slowly figuring out the makeup that went with her mood. And for the first time since meeting her and falling in love with everything about her, he saw that she was moody, and it didn't surprise him. He understood that over the course of her forty years of dealing with her own complex personality, she had cultivated a professional persona that concealed the Flo of moods and inner turmoil. He liked her even more knowing that she wrestled and coped with the depths of mood.

She thanked him for the documents and continued working, her eyes not even meeting his except perfunctorily as if through a veil. He left, wondering if the hug scene the day before played any part in her Japanese mask of today. He had too much work to plow through to spend much time wondering. And he had to leave early to meet Oscar and Emily for their movie date at Kendall Square—a nice three-mile walk at the end of the day.

He met Emily at a café off Hampshire Street. She was sitting at a corner table texting or e-mailing on her cell phone when he arrived. The place was crowded with MIT students, faculty, and young, hipster professionals. The décor was eclectic and underground. Nick and Emily often grabbed a bite there before a movie, so they knew the menu and could place their order right away.

Part of Emily's recovery, this time and before, involved indifference to her appearance. She sat across from him disheveled, with her brow creased and her mouth dry and unsmiling. She was the female version of a man who hadn't shaved for a couple of days and slept in his clothes. Her mood was grumpy, her answers gruff, but she warmed up a bit when he asked how her mood chart was going.

"I can show you," she said, and got it out of her book bag. It covered the weeks of her mood since her discharge from McLean. Part of her outpatient program was to keep the chart. "You can see how the mania starts to subside here at week four, and how I'm beginning to sleep too much."

"And you seem disgruntled, argumentative."

"I am. And that's because I'm dysphoric."

"What's that?"

"It's when the eagerness and happiness of mania—the creativity—turn into frustration and agitation, that is, dread of what's coming next—complete shutdown. Depression."

"Maybe it won't happen this time. You've been on Lithium all year. It might prevent the depression cycle."

"It's going to happen," she said, her voice filling with angry tears, but then it strengthened again with bitterness. "Every bipolar person who has taken the trouble to write about it says the same thing: shutdown. William Styron described it as the mind in deep stagnation."

"I hope we can prevent that."

"You can't. It's a nightmare that's real. It's torture. The only solution is getting out. Don't worry, I'm not feeling that way right now, I'm just telling you what's down the line. I've been there. And all you do is think about death all day."

His heart twisted in pain looking at her and knowing the road she had to travel all alone to somehow find positive reasons for her life, gratitude for its gifts, so that she could appreciate it enough to find meaning in it. He had seen her crazy, and as she wrestled now to keep her fragile sanity, understandably resentful of her lot, he despaired that she and others like her faced one of the worst fates on earth: possible confinement to a mental institution for life. She was free now, but what if things changed? What if her face always wore the confused, crazed, zoned-out expression of her acute psychosis? What if she lost coherence, logic, cognizance? He couldn't bear the vision of that and turned his thoughts in a different direction. Bipolar people were more fortunate than those with schizophrenia; many managed their lives productively, some brilliantly. And Emily so far had been high-functioning even when depressed.

"It was strange. I thought I was in Miami when they forced me down at McLean."

"You called out for Darrel."

"I thought everyone was the devil and I was terrified."

"I know, I was there. I felt all of it. I've had that dream—the sinister medical guys overpowering me for a lethal injection—but for you it was real."

She nodded, lips tight, tears brightening her eyes. Horrible!

"But Emmy, we know what triggered it, and that means there's a lot of hope. It doesn't have to happen again if you're careful."

"Yeah, stay dull and depressed most of the time. What a life."

"We have to be patient—it's only been a year that doctors have been helping you. Graduate school might give you a fresh start, inspiration. We have to wait and see. And keep busy in the meantime."

"What if I don't get in?"

"I don't know. Maybe you should travel and teach, have a big change."

She nodded. "I was thinking of that. I have to do something like you did in Brazil."

He nodded. "Travel and other cultures." But would she be safe? What if she broke down? He had been her lifeline.

"The thing is, Dad, a depressed person can't even be curious about what's fascinating out there. I could end up in Africa or South America and not be able to get out of bed."

So she knew it too, but he couldn't help hoping it would be different.

After their meal they went to find Oscar at the theater. He was coming out of the parking garage just as they approached from the street. From the distance, in his hat and parka, he looked like an old man, and his gait was arthritic. Nick immediately saw what lay ahead for him just a few years down the line. And how strange it was to know people for a lifetime. Many friends his own age, whom he had witnessed through their weddings and young family days, were now overweight, with body breakdowns or disease. He realized that if he lived long enough, say ninety, he would see Emily at that same decaying stage.

They watched *The Other Son*, which had the classic premise of babies switched at birth—one from a middle-class Israeli family and the other from an oppressed Palestinian family of the same class. The movie raised all kinds of humanitarian questions about the Israeli-Palestinian conflict, in addition to studying human reactions to learning the truth about the children you love and have raised but who actually come from the detested enemy camp.

After the movie they went across the street for a drink to air their responses, for the movie had held them in its grip. Like the film, they were proponents of a solution to the Gaza conflict, which meant action from Israel that was acceptable to the Palestinians, something not on the horizon. They all agreed that film made world problems visible faster than books or the media, though Nick wondered how many people went to see such significant movies with producer credits showing "French-Arab-Hebrew." It was the peacenik advocates from France, Gaza, and Israel who were making the recent spate of films showing Israel's inhumane treatment of Palestinians. "And it's peaceniks like us who go see the movies. So how does the word really get out?"

"It gets out slowly," Oscar said. "Journalists and filmmakers help."

"Have you seen *Incendies*?" Emily asked. "It's much more Hollywoodesque but really shows the insanity of ethnic violence in the Middle East."

"I can't keep up with you," Oscar said, "but I'd like to. Can I get it from Netflix?"

"Yes, and call me when you have it and I'll watch it too."

"Divine. We'll get a film club going. Are you on board, Nick?"

"Of course. I'll watch a movie any night of the week."

"He's a junkie. What about *The Skin I Live In*?" Emily said with fresh inspiration.

"The review sounded gross," Oscar said.

"It is. I can't recommend it, even though I loved it. It was incredible," she said. "But I wouldn't want to watch it again. Unless to study Almodóvar's genius."

"It was sicko, but so are humans," Nick chimed in. "It was a tour de force."

"I still think I'll pass," Oscar said. "But I did like *Bad Education*."

That led to more discussion on the Almodóvar films they had seen and the ones they had missed, which led to remembering other favorite movies and directors till the hour passed and they agreed it was time to head home for bed. Oscar drove Emily, and Nick walked back over Longfellow Bridge, affectionately called the Salt and Pepper Bridge because of its stubby stone towers with caps. It was a clear, cold night with a sprinkle of stars but no moon. The Charles glittered and lapped in its night's peace, and saltwater smells and the tinkle of boats moored along the river and farther out in the harbor wafted through the curving channel with a familial softness and promise of eternal revolutions from night to day. Yes, eternity was in the softly lapping waves, and Nick thought of all the people who had come and gone before him with the same yearning love to remain forever in the venerable city.

S IX

The memoir-thriller *Island Peril* made its debut in March, creating a buzz in the office as press and marketing staff pushed hard for two weeks, concentrating on traditional and social media outlets for the risky 100,000 copies that had been shipped out. But the ripple effect was rapid, winning applause for the company's marketing team; and Flo, who had spearheaded the book, glided along the halls with a broad smile for days, pleased to share with anyone she passed that the book was headed for a reprint before the summer. Nick was happy for her success. It was a classic example of how publishers and editors took ownership of their books, as if they themselves had written the stories. *Island Peril* was Flo's book.

Days passed with the usual sensation of heated rush in the office, projects progressing at different stages of development and completion. Staff working under intense pressure hurried down the corridors carrying papers, the photocopiers churned out manuscripts and layouts, and the meeting rooms never sat empty. New books were begun and old ones wrapped. Churchill's pace had no hiatuses, but few complained for almost everyone loved publishing. Nevertheless, when Friday rolled around, they were ready for the weekend, glad to say good riddance to the office.

A lot was on Nick's plate that particular Friday, including a prospective self-help author coming for a meeting followed by lunch. Hours would be shaved from the workday. Meanwhile, the revised manuscript for the next volume in their culinary travel series had come in the week before. These were coffee-table books that captured the beauty, history, and dining culture of tourist destinations. Local chefs contributed nuggets of information about their national or regional cuisine. Morocco was this year's choice, and the freelancer working with them had sent in unacceptable text. Nick had spent hours rewriting the eight section intros because no one else had time. Then Flo had asked to see the manuscript when she heard how bad the first draft had been. She had been sitting on it all week, and now Susie was complaining about the schedule.

Nick went down the hall and found Flo busy on the computer. Her red cardigan was like a flame that suited her dark coloring.

"Flo, are you done with the Morocco text?"

She kept typing while she spoke. "Oh yes, sorry I kept it so long. I finally got around to reading it last night at home." She swung around to her desk and searched for the manuscript in her pile. "I think we need to umpf it up even more. Of course I see what a wonderful job you've done—I compared the two manuscripts. But I still can't finish reading this opening paragraph. It's too long, too full of details no one's going to care about. This series used to have 20,000 words in each book, including captions, but we're not doing that anymore. Morocco should have 7,500 words max, and audiences don't even have attention span for that. They like their tweets." Her mechanical pencil ran down the margin of the first few paragraphs. She flipped to the next page, then through more pages, then back to page two. "Maybe begin with this sentence here." Her pencil hesitantly made a check mark.

It was random, Nick could tell. She had barely glanced at the new draft and was now groping for suggestions to shorten it.

As if hearing his thoughts, she looked up and dropped her pencil. "Nick, I need to go over it more carefully—is there time? I want this volume to be our debut for the series' smashing new look."

Her phone rang and she looked at its little screen. "It's Al! I've been waiting days for him to get back to me—can you wait a sec?"

He sat down to wait.

"Al!" she exclaimed, as if running into a long lost and cherished friend. "I'm so glad you called, I've been dying to get your expert advice on the royalties clause in Blaze Denis's draft contract. Are you coming to our meeting in an hour? I hope so. And he's staying for lunch. I'm praying *you* of all people can join us for the lunch. We need your know-how, your special touch with authors. His agent wants six figures."

Nick listened to her oozing voice. Her flattery. She did it with everyone, and since everyone at Churchill was talented and expert, maybe it wasn't so bad. Maybe it was all true, but it sounded manipulative. He wondered, just for a moment, how much beauty lay in the eye of the beholder. Had he invented Flo? How was it possible that love, the deepest and most important human emotion, could switch off instantly when someone you loved to distraction said or did something you intensely disliked? His blind love for Flo had switched off for that moment.

Her call went the way she had hoped, and she hung up with a breath of satisfaction. "Sorry about that, Nick. I've got to catch Al when I can. He's a hardworking dear but always on the run, and contracts take forever with him. It's not his fault—he needs an assistant. And this cool dude, Mr. Denis, is asking too much for his story, and frankly, even though he's been a hit on TED, we can't guarantee his book will sell. You're coming to the meeting right? And lunch?"

"I am. Can't wait to meet Monsieur Denis."

"I can tell he's not your type, but selling books is our business." She made a supplicating face at him. "Could I please have till Monday with Morocco? I promise to read it over the weekend."

Nick smiled. Of course she could keep it. He'd handle the threats from Susie. He got up to go.

Flo's bright smile beamed at him. "I don't know what I'd do without you."

He turned away, feeling like Al.

"I mean that, Nick," she said loudly to his retreating back, as if realizing the comparison he was making. No question about her perspicacity.

"I love my work," he called back.

At the meeting with Blaze Denis, Flo and the marketing team asked innumerable questions about the author's career, his book proposal, and his ability to give them his time when it came to marketing the book. "We'd be organizing a lecture tour at college campuses and women's clubs, some TV and radio shows, that kind of thing. And we'd want you to use your extensive social media outlets to promote the book," Flo told him.

"Naturally," the poetic-looking young man said with an unflappable smile and large puppy-dog eyes that made love to anyone looking at him. He was Parisian and had a sexy French accent besides his appealing looks. He lived with his American wife, Trudy, in New York. "I have a million followers on Twitter, and my Facebook page is like a love-in." His voice and manner were warm and affectionate; his words and way of sharing his life story of thirty-seven years couldn't sound more open, honest, and genuine.

And yet Nick discerned underneath all Blaze's humble recitations of his accomplishments, a larger-than-life ego. Similar to *Island Peril*, the young opportunist's story was a possible moneymaker.

"How did you get the name Blaze?" Nick asked in the same neutral tone everyone at the table was using.

"Good question," Blaze said, smiling with seduction into Nick's eyes so that Nick blushed for his banal tactics. "You see, Nick, it was my wife. After we met at a retreat in Hawaii, our first trip together as a couple was to a beach that had wild horses. The sight of them was awesome—I mean, we never see horses in the wild, only in stalls or corrals, or in movies. These horses were shimmering with life, their manes and tails long and flying in the wind when they galloped down the deserted beach. Trudy said, 'You're like those horses, you blaze—you are Blaze.' And it stuck. And frankly, I like it. It's a constant reminder to keep the fires going under me."

"Will you put that story in your book?" Al asked. He was an older, balding gentleman with a solicitous manner who handled a portion of Churchill's deals.

"I'll put any of my stories that you like into my book."

"How much of it have you written?" Al continued.

"At this moment I have a notebook filled with all my philosophy. Trudy watches me on TED or listens to me over breakfast or anywhere I happen to give a talk and jots down my philosophies."

"Everyone seems captivated by these philosophies of yours," Flo said. "Do you happen to have the notebook with you?"

"You know, as soon as I got on the train this morning it occurred to me I should have brought the notebook. So I texted Trudy and she's bringing it." He looked at his watch. "She arrives in an hour. And I hope in her hurry she doesn't forget it on the train." He laughed and looked around the table at all the expectant faces.

"You wouldn't want a Nick Adams disaster," Flo said.

Blaze raised his brows quizzically.

"You know, Hemingway's wife Hadley, who left the only copy of his Nick Adams stories on the train."

"What? Really? I think I've heard of Hemingway."

"I hope so," Flo said, a bit drily. "It's a Parisian story. It happened when they lived in Paris."

"Well, luckily we're in the digital age and Trudy's backed up my notebook." Blaze smiled, looking a little impatient that the conversation had strayed from him and pointed out his ignorance. "She's something, and I don't know why everyone's clamoring for a piece of me when it's Trudy who's the dynamo. And frankly, it's fitting with what I always believed about American women. It was my destiny to marry one."

"Blaze, why do you think people latch onto your philosophies, as you call them? How would you describe the response?" Dee from marketing asked.

"Funny you should mention it, because all those wonderful vibes were just this minute going through me, as if I were on the stage and feeling the magic of sharing with other people—magic for me, magic for them. All of you have really great karma. I'm glad to be here."

"But the philosophy—"

"Exactly—it's all part of the karma that happens when I'm with people, and in a way I'm bleeding for them, I love them so, without even knowing who they are or what their names are—it's that kind of uncanny communication. Things from my experience, my travels, my thinking, just start coming out of their own accord, and people seem to love it. They write me that the things I share from my past and present help them heal, help them feel free, help them let go of old, crippling issues."

"Remarkable. And you have no training in psychology."

He smiled sublimely. "What I offer springs naturally from the well within me, just the way it did for the Buddha."

"And you say Trudy has all these spontaneous wisdoms written down."

"The notebook's on its way."

"And for your book," Flo said with a professional firmness, "you wouldn't just be plopping down these statements, would you? What did you have in mind? Your proposal just says 'like on TED.'"

"Exactly. I want to recreate the magic of me and the audience, and naturally I would talk about my beliefs in mini-chapters, not just a series of statements. I'd give the background to each situation that happened that made that particular revelation come."

"Would you describe yourself as a guru?" Flo asked.

"People have called me that, but I'm just me, Blaze."

They adjourned after a few more questions about the vague proposal. Nick doubted they would get around to fine-tuning the contract that day. In fact, in the next instant, Flo and Al chorused that the next step was to look at the notebook Trudy was bringing and come up with a plan to shape the material in a way that captured Blaze's charisma with live audiences.

"Let's have lunch," Flo suggested to her guest and a few others in the room, including Nick. As they broke off into twosomes to head out of the conference room, Nick let Flo know that he needed to get back to his desk and would prefer to skip the lunch.

"I guess there's not much more to learn," she answered in an undertone. "We should call the book *Mirror, Mirror on the Wall*. But if he can do in his book what he does on the stage, then we've got a best seller in the self-help category."

Al came up, put an avuncular arm around Flo's shoulders, and gave them an affectionate squeeze. "He sounds promising, my dear."

"We have to see the notebook to know," Flo said. And when Al's hand stayed too long on her shoulders, his fingers like claws, she moved her head to stare at it, as if to say, What's detaining you? Al let go. Flo shook out her hair.

Well, Nick thought with a bit of disgust for both of them, her smarmy flattery on the phone did encourage him.

He went back to his office glad to escape the scene that included Blaze's foppish presence. He settled into his chair, his screen, his papers—his own universe at Churchill. And it was Friday, an additional perk. The weekend stretched ahead with promise for filling his notebooks, reading and walking, and maybe watching a movie from Netflix or at the theater with Emily. He was aware that his rapture of the weeks before had turned off. Shakespeare's sonnets sat on the corner of his desk untouched. He had brought them to work in case he found time to read one or two over lunch and be transported to the realm of Flo. But the week had sped by and he hadn't opened the book. At lunch time he wanted to avoid words, and usually his mind continued to cogitate on projects and priorities. There was no space for daydreams at Churchill.

Around six he was closing shop when Flo slipped through his door, dressed in an orange coat with decorative front seams that traced her womanly lines. She smiled at him. "TGIF."

"To you too. We earned it."

"I'll say. Putting up with Blazing Ego was worth my month's salary."

"Amazing that such a turn-on can be such a turn-off," Nick said with a smile.

"Diversity makes the world go round."

"You said it. That's what's so fascinating."

She didn't fill the gap for once, so he added, "What are your weekend plans?" He leaned back in his chair, relaxed, so as not to rush her away.

"Amazingly, absolutely nothing. Garrett's on a business trip, and much as I adore him, I look forward to having the place to myself, doing whatever I want, which includes doing nothing more than reading the *New York Times* in bed." She noticed the Shakespeare on his desk. "Oh, the sonnets. 'Shall I compare thee to a summer's day . . .' Which is your favorite?"

"I'd have to reread them. But, how about 'That in black ink my love may still shine bright'?"

"Of course—that was the point of them all. I wish someone would write poetry about me."

Someone is, Nick thought, feeling his neck heat over the secret he held but at the same time delighting at the tingling in his veins, the return of Flo to his bloodstream.

"Someone has or will," he replied. "No doubt of it."

"Thank you. I take that as a compliment." She moved toward the door and then turned back. "And what are you doing this weekend?"

"The usual."

"Which is?"

"Let's see. The last few Sundays I've been taking city walks with our new architecture book, or printouts from the PDFs."

"What a good idea. We should take an architecture walk together sometime. After all, we're neighbors."

"There's a lot to see." He nodded, at the same instant feeling chagrin that he hadn't taken her up on her suggestion by answering, Yes, let's, how about Sunday? What was wrong with him? He wanted to be with her, spend time with her outside the office, and she had just given him the opening. As his mind raced for a way to back up and propose a Sunday date, she hitched her satchel higher on her shoulder and gave him a farewell smile, something soft and sweet, a tinge regretful, to take home with him. What a disappointment he was, to both of them.

The following week every meeting and every greeting in Churchill's halls carried the exciting news of *Island Peril*'s rise on the charts. Sales were unprecedented for the company—twenty thousand sold in less than a month, with daily sales growing. Flo announced an office party for Thursday at the Westin, and colleagues came to work that day dressed a little better than usual—hair, fashion, jewelry planned for the after-work celebration. Flo wore bright violet slacks. Their ultra-fine ribbing gleamed like an iridescent seashell, and her eye shadow matched. Chunky amber beads hung down the front of her black top. She looked amazing. Nick had to wonder if a man wanted to possess the product or the woman inside. Someone had done a study he read about in the paper. They placed a group of women in a waiting room and then had a final woman enter wearing ordinary jeans, a T-shirt, sneakers, and a ponytail. The other women hardly noticed her. The next day in the same scenario, the same last woman to arrive wore the sexiest outfit imaginable, with her hair let loose and styled and her legs in fashionable heels. The other women, not recognizing her, vociferously criticized her appearance as soon as she left the room. Nick had looked at the two photographs of the ordinarily dressed woman and the alluring version of the same person. It was obvious that the latter elicited instant attention and sexual vibes, just as Flo did with her clothes, her perfume, and her feminine aura. Yet, now that she had ensnared him, he knew he would love her best barefoot and in shabby clothes.

Promptly at five the editorial office emptied. Nick was one of the last to leave. Outside it still felt like winter, even though it was March. People would stay cozy in their parkas at least another month. But spring was in the air, days were lengthening, and even though the streetlamps had come on in Copley Square, daylight still lingered, reminding him that soon the evenings would extend till eight, with more outdoor enjoyment and sunsets after work. People would stroll the streets and eat at the sidewalk tables, or wander down to the Charles to watch the sunset. The marathon on Patriots' Day would crown the season.

Liza called out to him, and he turned to wait.

"I thought I was the last one out," Nick said.

"That's my role," she said with a smile.

"Yeah, I know how you like this place on weekends."

"I grew up in it," she said. "I started out here as an assistant. I quickly found out I had a weekend office at my disposal to do my own stuff—I live five minutes away, like you. I'm alone, no family, at least not downtown."

"Funny how the 'burbs are a world away. I used to live in Concord and commute. I grew up there."

"I grew up in Dedham. Concord's really out there. But it's one of my favorite field trips. I love Sleepy Hollow, looking at those famous graves. They make the luminaries so real, so human. I love Thoreau's little headstone."

"Henry."

"Yes! Just 'Henry,' nothing else, as if he were a counterculturist."

"He was."

"Do you have a favorite?"

"Oh, I don't know. I think it's the phenomenon of all of them on the planet at once, their intellectual renaissance, the ferment of the times—that's what I like. The closest thing we have today is book clubs."

"A far cry."

"You're not kidding. It was a small, small world back then. Who's your favorite?"

"It changes," she said. "Recently Hawthorne because I've been reading him and chuckling. I didn't notice his irony when I was young."

"Oh yes, he's the real protagonist on every page, talking, talking, talking."

"And didactic and fablesque. He's got his own brand of religion. I don't know what it is, but 'all goodness' and not very real. Mainly I'm floored by his fluid and florid command of the English language."

"Yeah, it's amazing. People don't write in that style anymore."

"No, but we can still be floored by it."

"What do you write on the weekends—your stuff, as you called it?"

"Sssh." She smiled again, eyes twinkling at him, showing him a personal side of her that he hadn't seen before. She was one of those women in plain clothes with plain hair who would look entirely different if dressed like Flo, and again she reminded him of his sister Ann. Solid, capable, dependable New Englanders. "Our employee manual stresses that we aren't to use the equipment for our personal work. I love the printer for my drafts—fast and free. But mainly I need to get out of my house to write."

"Fiction? Novels?"

She sighed and gave little laugh. "Indeed, I'm on my sixth, or is it my eighth? Nothing published. I've never gotten an agent."

"Have you tried? I'm sure Flo could help you, or others. I know a few agents myself."

"Me too, but it must be a Freudian hang-up, because I'm always waiting to finish my latest before querying one, because I think my latest is my best."

"What's your latest about? Can you say?"

"Sure, it's finished already. I'm at the polishing stage. It's a novel based on a segment of Colette's life."

"Good idea. I'm here when you need a reader."

"Really?" She looked surprised and hopeful.

"Really," he assured her. "Can't you tell I love manuscripts?"

"I'll be ready in about three months. Watch out!"

He gave her a brotherly pat on the back as they came to the Westin entrance. Upstairs, the bar was already noisy with their colleagues seated on a long couch behind tables with others standing in the area. They were all there—Susie, Margie, Janice, Fran, Al, Moser, the top brass, and many others, names Nick still didn't know, faces he rarely glimpsed. Flo's purple pants wrapping her long legs and stretching around her feminine hips and derrière seemed the focal point of the party, its bright pulse, or at least to Nick, but he knew to others as well. She was deep in conversation and laughter with their white-haired chief. Her wineglass waved this way and that as she told her story, and at one point Sam steadied her hand when the wine splashed out. When her eye caught Nick's, she gave him a delighted greeting with her features and her raised glass. Why was it he couldn't imagine having a normal conversation with her, the way he had just talked to Liza? Was it that she ran at her own high speed in her own LP grooves that had no openings for his own personality and world to enter? Or did he clam up because of the secret love he harbored for her while pretending to be neutral? His thoughts went back to that first day they had met in her office. He had liked and admired her immediately and perceived at the same time how alone she was in her singularity, never to be blended with anyone else. And yet she wanted him nearby, close, experiencing her intangibility. She longed for a friend who saw her, understood her, and she knew intuitively at first and later by his presence that Nick could absorb her, all of her, without ever being able to define her, but absorbing her was enough.

These thoughts ran through Nick's mind as he found a seat by Fran, knowing that they had movies in common, since they talked about them at office gatherings. She was a kindred spirit in her late thirties and wouldn't mind chatting with an older colleague, especially one with a glass of soda water who wasn't loosening up with wine or beer, something he had once looked forward to himself.

After forty-five minutes of small talk with various colleagues and nibbles from the platters of opulent hors d'oeuvres Flo had ordered, Nick plotted his exit strategy—a trip to the men's room to kill a few more minutes, followed by a quick goodbye to the people seated near his coat, and then off he'd be into the delicious, voice-free night, the workday finally concluded.

In the long hallway leading to the restrooms, a feminine voice he knew so well pealed musically, girlishly, from behind: "Niiiick!"

He turned with his usual friendly smile and met her radiance as she laughingly tottered up to him, obviously tipsy, wine glass splashing. She came so close he could see her fine freckles, the unmasked face he liked best. "Nick," she repeated, her shiny eyes and solicitous lips so expectant of something from him that terror and a shooting thrill gripped his heart at once, sending shock waves through his mind. He knew through instinct the fateful moment had arrived and could not be stopped in its unleashed trajectory.

"Nick," she breathed again, swaying in, so that their chests just brushed and her uninhibited eyes melted into his, the faint whiff of wine on her lips. "Aren't you ever going to take me in your arms and kiss me?"

Oh yes, his arms instantly responded, filling at last with the ampleness of Flo, the body and form of Flo, the rich effulgence of her spirit and fluttery chatter, her secret turmoil and insecurity. His arms held tightly to all that precious, vibrant, living being he had admired for so long. How sure she must have been of his response to have dared such a move. And how glad he was.

"I love you," he said automatically against her hair, his lips kissing the tip of her ear.

"And I love you," she said, her face burrowing into his shoulder and neck. Then her head thrust back. "Let's get out of here. But please, kiss me first."

Their lips touched and tasted with a gentle greeting, a how-do-you-do, while their eyes searched, filled with wonder, disbelief, happiness. Could this really be happening? Had they stepped over the edge? Yes, because their fusion had been so long in the coming. Nick gave her one last tight embrace before releasing her, his heart going like mad.

"I'll leave first," she said practically. "Meet me at the library. Oh my god, we can stroll in the Garden. Do you know how many times I've strolled in the Garden with you?"

He smiled. She was a dreamer too. Maybe they were all dreamers at Churchill and that's what drew them to books.

Then she was gone and he wondered what the night held. Their hug and tender kiss was one thing, but carrying things further was out of the question. Garrett was at home a few blocks away. That circumstance alone had to be voiced. But Nick wanted to feel her in his arms again, that rich womanly abundance that overwhelmed his senses. That was the crux of it—Flo awakened all his dormant senses. Exuberance flowed in his veins, and he had not felt it in years.

It was still early, but the sun had set and dusk was deep in the Garden, the shrubs like shadows, the bare trees webbed against a darkened sky where a half-moon was on the rise. The antique lamp-posts stood tall and gracious, their orbs casting muted light over the sylvan landscape with its central curvaceous lagoon. Nick and Flo followed the quaint paths and crossed the storybook bridge, also lit with lamps. It was a cold night, and only a few others strolled through the park with the leisurely air of Nick and Flo, her arm pulled through his, their hips rubbing.

"I must be crazy," she said with a laugh. "How can we pretend at work tomorrow? Or maybe that'll be tantalizing. But if I hadn't been the aggressor, would you have ever let on? No. You're not impulsive like me, but there's something to be said for being impulsive—at least sometimes, like now, tonight."

"It's sure to be trouble," he said, squeezing her arm.

"Said just like Nick. But you're right, and you don't know the half of it."

"But you're going to tell me."

"Yes, but not this minute. This minute, all I want is to see your body."

"Ha. I hate to disappoint you."

"Fuck that—I can see it through your clothes every day, and I want it without your clothes."

"Ah, Flo! The clothes have a purpose." He smiled and tightened his hold, musing about how she wanted to possess his body while he wanted to possess her soul.

They came to the Beacon Street gate. "We're at the hill. Your home. Can we go in? Let's make the evening last a little longer," she said.

As they crossed the street her phone pinged like a sharp warning, and she read the screen. "Garrett. A reality check. How prescient. 'Coming home soon?'" she read the message aloud.

She punched back on the keys, saying the words for Nick's sake. "Home soon, party a gas, going for something to eat with others."

"OK," Garrett's text pinged back immediately.

"We can't do this," Nick said. "It's a world of lies and betrayal. You just told your first lie."

"That's what I have to talk to you about, but not this minute. Can't we go to your place and hold each other for half an hour? Nothing else, just snuggling on the couch to get warm. I know you're a snuggler just by looking at you, the best snuggler in all the world. Aren't you glad I broke through your wall?"

"I am, but—"

"I don't want to hear any Nick Turner buts tonight, always so prudent, always so correct. I want to drink some more wine at your place and feel good, feel carefree, out of time and place."

"I can't resist. And then I'll walk you home."

"Do you know, I can predict almost everything you say, like that: 'Then I'll walk you home.' I want to convince you to abandon your good sense, even though it attracts me. I love your integrity, but I want you to let go and live something with me you'll never live again in your lifetime, and that goes for me too. We shouldn't be afraid, of anything. Is this your building? I love this neighborhood, it's so sweet, so Boston."

He turned the key in the lock and they went upstairs to his flat, Nick's thoughts running ahead of their steps to what papers and writing he might have left out on the table, but usually he concealed his personal work in case the landlord showed up for some reason.

Flo exclaimed over the cozy, old-fashioned apartment and comfortable furnishings handed down from his family. Nick went into the kitchen to look for wine—nothing cold. "I can offer you red or white on ice."

"White. I don't want purple teeth."

"They'd match your pants."

"Aren't these pants wild? Have you noticed, I'm starting to branch out of my New York black? People dress so differently here. I'm starting to appreciate color."

"Plumage attracts mates."

"That's for the male birds. The hens are always brown and drab."

"Not this one." He handed her the wineglass.

"Thanks. And you won't believe that I rarely drink. The only times we've seen each other outside the office I've been guzzling drinks. But it comes in handy, like tonight. Just me? Aren't you having any?"

He shook his head.

"Do you have to keep your head?"

"That and a lot else. How about some music?"

"Yes, put on some of your excruciating arias."

"I have something I know you'll like."

It was a push of the remote control, for the CD was still in the player—Caetano Veloso with his soft guitar and mesmerizing voice. Nick had played the music the night before, thinking of Flo. She was settling into the couch and he joined her. She draped her legs over his lap while she sipped her wine and relaxed against the cushions. "Do we really have work tomorrow? Let's sail into the sunset—that's how I feel. All we do is work like ants. I guess we're programmed to, but to sail into the sunset . . . ocean wind on our faces, no need for words, though you're probably thinking how could Florence ever be without words? I talk automatically. The transmitters in my brain have no brakes. Your brain has too many brakes."

He laughed. "The brakes come with age." His hand contentedly stroked the velvety fabric covering her leg. He wanted to roll sideways and feel her filling his arms again. As he turned, the specter of Garrett spoiled his sensation.

"Hey, we need to talk—"

"I know, and we will, as soon as I finish my wine. And I want to see your body."

"I'm not ready for this."

"You would be if you had some wine."

"True."

"Like I said, it comes in handy. You have to stop thinking." She tipped her glass at him with arched brows. "A sip?"

He took a sip and handed it back. She swung her legs off the couch, kissed him, and then snuggled against his side, her left arm wrapping around him, her face near his.

"Have it your way."

He wriggled so his arms could encompass her, loving the combination of her girlish face and womanly body. He lost himself in another kiss.

"And now for business," she said, drawing back, "because everything has to be up front with us, always."

Nick heard the word *always* and didn't know what to do with it. Probably it had just fallen from her lips automatically. He waited. She was straightening up a bit to deliver her story, one that would affect him. He leaned over for one more kiss in case it was the last.

"And so," she said, "it's like this. Garrett and I have been together five years, and even though we agreed we didn't want to have children, Garrett couldn't have them anyway—a genetic defect. Now that I'm forty and in love with my little niece, I know I made a mistake not having one, even though my conscience tells me the world isn't a safe place for future generations. But I'm just as selfish as everyone else."

"You want a baby." He couldn't venture to say, You want me to help you have a baby.

Her eyes shone on him. "Garrett knows I want a baby, my own, and months ago he agreed. I said I would ask someone from my New York network, since it would be cheaper than all the artificial inseminations that put you into debt and never work."

He was stunned and put off by the turn in the conversation. The magic of the last hour had vanished completely, and a whirl of emotions and thoughts filled his head.

"I know you think I'm using you," she said. "But it isn't that way at all, I just want a baby, and I already know without asking that you don't. So if I love you and you love me, maybe you could help me."

Her words changed his soured feelings back to a more sympathetic place. But too much was on the table to process, including his job, for how could he continue going to the office with all this business suddenly being part of it? He pulled away from her.

"You don't have to say yes or no tonight."

"No."

Her eyes and cheeks crumpled; she was near tears. "Do you have to say no so fast? Can't you weigh everything out? Can't we talk about it a little more? Please don't say no right away."

"No." His arms folded over his chest.

She waited, holding him with her eyes, her hand lightly resting on his arm just for contact, just to stay connected.

"I wouldn't do that to myself," he said, "to my life."

"I know. And I knew you would feel that way—that's why I wanted to postpone serious talk and just be carefree for one night. I know everything—how you couldn't entrust the fate of your child to someone else's care, even if Garrett's a decent person and I'd be a loving mother. You couldn't live out the rest of your days wondering. It would be a torture—you'd die with that awful torment eating away at you."

"Yep."

"And even if, hypothetically, *hypothetically*, you and I could raise the child together, you couldn't come to terms with our age difference."

"That can be rationalized, but the other things can't be, and thinking on them would swim in circles without end."

"Good. I was wrong about age."

"Except I'm too old to love."

"But you said you loved me."

"I do."

Her lips turned down with slight bitterness. "You love me like a painting in a museum, or a sculpture."

"Maybe. But I was responding to your hypothetical context of being a couple. And in that scenario, I also have Emily. There isn't room for anything more."

"That's where you're wrong. That's where you have to break through. If you dare, you'll break through and have so much more than you have now, though I'm not saying you don't have a lot already."

"But we aren't talking seriously about the hypothetical. We're talking about you wanting me to help you get pregnant, after which you'll go about your happy family life la-di-da."

"Nick, I only said hypothetical because for *you* it probably is. For me it doesn't have to be."

Now his eyes searched hers incredulously. It was clear what she was saying—she'd give up Garrett for him, *um velho*, an old guy. But he couldn't make it all add up, not that fast, or he was afraid of allowing it to add up. Afraid of risk. Just what she had said, just what she wanted him to leap free from.

"Flo, let's have some space on all of this. I'll walk you home. I need the air and so do you. We can talk while we walk."

She didn't protest. And he thought how well she really did know him that she kept quiet for once and left him to his processing. When their coats were on, she faced him, smiled, and then gave him a long hug, which he reciprocated. It made their strange conversation have a positive ending.

Out in the night—nine o'clock already—he felt much better. How much he depended on air, the outdoors, for emotional uplift. With her arm through his they walked back through the Garden, this time without talking much, both busy with their own thoughts, possibly the same thoughts, such as: What if they were a couple walking through the park, a couple with a home somewhere and a private life together, even a child? What if they were a family? It was outlandish, Nick thought, but outlandish ideas started that way and then worked their way into the fabric of one's life, losing their original outlandish quality. Outlandish prospects turned into normal, humdrum life. What was he prepared for? It would take days to know.

Now it was his phone that rang, and the screen showed *Emily*. He answered. It was late for her to call—it might be an emergency. Flo leaned her cheek on his arm while he talked, and how he loved the feel of their closeness, as if it had always been and nothing in all the years ahead could threaten its sanctity. He turned to touch his lips to her hair.

"Hey, what's up, Emmy? Everything okay?"

"Sort of. You'll be happy to know Eric and I broke up."

"Oh, that's heavy—are you all right?"

"Yeah, but it's sad too. I mean, we both agree it's over, but we've lived together a long time—we love each other. That's the weird part. To say you love someone but break up."

"Believe me, I know what it's like."

"I wanted to know if it would it be okay with you if I camped out temporarily at your place till I find a new apartment. It might take a week."

"Why isn't Eric moving? You found the place, it's yours. But yes, of course you can stay with me. Are you coming tonight?"

"Yeah, if it's okay. I slept on the couch last night and I could do it again, but I really want to get out of here. It feels weird."

"Fine. Pack a suitcase and I'll pick you up. In an hour?"

"Thanks! Anytime's fine, I'm ready."

He put the phone back in his pocket, and Flo turned to him for a full kiss. "Just so you know, Nick, it's fine by me you have Emily."

He wished her words could have a stronger effect on him, but he knew the Emily wedge in his life was solid, deep, and permanent. It would take amazing work to loosen that for a relationship that wasn't hypothetical. He thanked her and smiled. Then they strolled on like lovers to the outside world, but in a matter of minutes, at her front walk, their lives would cleave.

Seven

Now, as April approached, the citizens of Boston were impatient for spring to gain a firm grasp and begin its colorful pageant that the annual marathon helped to celebrate. Eyes scanned the landscape for the fragile heads of purple or yellow crocuses, or the curling green leaves of a rising tulip, or the faintest softness in the wind that signaled the arrival of nature's most erotic season. Nick knew that from this point on, each week would offer a pretty sight for the eyes, especially the clouds of cherry blossoms floating into the distance along the curving Charles and the pink magnolias' profusion down the length of Commonwealth Ave. For now it was a delight to witness the chartreuse buds of the willow trees sweeping gracefully over the pond in the Garden, or now and then, where the sun shone fully, a bright spot of yellow forsythia. And birds—they were out in legions, their chirping animated, spritely. It was mating season, cause for exuberance in every living being, and the collective energy soared into the sky and treetops.

Nick's week at Churchill following Flo's fantastical proposal had been jam-packed with urgent deadlines, preventing any further meetings or discussion. However, their eyes met significantly whenever their paths crossed in the conference room or he dropped something off at her office. Twice they had discussed sample layouts on her desk without dropping their professional veneer, but in their bodies, so close as they leaned over the pages, secret knowledge ran like electrical currents. He knew how much harder it was for her to hold back words, and she couldn't just show up at his apartment after work because she knew Emily was camping there. But the dam would break imminently, he knew, and he had no idea how he would act or what he would say when the moment came. Caution might be his middle name, but he had lived long enough to know that the uncontrollable forces of love broke through all restraining barriers, in many cases like a bulldozer wrecking lives.

Emily had quickly found a group house to live in—friends with an opening—and on the weekend Charlotte and Emily's college friend Dan showed up, along with Nick, to help her move. Charlotte had borrowed a friend's pickup to handle the furniture. Eric had conveniently absented himself from the apartment. Nick and Charlotte gave each other a formal, barely grazing hug, which was their way of recent times, when forgiveness had settled all their difficult days into a past no longer felt by either of them. It was ironic that long ago their beloved child had contributed to the chasm that grew between them, but now it was her existence that drew them back together in a ghostly version of their former family. Nick suspected that Charlotte was too busy with her professional and married life to give much thought to her relationship to Nick. He, however, had most nights free for some reflection and in recent times had ruminated on their past, their potential and their loss. Something wonderful and irreplaceable had once existed. It was the special bonding ingredient that caused couples to marry and embark on life dreams together; why then did that unique quality invariably extinguish? Love might last for certain long-term couples, but it was a remembered love, a loyalty love, and more often than not a resigned love. And there was nothing wrong with that—like much of life, love and its many facets remained a mystery to humankind, never nailed down to satisfaction. But when Nick reminisced about his life with Charlotte, he regretted that they hadn't made it through those hard years when egos demanded recognition—a superficial recognition compared to the substantial roots of a marriage originally founded on love. Besides egos, the pressures and responsibilities of family life had led to quarrels, friction, and ultimately irrevocable frustration and resentment. Still, their foundation to last had been strong. They had lived in the depths of Rio de Janeiro together—had met there, worked with idealism in a slum where the conditions of human life were inconceivable to sheltered Americans. They had shared experiences that no others in either of their subsequent lives could ever know. And they had discovered the other sides of Rio as well—the nightlife, the dancing, the fun and abandon. Their Rio bond alone should have been enough to keep them together for life. But at the time it had been such a relief to end the relationship, the acrimony, the stress, the feeling of being trapped and suffocating.

With Fleetwood Mac blaring out of Eric's living room stereo, the foursome kept traffic steady in and out the front door of the tall frame house with a big front porch. Boxes, suitcases, grocery bags, and green trash bags filled with clothes went into the cars. Furniture was destined for the pickup, and if it didn't all fit, they would make two trips. Back and forth they went, walking fast with their heavy or bulky loads. Nick took a box from Charlotte to stash in his trunk.

She paused for a moment to catch her breath. "How's your job?"

"Great. I love it—always busy, good people. How's yours going?"

"The same. I'm happy but also thinking about retirement. Or doing something else. My next phase. I look around the school and everyone's thirty years old."

"I know what you mean. But don't worry, you look young too." He smiled. She still paid attention to her looks, even though she was dressed casually in jeans and a dark blue fleece. Her modeling days à la Flo were over, though she had never been into that kind of fashion, not as a teacher and not as herself. Hers had always been a bohemian style that favored handmade fabrics and designs, jewelry by artisans. Now she dressed more simply, as if accepting that her pinnacle had passed and it was fine to let the younger women shine, just as she had shone in her day. Like his, her face had that haggard look that came with age and showed up particularly when standing next to twenty-somethings like Emily and Dan.

"Let's go for a coffee after the move," Nick suggested.

"Good, I was thinking the same thing," she said, looking around to see where Emily was. "I'd like to hear your thoughts on Emily."

Emily came out of the house as if to prevent further discussion of her. She dragged a garbage bag that rattled with kitchen pans. Nick grabbed it up and heaved it into his trunk while Charlotte went back inside.

"I can't believe it," Emily said, hands on her hips. "Dan just told me that his parents are living together again. They've been divorced two years. Don't you think that's weird?"

Nick laughed. "Not so weird."

"What? After divorcing? Back in the same bed together?"

"It can happen," he said. "They once loved each other. It's complicated, but not weird, not when you're my age."

"Well, I think it's gross." And she left.

He followed her back inside, thinking that she didn't have to worry about her own parents getting back together again. They were safely divorced with her mother remarried. Even so, he couldn't help but smile that perhaps her extra-acute antennae had picked up his passing speculations about what it might be like if he and Charlotte lived together again, their past intact as they embarked on senior years. Maybe Emily was giving him a warning that it would be intolerable for her—gross.

He shook his head. How could he ever face her if he started a relationship with Flo?

Dan was surveying the living room for the next thing to move.

"Shall we get the couch?" Nick asked.

"Yeah, we're down to the big stuff."

They each took an end and eased the couch through two doors and down the porch steps to the pickup. Dan, a charter-school teacher, had been Emily's close friend since freshman year, when they had met in a writing class, both inspired by Bowdoin's literary legacy, Hawthorne and Longfellow. Nick figured Dan had secretly loved Emily, so that the friendship had developed and endured despite Emily's changing boyfriends, down to her recent relationship with Eric. Dan was part of her life, perhaps like a brother. Of course the dynamic could change if Dan met someone and fell in love.

Watching people on the subway and in public places, Nick saw that there was someone for everyone; people needed the comfort of sharing their inner worlds, and at a certain point looks stopped being the first criterion. And what about himself? What about Flo's proposition? He wanted to know if he had he drifted too far from the comfort zone of sharing human warmth to even imagine it anymore. The few months with Kathy a while back had been a band-aid to loneliness until he realized that he preferred being alone to spending time on the emotional ups and downs of a relationship, or one that wasn't compelling him. Flo was so different. An exciting terror seized him when he thought of her or stood near her, and the thrill consumed him. It spun his thoughts in circles. If he took a risk with Flo, the chances for disaster to his life were just as likely as the chances for success. It was an all-or-nothing proposition, and the all was terribly complicated, from the Garrett factor to Emily to his advancing age and her desire for a child. He saw himself facing her and saying, "No." And the next instant he faced her and said, "All." The no was safe, and the all was the wildest risk he could imagine, or not even quite imagine. And yet his senses roared with a fascination that he knew would outlive him.

"You okay, Nick? Want me on that end?" Dan asked from the bed of the pickup, ready to pull the couch in.

"I'm fine. Heave-ho." Nick gave the necessary lift and shove to move the couch into the pickup with Dan guiding its position.

They headed back inside for Emily's bureau, and then the bed parts and mattress. Nick felt his strength and energy. A pleasant alacrity flowed in his veins. He knew something big had just shifted in him during the move. He had finally, after a decade, stepped out of his past with Charlotte into the unknown but incredibly tantalizing future—his future. That's what had happened. Suddenly he had a future, and he saw himself with Flo.

"Dad, *Silver Linings Playbook* is playing—want to go? Bradley Cooper, Robert De Niro, *mental illness*."

He laughed. "When you put it that way, how can I resist?"

"What?" Charlotte asked, dropping a stuffed grocery bag onto the back seat of Dan's car. "What mental illness?"

"A movie about a young man discharged from the loony bin who returns home to his wacky parents while still experiencing erratic behavior," Emily said.

"We're all dysfunctional," Charlotte said.

"No we're not," Nick said.

"Well, to some degree we are."

"If you mean we all have foibles and idiosyncrasies, then yes, but dysfunctionality means something a lot bigger."

"I'm the dysfunctional one," Emily said dully.

"No, you're not, honey," Charlotte said, putting her arm around her shorter daughter. "You cope magnificently."

"You have no idea what goes on inside my head."

"Maybe it's a bad idea to see the movie," Dan said. "It might depress you."

"It's supposed to be uplifting. It's actually billed as a comedy. Do you want to come too?"

"Maybe. What day were you thinking of?"

"I vote next week," Nick said. "Wednesday?"

Heads nodded consensus. Their packing was done and they remained around the back of the truck chit-chatting a few more minutes. Every so often the sun broke through motley gray clouds to send down some bright rays. Then the gray cotton rolled over the golden heat once more, reminding Nick of London's weather, gray and chilly one minute and streaming with teasing sunshine the next.

"I say we get these cars over to Emmy's new place and unload so we're free for a pizza or whatever you're in the mood for," Nick said.

"Mood," Emily said laughing. "That word has come to mean so much. I'll lock up."

She went back for a final eye-sweep of the apartment and then locked the front door. As she came down the porch steps, she texted

Eric that the house keys were in the mailbox. "Bye," she called over her shoulder to the old frame house.

On Monday the office was a tense scene and Flo was in the spotlight, dressed in black, without a shred of fuchsia or sea green showing through a crack in her sweater or flowing from her neck in a scarf or in jewelry. She was pale, so that her dark brows and red lips stood out. She was on the phone almost without interruption, because *Island Peril* had been declared a fraud by a prominent reviewer in the Sunday *Times*. "If such a far-fetched yarn could ever happen in real life, which isn't plausible, then Ricky Harmon, an assumed identity, could not have been the innocent bystander he purports to be but would have to be part of the drug cartel, even if a petty player."

Flo was at the center of a possible publishing scandal and had dressed herself for a funeral. The bosses had come into the editorial wing to consult with Flo, who defended the book righteously. "We're not going to let Michael Gould ruin our book just because he skimmed it and prefers writers like David Foster Wallace. I'm going to call him and give him a piece of my mind! How dare he stir up serious trouble just because the subject turns him off. He even admits that in his review," she told not only the executives but also Nick and several other staffers.

Meetings and phone calls happened all morning while the company decided how to handle the spreading rumor—the Internet had picked it up with bloggers and commenters. Already, within a day of the review, people were asking if this meant the book would be recalled. "Social media has been our enemy," Flo repeated to colleagues she passed in the hall or talked to on the phone. "If it weren't for fucking Twitter and the Internet, Michael Gould's review would have passed quietly by."

At lunchtime she called Nick into her office. The top brass was once again seated at her round table and smiled and nodded courteous hellos. Nick wondered if he was being fired. It came as a total surprise when Flo stood up and gave him her news. "We're sending you to Rio to look into this. You speak the language, you know your way around, and you have excellent judgment. I hope your passport is up-to-date. Sam's contact at the consulate can rush visas—this afternoon, meaning could you run home now and get your passport?"

Sam cut in. "I hope you can help, Nick. We want you to talk to Chad Winters in person, get a feel for him, go over specific sections of his book, and also talk to the relevant Rio authorities about what happened—get documented information if possible. The consulate is providing us with some names, including a lawyer."

"We just need evidence one way or the other," Flo went on, pacing about. "It should take at most a week. And this afternoon, if this plan is all right with you, we'll issue a statement that we're halting further distribution until the company investigates the claims being made. What claims? I mean, literally, what appropriate authority has made any proven claim against the book? But we have to deal with the mounting clamor—it would make things worse to ignore it. And by the way, our ghostwriter, Baker, is nowhere to be found—his mailbox is full. Oscar thinks he's in Iraq. He's trying to track him down, but for the moment we're going to forget about Baker and go straight to the source. We're counting on you, Nick." She smiled wanly, coming to a halt next to him. "I know you'll resolve everything. I feel those vibes."

"It's the best we can do—and for the public," Sam added with sober approbation, and with that, the important gents got up to return to their offices. Nick had stood there listening the whole time; they didn't seem to notice, or care, what he thought. "We'll post a brief announcement on the website, and Flo, you can make a few comments to one of our trusted journalists," Sam continued from the door. Then the trio was gone.

Nick heard Flo's relieved whisper: "Thank you."

He smiled, all the surprise of the past minutes in his face. "I guess I got assigned."

Her brown eyes implored him. "I know we plotted behind your back. It wasn't fair. We should have plotted with you. It all happened so fast. I had one of my brainstorms, and then Sam had the consulate connection. He really liked the idea. I promise to make it up to you. For starters, I'm coming along to help." Her smile broke wide.

He laughed. "What? You little schemer."

"I know, I can't deny it. I'm sure you agree we'll make an incredible investigative team."

"I'll carry your briefcase."

"You're not my lackey."

"I am." He smiled and she smiled back. In an hour her somber black attire of the morning had morphed into a ravishing black sheath because her resourcefulness had paid off and was now radiating through her clothes, through her girlish, animated cheeks. Born to laugh, he thought, born to giggle. But life always got serious and stole that childhood inclination away.

"And by god, I am not going to let that schlemiel get away with any lies. If the book has lies, then goddammit, we'll correct them. *Peril* is still going to be a Churchill blockbuster." She let her body sway lightly against his and added near his ear, "For god's sake, I've been waiting too long for you to ask me out for a drink."

"How about tonight?"

"Perfect. We can map out our game plan. This is going to be

fun. When was the last time you were in Rio? Should we warn this beach bum we're coming or just show up?"

"Warn him, in case he's away on vacation."

"I thought Rio was vacation. So what'll we tell him?"

"We'll say now that the book's out, we'd like to discuss its publicity. I won't say bad publicity. I'll call him."

"And in the meantime we'll reread the book and circle the questionable passages."

"Liza can handle that in an hour—she edited it."

"Good, because Sam wants us out of here tomorrow and apparently it takes an age to get to Rio—no direct flights." She pressed her stomach and grimaced. "Why was I born with nerves? They get me right here." Then she picked up her phone and pushed the speaker button. Her assistant, Justin, just across the hall, who could hear everything audible, promptly answered, "Hi, Flo."

"Justin, could you come over for a few minutes? Nick and I are going to Rio to get to the bottom of *Island Peril*, and we're going to need some instant bookings, and Sam has a contact at the Brazilian consulate who can help."

"Coming," he answered, and they heard him hang up his phone.

"You know, I can probably handle this junket on my own," Nick said, suddenly wondering if he could handle Flo 24/7 and in a hotel when there was Garrett in the background.

"But, darling, it'll be much more interesting if I'm there to help." She grinned, her lips tipping slightly down—that faint bitter dip at the ends that manifested itself now and then. "Don't you want me?"

Then Justin arrived and she rattled off instructions while Nick went back to his office to grab his jacket for a quick jog home for his passport. But on second thought he decided to call Chad

Winters first, in case he got an answering machine. Chad's wife answered and said that Chad was at their Copacabana snack bar, but he had received the book and loved it. So had she.

"We're coming to Rio to talk to him about the book's publicity," Nick said. "Likely Wednesday or Thursday, depending on flights. Will he be there?"

Yes, Chad worked seven days a week and she helped him part-time.

"I'll e-mail you the details," Nick said. "We're going to need about two hours of Chad's time."

She agreed, and Nick buzzed Flo to say they were good to go. "I take it Sam et al. know you're coming too."

"Yes. And I'm truly sorry I was so devious. I get so many ideas that there isn't always time to involve the people I'm making plans for. And this trip is obviously strictly business—they know both of us are needed on this job."

"Ha," he barely breathed into the phone.

"I heard that," she said. "I'm getting back to work. I have a lot to do. We both do. I hope you're looking forward to going to Rio."

"In more ways than one."

He sat for a moment after hanging up the phone, marveling at the way things sprouted and spouted out of her spontaneously, with so little premeditation—there wasn't time for it. All in a flash, she had contrived her role in the mission to be alone with him, to have an adventure with him, and it amazed and thrilled him. He opened his cell phone and sent her a text. "See you at six, *génio*."

When Nick left the building that evening, it was still light. The days were lengthening. People—mostly the young—had emerged from their winter cubbies and now strolled the streets with a carefree air, their voices lifting up into the sheath of sky. He wondered if this season he too would be out on the vibrant streets with Flo, and what about Garrett?

The minute Flo came outside he kissed her—automatically, passionately, and luckily no one from the office happened to be there.

"Oooh," she said, face brimming with pleasure as they came apart and started walking rapidly away from the building. "Now I know what the romance writers mean by bruised lips. Yum." She laughed, tasting her own lips.

"It's very hard not to grab you," he said.

"Music to my ears, especially when I feel so fat. I have to get rid of my winter layer."

"Flo, you're not fat."

"I had bulimia when I was a teen. I've felt fat my entire life, even when I've starved myself."

"You're a beautiful woman. I wouldn't change anything about you."

"I'm so glad to hear that. I've always wanted to change everything about me." She smiled, taking his arm. "I'm just as insecure today as I was in my teens, only I've learned to fake confidence. It took years of reading self-help books, talking to therapists, and trusting that I could bring my talents into the world so I could truly live. Deep inside I'm a little mouse who likes the safety of her hole in the wall."

"That's common."

"You mean you feel that way too?"

"Sometimes, yes. But men are raised differently and have a better chance of believing they belong out there in the tough competition. Society accepts them that way, whereas women get scrutinized relentlessly. We ridicule them for physical things. The newspaper is always describing what Hillary Clinton has on or how she looks. What about the job she's doing?"

"Thank you. That's why I'm all for women. Even if they aren't all for me. Our road isn't easy. And some men have told me, if you can believe it, that it's just our mixed-up outlook that's the problem."

"Stay away from those guys." He smiled at her, their eyes so close, for in her heels she was his height. "Tell me, how do you walk distances in those heels?"

"I don't. I cheat. I have flats in my bag."

"Don't you want to put them on?"

"Yes, I do, but I also want to look exceedingly sexy for you."

"Nothing could be sexier than you in flats."

She put down her bag, dug out her flats, and held on to his arm as she changed her shoes. He watched the womanly curve of her back and hip through her coat as she bent to reach her foot. It was a thin, beautiful foot, with fine bones tracing almost to her ankles through her sheer black stockings. "Ah, so much better!" she said, straightening and beaming at him. "But I love heels—I'm really me in heels. And now I feel so short."

They kissed, testing out the new dimensions between them. She had to lift her head just a tad for their lips to touch. "I prefer kissing you straight on," she said, going up on her tiptoes. "There, eye to eye, mouth to mouth, brain to brain. You're really beautiful, Nick, those deep-set eyes, a little sad. I know exactly how you looked when you were my age."

"Younger." He put his arm around her and started walking again. "I don't even know where we're going."

"Neither do I. But it doesn't matter. Is Emily at your place?"

"No, she moved over the weekend. What about Garrett?"

"He's in New York helping his parents look at apartments. They're downsizing. And now that I'm traveling to Brazil, he's going to extend. We can go to my place."

Nick did not want to deceive Garrett in his own home. How could Flo want that? How could Charlotte live with Bill in their former house? "We have to pack tonight," he said.

"Which is much harder for me—women need wardrobes, shoes, but I can do it in an hour."

"Remember your bathing suit."

"I can't wait to see those famous beaches." She turned and sang into his face, "'The girl from Ipanema goes walking . . .'"

"'And when she passes, each one she passes goes, Ahhh . . .,'" Nick sang back.

"Did you want to be a rock star growing up?"

"No, I didn't play any instruments. I wanted to be the next Robert Lowell or T. S. Eliot. What about you?"

"Princess Diana."

"Perfect, but your talents would have been underutilized."

"Not true. I would have applied them in a different way, like she did—charities."

"From her jet-setting hot spots. Shall we get something to eat on Newbury Street?"

"No, I'm a free woman tonight and I can't snuggle up to you at Stephanie's on Newbury."

"Okay, my place then—no spousal ghosts. I even have some food."

"You mean you're going to feed me?"

She lifted her face demurely with half-closed eyes, as if luxuriating in the idea of being pampered. He stared at those beautiful lips, an art object all on their own, perfectly carved from smooth stone. His hand lifted to cup the oval face with its prominent chin. The soft cheeks, round mounds, would never droop, for the bones holding them up were too strong to let go of the flesh. But it wasn't her face he loved, it was the network of wires inside her that produced her personality so visibly in her face.

At his place, after he hung up their coats, he looked at her across the unlit room. She stood in her stockings, her fitted black dress showing her curves as she looked out his front window onto the tree-lined street now lit by lamps. Her hair hung to her shoulders, which rose slightly in her self-conscious hunch. He slid his shoes off and joined her, lightly pressing his body against her back, his face dropping into the hair at the nook of her neck and shoulder. Her head leaned back to nuzzle his, and his hands traced the lovely line that ran down her hourglass sides and hips. His mind filled with her feminine scent and softness; his senses knew without yet discovering the full, soft breasts nestled into the front of her dress, the delicate rib cage and rounded belly, the long thighs, the legs ending in goddess feet. His right hand moved the zipper down the back of her dress so his hands could slide in and find all that his mind and senses imagined, his desire heightened by the murmurs of pleasure that came from her throat.

The nights that lovers, especially new lovers, spend in each other's arms in bed are the greatest intimacy humans can know, Nick thought. Music sometimes touched that vein but in a yearning, nostalgic, incomplete way, while the sweet warmth of two bodies completely in sync under cozy covers attained perfect contentment. Flo felt it too and would not go home to pack. "We'll take a cab over to my place before dawn, and then we'll get another cab to the airport after I throw my things in a suitcase."

"Good—I'll have a chance to see your closet."

"I admit, I'm an incurable shopper. It's related to my phobias. You'll have to pry the hangers apart, the dresses are packed in so tight."

"I was picturing three or four closets."

"Two, albeit big ones, and seasonal storage under the bed. It's disgusting, and I hope you'll reform me. I want to be like you—unconcerned."

"I used to be more concerned. It fades. You're still young."

"If you consider forty young."

"At fifty something gives way, you'll see."

"You'll always be twenty-three to me, the innocent American plunged into Brazilian culture. That's how I see you, black hair and all—just like the photo on your book."

All night their bodies stirred, legs lacing, in the heavenly dozes of love. Sometimes they clutched each other in gratefulness. It was not the time to talk about Garrett or what lay ahead, which could only be rough; it was a time-out for both, a cocoon of their own, a cocoon that held their eyes and their voices, their sexualities and their love. Daylight and the real world would rupture the bliss soon enough. They held hands when they weren't making love, for their hands conveyed the electricity of their unspoken and treasured bond.

The real world hit at four, when Nick's alarm went off. Flo sat up immediately. "Oh, my god, there's so much to do—why do you think I come to work at ten? It takes hours to get ready. Well, Brazil is just going to have to see the real me, and so are you. We need to hurry, Nick. We goofed off last night and today we have to save *Island Peril*. You haven't even packed yet, and probably I should just meet you at the airport—"

"You don't need help?"

"No. I might not be able to cook, but I can pack. Where did you put my shoes? What do I look like? Where's the mirror? Fuck, I'm sure I look horrible."

"Flo—"

She was hobbling around the room in a frenzy, grabbing at her clothes. The sight of her white skin, womanly curves, legs, and the patch of fur that joined them took his breath away. But he would have to turn off his admiration and get moving. He swung off the bed and stood up. She stopped and stared at him across the dark room, brown eyes shining like a woodland animal's, mouth slightly ajar. His chest was hairy, a mix of gray and black, the hair tapering down past his navel. She looked at his legs.

"God!" she said. "Your bod!"

"Courtesy of the dark," he said, reaching for his shirt, suddenly shy.

"You're as bad as me," she said.

Then she resumed her frenzy of finding her belongings, thrusting her jewelry into her purse, and pulling on her coat. "Where's the taxi stand?"

"Charles Street, one block down. I'm coming."

And he was as fast as she because he didn't have to put on stockings. They left the apartment and quickly found a cab. She got in and its red taillights sped off. He saw the back of her head through the rear window—erect, brain running fast with her to-do list. She would be home in three minutes. They'd be together again in a couple of hours, and then together nonstop for a week. Was he prepared for that? Charged to capacity! He turned back for home. Charles Street was deserted, though the ghostly storefronts were lit. He turned up his side street and began to jog the incline. Too much had happened at once and he was glad to be alone for a couple of hours to start processing it. First he would unleash what was stuffed right behind his face: an incoherent torrent of emotion that would rush out in lines he had no control over; they would simply flow like white cascades onto his page. She would always be there, five feet in front of him, vibrant, in living colors, smiling, laughing, twirling in her latest dress, and loving to be admired, loving to have his intent gaze on her, his mind trained on her, his hands fashioned and carved to handle her, and yet, inevitably, without ever being able to own even a molecule of her to make her feel safe. But that was all right, he thought, as long as he was there to share her space and anxiety, not to mention the spontaneous wellspring of love and affection that bound them.

He took the hallway stairs two at a time in his rush to get to his notebook. He had one hour before he had to get serious, one hour for the spiral universe that contained his love for Flo.

EIGHT

The flight to Rio was long, with a layover in Panama, but fortunately the consulate connection had not only expedited visas but also arranged with the Brazilian airlines for business-class seats. Nick and Flo talked about the challenged book and how, if it was grossly embellished or even falsified in places, it might still be saved. Nick had printed out from the Web several articles on recent publishing scandals, and they compared their situation to these cases. In the end, they agreed that scandals happened and publishers dealt with them, often by putting the bad book in its grave. The world went on, unaffected.

They also talked about themselves, their pasts. Flo told Nick she had been so devastated by her parents' divorce that she vowed never to have children of her own—divorce rates were just too high. She had been in a number of failed relationships with every kind of man, from bohemian painter to Wall Street banker to retired corporate lawyer pursuing art collecting. Then, in her mid-thirties, she serendipitously met Garrett in Central Park —"serendipitously because I wasn't in the park to exercise like everyone else. I was there to cross to the West Side, which on the weekend is like taking your life in your hands with all the joggers, bikers, bladers, and other aggressive fitness freaks. In fact, I had to leap out of Garrett's way and fell headlong onto the street. And that's how we ended up getting married. He had to make it up to me." She laughed. "Seriously, Garrett wasn't like all the other narcissistic men in my life. He was a funky entrepreneur and a green freak. He wasn't even riding his bike like a madman. I was the one who made a mistake and got in his way. Garrett's a good guy. And I'm sure your ex-wife is the same, since you loved her once upon a time."

He nodded. "Charlotte's good. We were different people when we met."

He asked her more about Garrett. He wanted an image of the man whose life she shared, besides his picture in her office. She leaned back with half-closed eyes to recite his essentials, some of which Nick already knew. Garrett was several years younger, from an educated family in New York, and after graduating in business from Cornell and working aimlessly in restaurants, he had started an organic food truck, with his parents' backing. It became a hit and led to a popular eatery followed by two more branches. He had sold the business when they moved to Boston and was still looking around for his next project, talking to various start-ups and young entrepreneurs. He had a wad to invest.

Nick broached the topic that was the easiest to avoid: What were they doing? What were they getting into? What about Garrett? Affairs never had happy endings for anyone. Affairs were horribly destructive.

Flo looked into his eyes purposefully, her voice assured. "I'm yours if you want me, Nick. I hope you want me. I want you. I can weather anything for that."

"I want you too—you know that. But it's complicated."

"Garrett."

"Yes, and more."

"I know—your job, our housing, Emily. God, Nick, if we can handle the insane publishing world, we can handle our personal lives, especially if we work together. I'm going to tell Garrett as soon as we get back, or as soon as I can this week."

"Good. Harder for you than for me. I'm sorry."

"Don't be too sorry. We have to have fortitude to do this," she said. "The way I look at it, Garrett's young, he's good-looking. He'll meet someone else, someone who loves him." Her brown eyes sent their lights into his, the expression naked. "I talked myself into loving him because he was so different from my other mistakes. But with you, my whole body went off in a chemical connection. I know I like to flirt and make people desire me, but there's only one man I want near me." She mouthed her last word: You.

He was moved and murmured her name. He lifted her hand to his lips, inhaling the pale, smooth skin. He would love it were it spotted and ruined with age.

Her eyes again sent sparks into his, as if she read his mind. He smiled affectionately. "I love those animal eyes."

"Animal?"

"Bright, in the wild, alive to sound and scent, vulnerable."

"Mmm. Are those really my eyes?"

"Like a doe's, like a squirrel's, like a cat's. Exuberant one minute, cunning the next, defeated and disappointed, hard with intelligence, conspiratorial, perceptive, seductive . . . I have a list somewhere."

"You made a list? I want to see it!"

"I bet."

"You've gone around taking notes on me—"

"Whole notebooks."

"Nick, you're so deceptive. All this time, all these months, I thought I was the only one who was interested. I had to slosh wine to plead for that first kiss."

"You were married. Otherwise . . ."

"When can I read the notebooks? No one's ever written one word about me."

"I'm sure they have."

"Promise me you'll share. I'm finally a damsel on paper, an inspiration to someone—it isn't fair if I never get the pleasure of seeing words that describe me."

He kissed her. "I'll give you something when it's ready."

"Something. Ready. That means it's more than notes."

"I wrote a few poems."

"Poems," she murmured and leaned back contentedly, her right hand sliding over to his leg and resting there. His left hand covered it.

"I want to talk to you about Emily," he said. "She's the counterpoint to Garrett."

"Of course," Flo said. "I want to know everything about Emily, I want to know Emily. I'm not jealous that she comes first. I understand she comes first."

"It's not who comes first, just who needs help at any given time."

Flo nodded, and he searched for words to capture everything he had experienced from the beginning to now as a parent, and of course that was impossible. She would learn it all in time, by increment. Haltingly at first, he told her about the first time he had seen Emily's face chattering insanely at him, madly, the Mad Hatter. "I was watching and listening and trying to process all at once the person before me, who was my beloved daughter and out of her mind, jabbering incoherently, face like iron, somehow dehumanized, and lost. That's the worst, when a person's lost." He went on to describe Emily's traumatic trip to Miami with Darrel and his ongoing fears for her safety, her life. "So much more happens to other families," he said. "I always remind myself of that."

"That doesn't reduce the impact," Flo said.

"No. And none of this is new for me anymore. Anything that happens now I've already lived with or tried to prepare for. I'm resigned to accepting life for what it is. Though it still hurts to know Emily has a certain life to cope with, or fight for, with no assurance of safety for her mind."

"Safety's an illusion," she said. "I had a breakdown my last year of college. Columbia Presbyterian for me. I've had a lot of help in my life, and I'll probably need more if *Island Peril* goes down the tubes. But I know firsthand what you're talking about, that's what I wanted to say."

"Thanks. What happened to you?" he said.

"Everything. 'Sorority lifestyle' is my standard line, and to some extent it's true. It was a catalyst, especially because, as you've probably already discerned, I have a propensity for melancholy."

"No, I didn't notice that, or not exactly. I've thought moods, complexity."

"Same thing. It was hard work, Nick, but I've achieved self-esteem—barely, possibly phony, but I try to believe it's a trembling 'real.'"

He squeezed the hand he was still holding. Life wasn't easy for anyone, including children. And women faced a unique set of challenges that made their path to well being a tougher journey. Still, life usually kept you wanting to live despite all its inexplicable hurdles and tragedies.

"So," he said.

"So it was something close to what happens in my book—you might have guessed already."

He had wondered. It was all too easy for that to happen. How odd, though, both Emily and Flo mixed up like that, and even odder that both had moods, and odder yet his unwavering love for both. What was the innate connection?

"It was a one-time, crazy deal, high-end beyond your imagination—the real jet set of royalty and celebs, where I got to be a princess. My friend and I deliberately contrived to be the weekend consorts of some playboy wastrels from the Gulf. We dressed up in rented gowns and jewelry and got paid ten grand each. Ten grand. But I paid dearly for that in the hotel rooms." She shivered. "The money revolted me afterward. Guilt. Staring me in the eye, even though I spent it. I still feel the horror and shame of it." She shook off the memory and then looked at him with helpless eyes. "I was crazy."

"No, you were just coming of age, naive, caught between childhood fantasies and cruel adult reality. Judgment comes from experience."

"That's a nice way to look at it. My shrinks never came up with that." She was quiet for a moment and then added with a slight bitterness, "Now you'll think I have bad genes."

"I would never think that. We all have good and bad genes." He took a breath, not wanting to disappoint her but also wanting to be open and honest. "But that's something we need to talk about."

"You mean not talk about. I know you don't want a baby and I do."

"I'm too old to have a baby."

"It must be my biological clock driving me to fulfill my female purpose."

"I had that drive too—about making a child with someone you love."

"I want ours. The mix of us. I never felt that way with Garrett."

Her eyes closed dreamily as her head reclined on the seat. He studied her face trying to feel something for the idea of their mix, their blend, but all he could see was a little toddler, a child going through the long years of elementary and middle school with birthday parties, school events, weekend sports, homework, and parental involvement each and every day, because that was the only way to raise a child you loved. Not only did he want his own life now, but he also couldn't imagine being an old-man father. He occasionally saw one pushing a stroller on the street. He could tell the difference between a grandfather and a father, because a grandfather with a stroller was always accompanied by a white-haired wife, whereas an old-man father was always alone, giving his wife a break. And what if Emily had a child in the next five years? Their children would be of the same generation. He couldn't wrap his mind around it.

"It's about raising a child," Flo said, opening her eyes, "being a mother. I could adopt an orphan from Honduras and I'm sure I'd be happy. But in this case, my vanity's driving me. I'm yearning to extend myself in some way."

And that was exactly what was missing in him: the desire to extend himself, or feel the anticipation of a new life that revealed their combination. No, he was wrong, it wasn't entirely missing in him. Her talk of it forced him to imagine the three of them, the family, and something beautiful was there, the evidence of their love bond. Just as it had been with Charlotte—Emily the evidence of their devotion. But how could humans do that kind of thing twice, or at least so late in life?

"They can," he said aloud.

"What?" Flo said, looking at him.

"Humans," he answered, laughing and kissing her. "They can."

"Obviously an inside joke."

He laid his hand tenderly along the side of her face. Maybe the deepest expression of love was the evidence of it. "I need time."

"That's fine, sweetheart. So far you haven't taken excessive time, so I'm content to wait. But I think we're all agreed on the first point, that we're together from here until eternity."

"Yes," he answered. "We're together, *juntos*."

Late afternoon of the day they arrived in Rio, *cidade maravilhosa*, they found Chad Winters at his bright yellow kiosk facing the Copacabana beach. It was a contemporary structure in the style of the old-fashioned, thatched-roof hut common in the tropics. It sat next to the famous black-and-white-tiled sidewalk in the pattern of waves. Yellow plastic chairs and tables were scattered in front of the bar, and an enormous cluster of green coconuts hung from a hook to the side of the counter. Gray-haired, hefty Chad served drinks to two young men in speedos, while a good-looking, curly-haired teenager stocked shelves with packaged goods.

"He looks pleasant enough," Flo said, peering through her glamour sunglasses as if through binoculars.

"He seemed nice enough in his book—full of enthusiasm."

"But that was John Baker's voice."

"True. Chad might be a mobster for all we know."

The shoreline's famous sandy curve was populated with half-naked, baked-brown bodies. It faced a breathtaking seascape with oddly shaped, jungly green islands rising up from the sea with a mystical, planetary feel, the phallic thrust of Sugarloaf predominant. The mountain's hulk formed an axis with Christ the Redeemer presiding over the city from a granite peak behind the city's strip of high-rises. The astonishing view reminded Nick that part of what had so attached him to Rio in his early twenties was its singular and infinite allure in setting, people, ambiance, and culture. Miles of open beaches and daily sunsets over the mountains could fill the soul with wonder for the greater, inexplicable universe that seemed to connect to Rio. And the city had been a melting-pot from its beginning, with piracy and smuggling rooted in its history and culture.

"Okay, buddy, shall we go nab him?" Flo said at Nick's side, her head just about even with his.

"I'm ready."

They walked the wide, patterned sidewalk toward Chad Winters's kiosk, their sunglasses reflecting the gleaming sand, sky, and water. Traffic sounds rent the air to one side of the promenade and ocean waves and breezes lent a dreamy, transcendent touch to the other. Chad's sharp eye spotted their approach and he quickly washed his hands, gave instructions over his shoulder to his helper, and then stepped out of the kiosk just as Nick and Flo came under its shady awning. They shook hands and introduced themselves. Chad's open-faced, friendly manner, in keeping with a successful businessman, concealed any observations he might be making. He waved them to a table. "Make yourselves comfortable. Paulo, bring us some coconut water."

As Flo sat down, she pulled *Island Peril* out of her satchel and put it on the table, while her light voice chatted sociably. "This is my first trip to Rio. What an adventure. The landscape's so startling."

"We call it Eden."

She stared out at it, considering the comparison. "I'm sure it is, but the traffic, all the congestion."

"We're building up for the games."

"I know, and frankly, I can't see how you're going to handle all the visitors. On the other hand, you've got the perfect location for your business."

"If I can keep it."

"What do you mean?"

"I mean this is Rio. Someone with better connections might want this spot for the boom times."

"How could they get away with that?"

"It's a way of life here."

The young helper with gleaming black curls and a serious face delivered their drinks in frosty glasses. Nick thanked him in Portuguese, adding *"Você está pronto para as Olimpíadas?"*

The boy smiled, which transformed him from a wooden automaton to a real person. *"Sim, é difícil esperar."*

"You know the language," Chad said.

Nick nodded. "I was here in the early eighties with the Peace Corps."

Flo steered them to business, turning on a mini voice recorder she had placed on the table. "Chad, we need to record this for Churchill, I hope you don't mind."

"It's fine."

"First of all, congratulations on your book. It's been selling like crazy." "Yeah, my wife follows it on the Web."

"And now more reviews are coming in."

He nodded. "I read some of the blogs. I know that's why you're here, and all I can say is, my story's true." He chugged a third of his drink.

"I'm glad to hear it," Flo said. "Nevertheless, we need to handle the attacks, and the best way to do that is to show you the places in the book where credibility has been challenged. By the way, did you file a police report after the ambush?"

"Of course I did—it's in the book—but it was only a formality. The police here are part of the problem."

"Then why aren't you worried about retaliation?" Nick said.

"All the names are changed. I'm Ricky Harmon." He laughed at that. "I like it—and I liked working with John. And he knows what it's like here too. Corruption's a way of life—no one cares what anyone says. It's like, 'So what, this is Rio.' And now the story's old—it happened four years ago."

"What a shame," Flo said. "I mean about Rio." She opened the book and pushed it over to him. "Here, could you look at page 105?"

He got out his reading glasses and bent over the page.

"Were you happy with John Baker's version of your story?" Nick interjected.

"To be honest, Nick, I never had time to read the whole thing," Chad said, looking up. "But my wife did. She couldn't put it down."

"But you signed contracts, first with John, then with us. And ours has clauses about the content."

"Yeah, but I left the content to John. He's got great credentials. He gave me his résumé. I know I should care enough about my own story to read it and glory in it, but jeez, I'm scraping by here. I had debts after the fire, and the games will probably price me out of this place. I'm counting on the book for some income."

"The bad news is, the book might be recalled for lack of truth," Flo said. "We've promoted it as a factual memoir, not a novel. Please, I'd like you to read this passage."

For a few moments of silence Chad read where her finger pressed on the page. It described the night he first saw flashlight signals on the beach. He had already noted increasing helicopter traffic to the island and not for his resort. Instead, the chopper rounded the hilly bend of his beachfront and disappeared. The night of the flashlights he crept down to the beach and watched his regular politician guests board an unknown motorboat on the calm, star-bathed water. It pushed away from the dock and quietly aimed for the promontory protecting Chad's cove. The surreptitious activity connected in Chad's mind to the recent helicopter traffic moving in the same direction.

After his guests finished their weekend on the island and returned to the mainland, Chad filled his own speedboat with fishing gear and casually motored out past the promontory. With patience, binoculars, and several more reconnaissance trips, he eventually spotted a possible sign of civilization in the green jungle about halfway up the hill. He returned in the dead of night to investigate, fully aware that if a drug cartel had a hideout nestled into the hillside, armed guards could be lurking in the forest.

"Yeah, I did go out there, and yeah, I was scared of gunmen. But you see, I also had dollar signs in my eyes, stupidly, but so does every businessman."

"What dollar signs?" Flo said. "The book doesn't talk about dollar signs in your eyes, only your complete naïveté about the island's perils."

"Well, maybe I shouldn't say this, but it occurred to me that if I knew about the hideout, I could get a payoff."

"Why would the cartel allow blackmail when it would be easier to kill you and your wife?" Nick said.

"Killing me might hit the news and put an end to their convenient location, which happened anyway, with the fire."

"But didn't they try to kill you? Isn't that how you lost your ear?" Flo said.

"No, I wasn't their target—Antonio was—he's Raoul in the book, the guy from the mayor's office."

"Let's stick to the names in the book," Flo said.

"Fine."

"Were you thinking you could trade something for the payoff? Be a runner?" Nick said.

A beat or two passed before Chad's deep voice grunted. "Sure, it crossed my mind. What can I say, Nick? You lived here, you know how it is—dealing's a way of life."

"So, hypothetically, you could provide intelligence from your lodge or serve as a courier with your boat, or even make deliveries to the mainland when needed—"

Chad's head was shaking. "No, I never thought it out that far." But his eyes showed he was now wary of them; his hand ran over his prosthetic ear nervously.

"Were you a drug runner?" Nick said.

"Absolutely not." But his stony face suggested otherwise.

"So," Flo said, taking the book back and turning the pages to the next Post-it note placed by Liza, "you did in fact go there and anchor your boat where it couldn't be seen. In the darkness, though moonshine and stars were a big help, you found the rough trail through the jungle and snuck up without encountering a single guard. Partway up, the land cleared in a plateau completely protected by vegetation, and you found what you were looking for—not a pirate's cave but a hacienda, or whatever the Portuguese word is."

"No, it was more of a simple lodge. Building out here isn't easy. Except for wood everything has to be brought in. Electricity is by generator. Water's by stream or well."

"That's not what the book says," Flo said sternly. "The hideout is like Shangri-la."

"With a helicopter landing pad," Nick said, taking the book and reading. "'At that moment, Raoul stepped outside the low-lying compound with a pilot I recognized and crossed to the chopper on the landing pad, confirming my hunch that some kind of smuggling was going on, most likely drugs.'"

"Yeah, that's more or less what happened. But it wasn't a

compound and there wasn't a landing pad, just the ground. They had a chopper."

Flo took the book back from Nick. "And you regretted not having your cell phone to take pictures," she paraphrased.

"I actually had it, but it was an old model that didn't have a camera."

"What were you thinking at the time?" Nick asked.

"Just what I said before—I had the goods on someone, secret knowledge."

"What about the danger to your life?"

"Yeah, I was scared—isn't that in the book? But I was more focused on what I had discovered."

"So if you weren't a drug runner, were you thinking you might inform the police or a journalist? It's all murky."

Chad's eyes widened as his head shook. "But the police were there, involved. I wouldn't go to them. And I don't know any journalists."

"A journalist wrote your book."

"Okay, so you're right. That's the avenue I picked. Though he proposed it."

Flo cut in. "The book says, here, where it's circled in yellow, that the only thing you cared about in life, besides your wife, was your dream enterprise—the diving resort that you were developing year by year with the meager savings earned from tourism."

"That's right, I put everything back into the place and more, and lost it all. My insurance was a joke."

Nick again thought how much it took to have a contemporary kiosk, even a small one, right on Copacabana's beachfront. He leaned in. "Did you ever approach one of your weekend guests, maybe Raoul from the mayor's office, with your knowledge of their activities? Did you and Raoul ever talk about a deal between just the two of you? Why did Raoul get killed?"

"No one will ever know."

Flo exchanged a look with Nick. How did Chad know that no one would ever find out?

Seeing their interpretation, Chad added with a heavy sigh, "What I mean is, it's all a mystery. And best left that way."

"Then you're definite about never suggesting a payoff or a collaboration with the cartel," Flo said.

"Nope, I kept silent. I wanted to run my business. In the back of my mind I knew I had knowledge I could possibly use one day. But that day never had a chance to happen. Things unraveled too fast after my discovery. Maybe they even saw me on video."

"According to your book," Flo said as she turned the pages to the last Post-it note, "something internal cropped up, creating a fatal conflict between Raoul and central command, or the ruffians, up on the mountain. This led to torching your place and killing Raoul. He was alone with you that night."

"That's right. I figure he had been kicked out of their camp, or maybe he had escaped. He showed up as soon as it was dark and looked in bad shape, as if he had been beaten. I didn't ask any questions—that was how it always was with us: don't ask. My wife gave him dinner and we all went to bed around ten. The marauders came around midnight and torched the lodge. They wanted us off the island, and they wanted Raoul dead."

"We keep coming back to the question, why Raoul? What did he do? And why does it seem like he's linked to you?" Nick said.

"It's just coincidence. These gangs are always betraying each other and killing in revenge."

"What if it wasn't a missed shot? Your ear, I mean."

"Maybe it wasn't. Maybe I was wrong in thinking they only wanted me off the island, and the fire was enough to accomplish that."

"In the book you go to the tourism bureau after the fire. Why not first to the police?"

"Because the tourism bureau was my original liaison to leasing my property, which the government owns—it owns the whole island."

"Which supports your hypothesis that political corruption was integral to events," Flo said.

"Yes."

"Chad, there are too many possibilities for how this story really played out," Nick said. "It infuriates the critics. Where's the gang now?"

"I have no idea. But if my ear was a missed shot, they could easily have followed up, and they didn't." He looked triumph with that, as if he had just come up with proof of his innocence.

"So all in all, you're saying the story in the book is true," Nick said. "Even though it doesn't add up that you're alive and have enough resources to own a refreshment stand in Copacabana. To sharp readers, it makes more sense that either the drug lords paid you off to abandon the island and forget everything you witnessed, or they aren't alive themselves anymore and the mayor's office gave you the payoff. Or you still work for them."

Chad tried to interrupt, but Nick talked louder. "The book ends by telling us that the bad guys had to abandon the island because the murder and fire got into the papers. Who do you think leaked it?"

"Obviously not me or I'd be dead."

"But you went on to retell it in full."

"After it was public knowledge."

Everyone was quiet for a moment. Nick was thinking that if they had hoped for some kind of confession about the true story, they weren't going to get it.

Chad broke the silence with an upbeat voice. "John read the story in the paper and tracked me down. You have a book, he said, a thriller-memoir, a best seller."

"He should have made it a thriller. The memoir part is what's killing us," Flo said.

"So what's going to happen?" Chad asked.

"We don't know," Flo said. "We need to talk to a few more people, including your ghostwriter, who's currently off the radar screen somewhere in the Middle East." She gave Chad a trenchant look. "The truth is of utmost importance, Chad. Investigative journalists from top magazines are going to take on this tale and dig for evidence if we stand by the book."

Chad hung in there, body pulled back as if braced to take her words, and once again he asserted that his story was true, with a few omissions and embellishments.

"In that case, we're done. With you, I mean. We still have other people to see," Flo said.

"Who? Where?" he asked.

"We need to cover all bases before we return and make a decision about the book," she said evasively, as she packed up her satchel and put on her sunglasses.

They all stood up and shook hands formally. Chad walked them to the edge of his awning. "Well, I hope things work out with the book," he said. "And you should be careful when you go around asking questions. Remember, this is Rio."

Nick touched Flo's elbow to hasten them on their way. He had no doubt that the man was involved with the undereconomy of bribes, trade-offs, and corruption; that was the only way to gain a business on Copacabana beach. Chad was part of the city's crime-ridden network, and so were the authorities whose doors he and Flo planned to knock on the following day. They should tread lightly, as if innocent.

Nick and Flo headed back along the black-and-white swirling sidewalk in the day's last glow of sunlight. It was warm, and the beach had become busier with after-work joggers and other sports aficionados. Nick could imagine a refreshing dip followed by a snooze on a beach towel next to Flo.

"I don't believe that bandit," Flo said with a flash of anger.

"He's a decent actor."

"Goes with the territory. Let's talk to the lawyer tomorrow and find out if it's even worth asking the authorities for records."

"It's not worth it. That's what Chad just told us."

"You mean his warning to be careful?"

Nick nodded. "If he's involved with them, they aren't going to tell us, and whatever really happened is not going to be in the records. But for the sake of Churchill's integrity, let's visit the lawyer."

"The person I want to grill is John Baker. What the fuck did he think he was doing?"

"He liked the story and decided it was more convenient not to question Chad's facts."

"But he knew what he was doing!"

"I'd like to know if writers are consciously devious or unaware of their dishonesties."

"I hope I'm not like that—consciously devious."

Nick laughed and took her arm. "Let's get into that surf, honey."

"Oh my god, I love how you called me honey! But dammit, I read that raw sewage pours into that beautiful sea. And did you see all the trash as we drove in from the airport?"

"It's a developing country in über-chic disguise."

"Did you love living here?"

"I did. It was wonderful—not as upscale as now, but the same anything-goes flavor."

"Would you live here again?"

"Maybe for a year, to read and write. But that's dreamland."

"You never know. Though I'd try to convince you to read and write in Normandy." She took off her sunglasses so he could see her smile and how it spread to her eyes, warming their dark kernels to a lighter chocolate. "I do know I'm not ordering any fish from that sea."

He smiled back and took her hand to cross the busy Avenida Atlântica. "Tonight we'll concentrate on dancing."

"Dancing . . . I was always a wallflower."

"Watch those lies."

"Honestly, I didn't even dance at my wedding. Oh, I pretended to, when the bride and groom have to start things off with that first silly dance. But really, my generation never danced like yours."

He stopped at the curb and pulled her into a tight dance embrace, pelvis to pelvis, his lips almost on hers. "We're going to have fun tonight, baby. This is Rio."

Back at the hotel they napped; the trip to Rio had cost them a night's sleep owing to the long layover in Panama. They got up around six and showered, soaping each other, and taking turns under the hot spray to rinse off. Nick got out first, leaving Flo to luxuriate longer in the steamy warmth. He dried off and then checked his e-mail at the small desk facing the bed, thinking how they were living as a couple and so naturally, as if they had been together a long time. Justin had booked two rooms for them, but they knew they'd never enter the other room, down the hall.

"Hey," he called out, "Emily got into grad school."

The bathroom door opened a wedge. "Hooray! She must be thrilled."

"She is. Me too. She's been in limboland too long."

He typed back a fast congratulatory reply, half listening to Flo's voice wafting musically from the bathroom as she dried off.

"I'm so eager to meet her. It fascinates me that you have a daughter and the two of you are close. I wasn't close to my father. He was a workaholic, always in the office, and whenever he was home, all he wanted to do was sit in his armchair and drink a few martinis—enter oblivion. After the divorce I saw even less of him."

"I wasn't close to my father either," Nick said as he closed the computer and got up to look for his clothes. Flo glided out of the bathroom at the same time, catching his eye with her diaphanous robe, which stirred like the vapors pulsing out of the bathroom behind her, her aura a faintly perfumed cloud. With a happy groan he flopped backward on the bed.

Flo came over him on her knees, her damp fragrant hair dangling down, her carved, dusty rose lips curled in a curious smile. "What?"

"Your perfume." He wrapped his arms around her, drawing her down and burrowing his face in her cleavage, the source of the scent. "Mmm, you smell so good."

"Ensnare," she said. "Glad to see it lives up to its name."

They had no plans, no pressure, no homes or office, no families, and they made love without any rush or nagging worries. Comfortable in each other's arms afterward, he wondered if the infinite love and fascination he felt could ever diminish. How? How could he ever for one minute be tired of her? The ways she delighted him were beyond his comprehension. He moved his head closer to tell her he loved her as he had never loved anyone before.

Her face pressed against him as if relieved and grateful, as if daring to trust love, or daring to believe she could be cherished the way she had always longed to be cherished, since her first consciousness in childhood. He knew—he could feel in her body— how much she wanted to be cuddled and held, nuzzled, made to laugh. He also knew, as he held her warmth and wholesomeness in his dependable arms, that she had found the right man in him. Awe filled him for the web of rightness between them. It was as complex as their individual lives, but the threaded intricacies needed no analysis, because a simple trust in love transcended rational thought. It mattered only that they were in the same room together, or walking along the beach together, or sleeping soundly next to each other; that their breathing was in the same space, a space that was their own languageless universe.

Her fingers traced his face. "You have tears in your eyes."

"Hmm." He smiled. "Tears of love."

"You're so real," she said. "That's what I love about you. That's what I want to be like. At work I play games, I'm phony. I've told you hundreds of little lies. I've hidden things."

"That's just work—boardroom secrets and smiling lies to conceal them. It happens everywhere."

"When are you going to stop making excuses for me?"

"In a few years."

"What will it be like when you blow up at me one day?"

"Or you me."

"It's bound to happen. When my closet overflows into yours."

"I'll help you prune it."

"Don't you see how dependent I am?"

His arms clasped her tight and rolled her onto her back, their bodies sealed. "Don't you see I love the entire puzzle of you?"

"Ha, and good luck ever putting it together. Crucial pieces are missing."

"I wonder which ones."

"The ones your logic and acceptance make up for, at least right now."

It was true they were different beings, he thought, but at the same time like one set of eyes and mind in their perceptions. And by osmosis, not by words, they understood each other.

Nick would never forget their night of dancing at the samba club in Lapa. They laughed so much. They drank the local beer between dances, and after her initial inhibition Flo let loose and took to dancing, her hair and dress flaring out as Nick led her in twisting, bending, flinging movements he'd learned long ago while living there. He loved it most when their bodies crashed and nudged sexily, and when he rocked her back against his body and hummed the music in her ear. The slow songs inevitably led to kissing.

At the end of the evening, as they moved through the dancers and tables to the outdoors, Flo wrapped her arm around Nick's back and said, "I think we should do our sabbatical in Rio."

"You can learn Portuguese."

"I plan to."

The next day they met the young lawyer, Pedro Lopes, recommended by the consulate. He was handsome and perky, and probably liked to dance the nights away, for he moved with agility and zest. He and Nick made small talk in Portuguese as the three of them got settled in the elegant office, each taking a comfortable leather armchair around a coffee table. Then Pedro switched to English while nodding agreement to Flo's voice recorder.

"The consul general told me about the book and I've had a look on the Web at the reviews and blogs. I'm happy to make inquiries and send you a report, but frankly, I wouldn't be surprised if Winters, or his ghostwriter, took liberties with the truth." He paused to smile affably and wait for their nods of agreement. Then, with his hands in a prayer gesture under his chin, he continued. "What are memoirs anyway? They're how a person remembers something. Truth and the imagination intermingle, inevitably. In other words, these kinds of personal stories are never reliable sources for truth or facts. My advice to you, without having read the book, is to let it stand, simply because memoirs, by their nature, aren't historical records, even when they purport to be. Haven't you noticed how more and more relatively distinguished online news agencies are publishing half-truths, sometimes complete lies? Fact-checking's a thing of the past. There's no time for it in the digital world. In my opinion, Churchill should make a few public statements and take the criticism. It won't last. Of course, if your company's completely focused on its corporate integrity—which frankly doesn't mean much today—then recall the book." With a fixed smile he concluded, "The bottom line is, no one cares anymore. Ha! The world's become more like Brazil."

"Then is it worth bothering to ask the authorities for the official criminal records?" Flo asked.

Pedro's brows rose in amusement. "And what are those? No, why bother?" He made movements to end their brief meeting. "If I were you, I'd go home, the sooner the better, and enjoy the success of *Island Peril*." A peculiar gleam darted from his eyes to theirs, as if to say: Do you get my meaning?

Outside again, Nick and Flo walked quickly back to their hotel.

"Do you think we're in any danger?" Flo said.

"No, not as Americans with a paper trail involving the Brazilian consulate. But we're supposed to stop asking questions."

"You know, the book would be a whole lot better if Chad's real story were there. It's more exciting."

"Indeed. But we're stuck with what we've got."

"Culpa mea."

"No one's going to complain about the profits."

When they opened their hotel room door, they found a folded note on the floor. Nick opened it and together they read from a computer printout, untraceable: *Yankees go home.*

They rebooked their flights for Sunday and spent the rest of the weekend wandering Rio as lovers, doing the usual tourist attractions, such as riding the cable car to Sugarloaf and watching the sunset from the Arpoador rocks. They walked the beach for miles, oblivious to the soccer and volleyball players and other movements and muffled sounds of human life and surf around them. They were in their own world and talked without reserve, Flo's voice carrying on the wind like its own kind of breeze.

They did not visit Rocinha, Nick's favela, though if he had been alone he would have, and also his old neighborhood and ninety-year-old landlady in Leblon. Their time was short and their love was new. Flo, who had suggested such visits, turned her lips down in their slightly bitter way when he declined. "You just don't want your old friends to see you with me."

"It's a bit of that," he admitted, and tried to explain how those people had also been close to Charlotte and for years they had all kept in touch like an extended family. He and Charlotte had brought Emily to meet everyone in the early nineties. "Next trip," he promised, "when we're married."

"Well, if you put it like that, fine." She grinned.

They flew home knowing what Flo would tell the bigwigs: they could recall *Island Peril* or make a statement and take the criticism. They would make every effort to reach John Baker before they faced the public. During their layover in Panama, Nick typed up a report and Flo edited it. On the flight to Boston, it was clear that their romantic interlude was over. Their carefree spirits in Rio, even in Panama, had vanished, and life had returned to business, to reality. Garrett loomed. So did Nick's professional future.

"Let's talk about how we're going to handle our jobs," Nick said.

"I've been thinking about it," she answered. "Can we let it slide for the short-term? After Garrett and I settle our separation, we can figure out our jobs. Total secrecy at Churchill till then."

He agreed, though he already knew he'd be the one looking for a job, a task he dreaded. He would call Oscar for lunch and talk it over. Though older and retired, Oscar still had extensive networks and continued to build new connections.

Flo leaned her cheek on Nick's shoulder. "Let's not worry right now, Nickie. Why don't we set up a dinner date with Oscar later this month?"

Nick laughed lightly. "You're clairvoyant."

Nine

The first week back in the office, Nick faced more work than he could handle. His brief absence from Churchill's relentlessly turning publishing cogs had wreaked havoc on his system for order. The books he managed all demanded immediate attention in different ways. Staff editors and designers were clamoring for urgent decisions on projects. The backlog of e-mails from all corners of the publishing world looked like a long, bolded chain on his screen, screaming at him to catch up. He was in the overwhelmed mode and knew from experience that the only way to cope was to chip away, nonstop.

Island Peril's unsettled fate loomed in the halls. Flo was handling the discussions with the executives. Nick was back in his subordinate position. He didn't see her or catch a whiff of her perfume those first days back, but often pleasure rushed through him as he recalled their moments of intimacy. Invariably, in the wake of such delicious thrills reality rose up. She had returned home to her nest with Garrett. She had almost certainly kissed him, perhaps allowed his overtures and made love to him. It seemed inevitable. Sex was the first thing Garrett would want when his beautiful wife returned. Nick shook off these upsetting thoughts. Flo faced much more than he. She had to find the right moment to announce her decision to end the marriage. She had to confess her duplicity. Nick took solace in their brief text exchanges: *Miss you. Love you. Hang in there. We'll be together soon. Kisses.* Some of the texts were sexier.

On Thursday, Nick saw John Baker walk past his office, accompanied by the receptionist, obviously on their way to Flo's. Flo had arrived early that morning, dressed in a black raincoat with a chic sixties look that fanned out slightly, smartly, expensively. Nick thought it must be a new acquisition, for later, when she walked John back to the elevators, her musical voice fluttering like piano keys, she still wore the coat. Later yet, on his way to a meeting, he saw her down the hall still wrapped in its elegance as if she just couldn't take it off. It made him smile with love for her little idiosyncrasies.

The next afternoon Nick was invited to an *Island Peril* meeting in Flo's office. The bigwigs sat in a row on her couch—Sam, Tom, and Calvin. To Nick they looked like schoolboys on a bench facing their principal. Flo sat at the round table, elbows relaxed on the surface, freeing her hands to move as she spoke. Nick took a seat across from her as greetings were exchanged. Flo's bright face focused on him. Who in the room, Nick thought, would ever suspect that the two of them knew each other in bed?

"I was just telling our intrepid triumvirate that we missed the boat this year, but next year we're going to be ready with a Boston Marathon book prominently displayed in every tourist kiosk around town. Something like Plimpton's sports books. Is this a project you could spearhead for us, Nick? Churchill's Boston Marathon 2014? We'll need a writer—maybe a past winner. Let's set up a meeting with marketing and do some brainstorming. And could you print out the competition from Amazon? I bet there isn't any, not of the caliber I have in mind. And by the way, I haven't had a chance to tell you—this has been the busiest week I've had since joining the company—a story came in, a diamond theft that involves a murder." She gestured to those on the couch. "I already shared it with Sam & Co., and I'll e-mail you the proposal. In a nutshell, back in the eighties, a young Russian, Vladimir, duped a rookie diamond dealer here in Boston. He convinced the guy he had a Saudi client with a suitcase of cash. But as soon as Vladimir got his hands on the diamond, he sold it in New York and got caught. Apparently the diamond business is a racket, and the rookie who gave him the diamond got murdered for losing it. Well that's what you get if you lose someone else's diamond. Anyhow, Vladimir was already in jail when the killing took place, so he wasn't guilty of that. He was just a kid, twenty-one, and got locked up in our prison system for twenty-five years. Don't look at me like that, Nick, it's not *Island Peril*! Vladimir has an agent from William Morris, and everything checks out in court documents you can read for yourself online."

"Great," Nick said. "I'm psyched to read the proposal."

"And more good news—I've saved the best for last. We've decided to keep *Island Peril* and hold a press conference with our favorite journalists. In addition, Oscar's going to come back from the dead and interview us for a YouTube video. It'll look like a talk show but run for three or four minutes. I plan to tell the world that if Nan Talese can do it with *A Million Little Lies*, I mean *Pieces*, Churchill can do it with *Island Peril*."

Her flair and natural smile made everyone else chuckle. "Don't worry, Sam, I know how to be discreet."

"I'm sure you'll pull it off, Flo," he said.

She stretched and stood up. She wore a lilies-of-the-valley spring dress with bare arms and visible cleavage, her breasts like soft pillows; her winter wardrobe, her dark jumpers and tights, had been put away, even though Boston was still chilly. "What a neighborhood we are," she said. "Houghton with Jonah Lehrer, Little, Brown with Kaavya, and now Churchill with Chad Winters." Her smiled gleamed at them again.

"I appreciate your humor," Sam said, "but let's make Churchill's reputation our number-one mandate."

"Yes indeed," she answered, straightening books on her windowsill that were already perfectly aligned. "Luckily, these days such episodes fade overnight. They get swallowed up in the next minute's news feeds. People want the latest headlines, the latest blogs and tweets and, more than anything else, YouTube's coverage. The twenty-somethings spend half their day on YouTube. And ethics is a thing of the past, or maybe incites debate for one day with the seniors, after which we move right on with our personal agendas. And, as we noted in our report, online journalism is openly accepting falsified stories. Fact-checking's just not possible, given the speed and transience of digital media. Meanwhile we still care about profits and losses, and *Island Peril* remains a winner, with *Diamond Murder* about to follow in its heels. And then the marathon book." She clapped lightly to get their momentum going. "Let's hustle. Don't you just love this business?"

Faint groans responded.

"Oh, come on, you can do better than that," she said, laughing.

"No," Sam said. "I don't love it the way I used to. Social media, digital everything, cheap values . . ." His white head shook. "Nope, I like the old world of print."

"But Sam, print is still here, and we're going to stay on top of the game the way Churchill always has. By the time publishing's completely digital we'll all be dead."

"Just keep the ideas coming and we'll take one day at a time," he answered.

"No, we have to look ahead, be visionaries, and be ready with our books when the times demand them. Have you read the front page this week? Or listened to NPR? Egypt's about to erupt again. It's obvious that Morsi's a goner. We need an eyewitness book on everything that's happened since his election—momentum and analysis. We need to get hold of one of the jailed journalists. Nick, could you call Al Jazeera while there's still an Al Jazeera in Cairo and see who's there? And if we can't get an insider to write it, then let's get a foreign correspondent. Who do you all lunch with at the Harvard and Yale clubs? Let's get the network going. This topic is hot and will explode any minute. We have to be ready with a book when the coup happens, or an analysis for immediately afterward."

Her face had pinkened with excitement that was contagious. It was clear that the idea had just come to her. The others responded, stirring in their seats—Egypt, Al Jazeera, revolutions, Middle East transformations, someone's live story on the events, their history and meaning. Yes, they'd get the network going. This was the kind of material that stimulated Sam in particular. It had relevance. He rose to his feet, once again feeling like a presence in the industry. The others followed. They were tall, distinguished men, publishing aristocrats from another era, an era that had vanished overnight only a few years before, when the Internet took hold of world communication. Nick knew their careers would end soon, as digitization moved faster than brains in an ever-expanding infinity of information. Generations born before the 1960s couldn't keep up with the dizzying pace, nor did they want to. Such was life. Each generation preferred its trends and progress, and with longer lives there were too many years of being left behind. In many cases, people chose to throw in the towel and step out of the eternal forward orbit, which was the same as saying, "My life, the flourishing part of it, is over, even though I might have thirty more years on the planet." Nick, working at Churchill, had already experienced such inklings of his own future, but being younger than the triad by a dozen years, he was still in the times, just barely. The professional world all around him, at Churchill and on the streets, was mostly young with only a small percentage of gray heads.

Soon after the meeting Nick received a text from Flo. *I told Garrett last night. Earth-shattering. I'm a free woman.*

He went down the hall to her office and closed the door. She was seated at her desk, reading her computer screen. She nibbled potato chips from a snack bag in her lap.

"Nick! You got my message." She jumped up, spilling her chips. "Oh no, you've caught me red-handed eating junk. But I couldn't resist. I needed comfort food—too much has happened in twenty-four hours."

She threw herself into his arms and kissed him. "Do I taste like chips? I'm so happy, delirious—you and *Island Peril,* all in a day— but poor Garrett. I don't know how I got through that, but I did. It was surreal . . . I could hear a clock ticking even though there wasn't one in the room. Can we get together tonight?"

"Let's pack up and leave now. It's five."

"I can't. I still have a shitload to do. It's the diamond book. We're bidding, but so is Simon and Schuster. I mean, this deal takes guts. It's going to take way into six figures."

He shook his head incredulously.

"But I know what I'm doing. Can I call you in a few, I mean a few hours?"

"Anytime."

"Garrett took off for New York—the house was toxic."

"I'll come your way."

"That's so sweet of you. You're always so thoughtful. I'm truly bushed. This week has been relentless stress, as my burning stomach keeps reminding me, so why do I go and feed it chips? I didn't know how *Island Peril* was going to turn out until today. I gave them so much research on memoirs and the truth. We might as well write a book on the subject. And do a memoir series. The verdict's in—facts don't matter." She burrowed against him. "I'm so grateful I didn't lose that book and probably my job."

"They need you. You're part of the new age."

"I see myself more as the bridge."

"You look pretty in that dress."

"You like it? You're the only person to say so. I have to confess I've been shopping every night this week. It's a sick compulsion. Putting on new clothes, longing to feel attractive. It's a medicine for my nerves."

"If it works . . ."

"It's damn expensive."

"Maybe hugs can do the trick in the future." He pulled her close, absorbing the feel of her inside the lilies-of-the-valley dress, the fabric smooth and soft, fresh and fragrant, like her.

"I think they might."

"Good." He gently let her go. "I'll see you soon. Give me call."

"I will." She smiled and watched him leave.

Back in his office, he finished up some work and then gathered his belongings for the weekend. His cell phone pinged, showing a message from Emily. She was in his 'hood and could stop by.

He texted back: *Just heading home. Até já.*

K, she answered. *Eu tenho a minha chave.* She had her key.

Moments later he was out on the street heading for the Garden via Commonwealth Ave. Preparations for the marathon, a week away, had begun. Materials for the upcoming roadblocks had been deposited at curbsides. More than twenty thousand runners and half a million spectators would converge on the tight downtown core to view or be near the finish line at Copley Square. Nick knew the routine well: streets would close, partying would begin the weekend before Patriots' Day, and Boston would be overrun with strangers and revelers, besides avid locals and families of runners who arrived on the day of the race. He liked the marathon's vibe and usually spent an hour or two wandering the last blocks of the route to watch the runners bobbing along in their tracksuits emblazoned with ID bibs, bodies sinewy and proud, faces rather ravaged from the exertion. He marveled at the athletes' passion to succeed at such a physical test of endurance, something completely absent in himself, despite his love for sports and the outdoors. The runners were another breed, another category of human self-discipline and ambition.

Emily was making a cup of tea in the kitchen when Nick let himself in the door. He dropped his backpack and they hugged. He hadn't seen her since his return from Brazil, though they had talked on the phone about her plans for graduate school.

"How about some dinner?" he proposed, opening the fridge. "Did you see I have that açai juice you like?" He took it out.

"I saw it, thanks, but tea's fine. I have to get home soon, but I was over here for the dentist and wanted to say hi." She smiled as if distracted and said politely, "Any news on the book?"

"Just today. It's a go." He found a glass and poured some juice for himself.

"I guess that's a relief."

"It is. Though kind of funny, don't you think? The book I so disapproved of is now the book I want to save, so my job is safe. Even though that's another iffy story."

"What do you mean?"

He shouldn't have said that. He didn't want to get into a Flo discussion right now—his future, and how the relationship would bomb his job. He smiled at her, noticing that she looked well. Her hair was brushed and the disgruntled face of a few weeks before had given way to her usual tender, sweet expression. But behind her glasses her blue eyes had an imploring look. Something was on her mind.

"Everything okay, hon?" he said.

"Actually, I'm feeling upset about something."

Uh-oh, he thought, had she found out about Flo? Before he could tell her himself? But how?

"We can talk about it. Let's sit down," he said.

"Okay. But first you have to promise not to tell anyone else. You have to promise this is just between us."

"Okay, I reluctantly promise."

They sat on the couch. She held her tea in both hands as if needing the cup's warmth for her chilled insides.

"It's Oscar. We went to the movies last night and had a coffee afterward. When we said goodbye on the street, he kissed me, which he always does, only it wasn't like an uncle or a godfather this time. And I needed to tell you, because I don't want to see him anymore." She shivered with the memory.

Nick felt a surge of adrenaline that made him want to punch Oscar.

"And don't tell him I told you!" Emily added, seeing his face. "You promised."

Reluctantly. He couldn't find words right away. Too many thoughts rushed through his mind at once—her escort fiasco, her current fragile state of mind, Oscar's awareness of it, her young loveliness, her female vulnerability to male predation, and his own horrible pain over being unable to make her life carefree and perfect.

"Emmy," he finally said. "What a bastard!"

"Believe me, I never encouraged him. We're friends—I like him, or I did. He was someone I could talk to, and I like all his stories. We watched a DVD a couple of weeks ago at his house and met for lunch one other time, just the way friends get together. In fact, I've always been ultra-careful to keep my personal space clearly drawn, because I've learned that men want only one thing. Which is an insult to women. We have minds and talents besides our bodies, but in the end men just want sex."

"Unfortunately, you're mostly right. But not all men are predators. Look at your friend Dan—all these years of friendship."

"We had an affair freshman year but somehow managed to stay friends."

"Oh. Well, I'm not going to defend men. I wouldn't want to be a beautiful young woman and have to deal with them."

"Did you ever have to deal with predatory women?"

"I like your past tense."

"I didn't mean that. You still look good, but it's obvious from your hair and some of your lines that you're old, I mean older."

"Well, it's my experience that women pursue men differently from the way men pursue women. Women want sex too, but they also want the person, the character, the meaningful stuff, whereas, just as you said, men are driven by the sex. And it pisses me off that someone as close to us as Oscar—someone who's known you since you were born and knows all your recent history—could lose sight of reality."

"It's not like he's a pedophile. I'm almost twenty-six."

"No, I didn't mean that. You're a lovely young woman with a mind and personality, but Oscar's my friend, my generation, practically your godfather. It's too weird."

"Maybe it was a fleeting aberration."

Nick nodded. "It shows how human behavior is totally unpredictable. The sexual impulse can obliterate everything. What did you do when he kissed you?"

"Nothing. I said goodnight as if nothing had happened and left."

"Avoid him."

"I plan to."

"Emmy, please don't let anyone ever guilt-trip you into thinking you owe them your body. You don't owe that."

Her sensitive face absorbed his words. They both knew it was easier said than done. Those live situations were always tricky to handle, and when women set their boundaries, they often lost the male friend, proving that sex instead of their deeper selves was the main objective.

Nick couldn't help but compare Oscar's attraction to his own for Flo, even though a forty-year-old woman was different from a twenty-five-year-old, who was like a family member. Middle-aged women also lusted after younger men, more openly than in the past, and society labeled them "cougars." Well, men got called "dirty old men" or "leches." Still, the double standard was strong: older men commonly started a second marriage with much younger women, but older women remained alone or with a new partner their own age or older.

"Hey, this is probably a good time to tell you I'm seeing someone named Flo, from the office." He surprised himself by voicing this news.

"What? Your boss Flo? The one you went to Brazil with?" Her face was incredulous.

He nodded. "It's bad, because she's married."

"What? How could you do that?"

He sighed. "I did. I didn't plan to, but I did."

Her eyes shone with a film of tears. "Mom did that to you, so how could you do that to someone else?"

He raised his hands as if surrendering to the cops. "I agree." His mind groped for a reasonable excuse, but nothing stuck. "With love, so many other forces come into play," he said, "especially rationales for plunging ahead with imprudent desires—just like with Oscar. People are just people with all their foibles, and nothing in life, especially in love, is black and white."

Her voice was a little hard. "So you love her."

He nodded. "We plan to live together, eventually." He couldn't say "marry"; he could share that intention later. "That's why my job is in jeopardy."

"You're crazy, Dad. Why did you let this happen?"

He had known it would be hard to tell her the news, news that should embody the same joy as the love itself, but because of human nature didn't and couldn't. He knew Emily wouldn't like Flo at first, inevitably, because Flo would be a newcomer to the family configuration and attached to Emily's one and only father. Their closeness would be affected.

Luckily, Nick thought, Emily was a reasonable person. Already her anger was subsiding. "Well," she said, trying to smile, "even if I think it's wrong to cheat on someone's spouse, I'm glad you love someone, because you've been alone a long time and everyone should have a partner to talk to. When do I get to meet her?"

"How about next weekend? I was thinking we could watch the marathon for an hour as the winners come in, and then go for lunch in the North End. I know Flo's eager to meet you."

Before she could answer, his cell phone rang and the screen showed New York City's area code: Flo. "I'll be fast," he told Emily as he answered the call.

A male voice responded. "Hello, Nick, this is Garrett Healy, Flo's husband."

Nick's heart clenched. He glanced at Emily's watchful face as he got up and moved off to his bedroom and closed the door.

"Hello, Garrett," he said shakily.

"I think you know why I'm calling."

"I think I do."

"Flo told me she's in love with you and is ready to abandon everything with me to take up a new life with you. I want to know if you're on the same page with this plan."

Nick squeezed his eyes shut as if darkness could make the horribly awkward moment feel better. "I am," he said. "I'm really sorry."

"Lame words, dickhead. You disgust me. Fuck you." He clicked off and Nick stood there stunned, imagining Garrett experiencing all the pain and anger their duplicity and shallowness had caused. He had once been in Garrett's shoes, shocked by Charlotte's betrayal and mystified that their world could be shaken out like a dirty rug, the years of accumulation scattered and lost forever. Flo's marriage was simpler—a few years and no children. But that didn't lessen Garrett's broken heart, broken life.

He went back to the living room, to Emily's intent face and questioning look.

"Her husband," he said.

"I figured. How could you be in such a messy situation?"

He shook his head: he had no answer.

"What's she like?" Emily said, getting up and putting her mug in the dishwasher.

"She's a flower, pretty rosy petals and a lovely scent."

"God, you're so corny."

"I am. I want a simple life till I die, and I have a complicated one."

"Partly because of me."

"The you part is just fine, honey, and don't you ever worry about that." He smiled and gave her a warm hug. "I love you to death."

"I love you too," she said. "How old's Flo?" Her face braced.

"Forty."

"Oh. That's not so bad. I thought you and Oscar might be having parallel senior experiences, and yuck."

"The same thing crossed my mind. And I'm not a senior yet."

"Don't you realize she's going to want a baby and that's going to be weird?"

"She wants a baby. But I don't."

"Too bad. If she wants a baby, you're going to have one. I can't believe you're doing this. You're going to be one of those old-man dads. And if I ever have a kid, it's going to be really weird."

"Hey, this kind of thing has been happening since the start of life." She zipped up her leather jacket.

"Where are you going to live?"

"We don't have plans yet. Everything is new."

"Well, this place is too small for two people, let alone three."

"It is. We'll have to look for something."

She moved to the door. "I have one more thing to add about

the Oscar incident."

"What?"

"It's that people biologically want to be admired, looked at sexually, desired, but that doesn't mean they actually want sex. I know I want to exude sex appeal and get signs that it's working, but I don't necessarily want to have sex because it's working."

"You nailed it," Nick said.

"It's a terrible paradox, wanting men to feel attracted to me but then never knowing if they are unless the attraction gets exhibited. Like with Oscar and a zillion others before him."

"I hope not a zillion."

"I just mean the pattern is always the same—it's a human pattern."

"And women suffer more as a result. There's rape. Even when they aren't trying to attract notice."

"Right." She stood straight like a little soldier as she delivered her next words. "I wonder if I can ever be fully who I am with a man, because in the world of humans, the man comes first and the woman is just a sexual object."

"You should come first, and so should your partner—though that kind of equality is probably an unattainable ideal. Usually one or the other has more weight."

"Usually the man."

"I'm afraid you're right." Even with Flo and her center-stage presence under full limelight, he was their anchor, partly because of his steady nature and partly because of his gender. She was an independent, savvy, and successful professional, and he easily deferred to her superior editorial talents. But in their life as a couple, he knew she would ask for his judgment, his help. And he expected to fulfill that role—a role that had come with his birth.

"I don't want to depend on men. I've depended on you all my life," Emily went on, her hand turning the doorknob. "So it's probably inevitable that I would look for men to take care of me. And I don't want to do that. Nor can I be less important than a man."

Nick nodded agreement. "You're right. But remember that it's natural, it's fine to seek support in family members, from parents to partners. That's part of being human."

"Hmm. I'll have to think about it."

Obviously she was wrestling with the proverbial male-female dichotomy, having just been bothered by an old geezer while at the same time liking him and even seeking his approbation. Nick wondered if she was weighing the possibility of same-sex relationships as an alternative to male-female inequalities. He wouldn't bring it up unless she did, for that was her business and she was fully capable of working it out.

They said goodbye with a final hug and promises to be in touch about meeting up for the marathon the following weekend. Emily stepped into the hall but then turned back with her lovely smile to say, "I look forward to meeting Flo." It was the peace laurel from a mature young woman. Nick smiled back, knowing that one day Emily and Flo would be great friends.

Back inside, he made a quick dinner from leftovers in the fridge. All week, waiting for Flo, he had spent his free time polishing his poems, many about her and some about life itself, all of them inspired by his experience of falling in love with her, including the latest poems, set in Brazil. These expressed his sheer elation, Pablo Neruda style. Soon enough, he well knew, the rare opening to the songs inside him would seal back up, the emotional surge over, the channel to the fathomless unconscious extinguished like a candle flame. That brought to mind an image of himself as a young man writing late at night by a candle's dim light. Darkness had felt deep and protective, allowed his words to flow without inhibition. Creative writing had a secrecy about it. The self got exposed, like slicing open the body for all to see and possibly ridicule; darkness provided cover.

Nowadays Nick wrote with bright light pointing down on his work. He hadn't lit a candle in years. Perhaps he would tonight as he read the poems aloud and fine-tuned the music to his ears. Already his imagination was leaping ahead to the book he would make for Flo: its title, the cover image, the dedication. It was easy these days to put one's work between covers for a personalized gift; he had already researched and found the online printer he would use.

Around nine Flo's text pinged and he opened his phone and read: *Surprise!*

At the same instant his doorbell rang. She was downstairs and he buzzed her in. When he opened the door, she was just coming up the last stairs, lugging her satchel. He quickly took it from her.

"Flo, I would have come to your place. Or picked you up. Did you walk here in those heels?"

She leaned against him in relief. "I should lie and say yes like a martyr, but no, I cabbed. And I actually nodded off for the five minutes it took to get here. I'm positively dead, Nick—what a week! But I think I got the diamond book. The agent agreed to $200,000 and I sent a draft contract. We're going to need a translation. Vladimir speaks perfect English after all those years in prison, but he wrote the damn book in Russian."

He helped her out of her jacket. "You were born to do this work, my dear. You're indefatigable, tenacious."

She kicked off her heels and sank on the couch full-length. "I don't know. I think I detest it most of the time, but it's a job, one that's at least interesting. Books. I love them. But would I work if I didn't have to?"

"Yes," Nick said as he casually cleaned up his poetry project on the dining room table.

"You're probably right. Did I interrupt your work? I'm so sorry! I don't have to stay."

"I've been waiting for your call, darling." He went over to kiss her, which entailed dropping to his knees.

"Good, because I don't think I can get up again. And it's so cozy here. I want to live here."

"It's too small. Aren't you hungry?"

"I was starved when you saw me at five, but then I went downstairs again and bought more junk at Starbucks. I feel hideously bloated."

"I think your stomach would be happier with a healthy diet."

"I know. I'm incorrigible. But I plan to do better."

Nick sat down in the armchair beside her and told her Garrett had called.

"What? How awful for you! He must have gotten your number from my cell phone. Oh my god, that means he read our texts!"

She reached for her phone to see the horrible evidence, but Nick slid it from her hand.

"Don't torture yourself."

"You know I'm going to look at it."

"Why don't I delete the chain right now, to spare you?"

"No, I want to see what he saw."

"What's done is done. We were bad."

"Were we really?" Childlike hope that they weren't really bad hung in her voice and brimmed from her eyes. When he didn't answer but just looked at her with kind love, her lips turned slightly down in their professional hardness. "Go ahead. Delete it."

He was only too happy to erase the incriminating chain. He opened the app and ran his eye down the list: *Miss you, love you, longing to be together,* and then her sexy one about craving his bod.

He groaned.

"Tell me what it says!"

"It's gone, you were feeling hot."

"Cripes! I know which one it was! I can't believe he saw it! All week I was sitting at my desk tortured with horniness for you. I tried to find pictures of you on the Internet. Then I remembered I took a bunch in Brazil, so I looked on my iPhone. Oh my god— he probably saw my pictures too! And all the ones other people took of us hugging and snuggling. Oh my god!" she repeated, hiding her face in her hands.

"It's okay. It's over."

"No, it's not okay. It's mortifying."

He sighed. It was a bad business, but they had chosen it, and the worst moment was over. He said as much, hoping to calm her, and then changed the subject to Emily and how he had told her the news. "She's looking forward to meeting you. I suggested the marathon and lunch."

"Perfect! I'll finally get to meet Emily. She's going to hate me, of course."

"She'll warm up."

"I know. I know how it is. Remember, I have stepparents, on both sides, and I adore them, but before I got to know and trust them, I'm sure I was a witch."

"I don't think Emmy will be a witch."

"Of course not. She'll be courteous, just like her dad." Smiling, she took a deep breath, as if imagining their new configuration. "I can't wait for you to meet my family, especially my mother—

you'll love her—and my brother, Jim, and little Claire de Lune. She's such a doll-baby! She can come visit us sometime. We can take her to the museums. What sweet dreams I'll have tonight. I can stay over, can't I? I won't disturb you—in fact, I don't think I can get up again. I'll sleep right here on the couch if you'll lend me a blanket and pillow."

"Come on, I'll help you to bed." He gave her a hand to pull her up.

"I hope it doesn't lead to instant chemistry, because I'm too tired. I mean that, Nick."

"Same."

But they both knew that after almost a week apart they would not lie there without touching. They would settle down intending to sleep in each other's arms, their legs naturally entwining. The mere feel of her length against him would send instant electricity to his brain and from there to every other part of his body, until he tingled all over with pleasurable, acute desire, instinct for a physical destination.

"It's hopeless, Nick," she said, going into the bedroom with him. "We're doomed."

"Not a bad doom."

He woke up around four o'clock to escape a bad dream. It had started out almost celestially with a harbor like Rio's, a shimmering seascape in a foreign place. He was so mesmerized by the beauty of the sky and water, the sound of gulls, and the atmosphere of carefree abandon that he had seated himself on the bow of a low-lying speedboat in order to gaze for a while. Suddenly the boat took off across the bay toward the open sea, not unlike the setting at Copacabana. The boat was moving fast, with Nick at its prow, close to the water's foaming surface. He had to hang on to the boat's edges, but there was no rim and fumbling for a grip wasn't working; the boat felt like grease. Now the sea was so vast that its rippled blue blended entirely with the blue sky. With the wind rushing in his face from the boat's trajectory, he couldn't discern where the sea ended and the sky began. Suddenly red sharks dipped and dove on both sides of the boat, smelling him, evilly eyeing him, already tasting him. He hung on, hands slipping, body sliding precariously toward one edge and then the other. He knew he would end up in the sea. He was facing his fate—any second now he would go overboard. Suddenly the boat slowed and pulled in to a dock, safety, and Nick, dazed and wobbly, got off and asked the captain if he had known he was on board. No. Nick moved away slowly, thinking how curiosity killed the cat.

Replays of the red sharks and their cruel eyes just waiting for his meat woke him up. Flo was sleeping peacefully, her hair all around her face, a strand glued to her lips. He gently pulled it back behind her ear and kissed her temple. Then he nestled back down against her warm, soft limbs, lightly wrapping his left arm around her and breathing in the earthy scent her skin. What contentment he felt to know that this woman and all her vibrancy and eccentricities would be with him the rest of his life.

TEN

Patriots' Day arrived. It was Boston's premier city holiday, not because it commemorated Revolutionary battles but because for more than one hundred years the city had hosted the Boston Marathon, a world-famous and well-loved competition. It was a festive day when hundreds of thousands of people of all ages and from neighboring towns and greater distances came out to watch the runners complete the race. All year these determined athletes had been preparing for this day through strict self-discipline and anticipation. Now the day, remarkably sunny and temperate, had arrived. Nick could imagine the runners' mixture of intense anxiety and euphoria as they prepped themselves for the hardest test the body and mind could undergo as a working unit and as a single challenge. It took a certain kind of person to live solely for the great race, a competition with others but mainly with the self.

Nick was up early and after a quick cup of tea headed out to scope the scene. He took a circular route that covered the Common and all the principal streets surrounding it, everything cordoned off, with lines of buses along the curbs. People, strangers to the city, some of them all-night revelers, wandered contentedly around, not yet staking out a position for the race; it was only eight o'clock. The corner pubs had just opened, and Nick could see through the doors to the hard-core drinkers seated at the bar, mugs of beer in their hands.

The race would begin in Hopkinton at nine, with the fastest runners starting out at ten. The plan was for Emily to come by in late morning and walk over to Flo's with Nick, and from there to the finish line, or as close as they could get to it, given the crowds. Flo was excited about the race, her first, as she'd been out of town the year before. Her mind was focused on shaping a marathon book for 2014, "and what can be better fodder than being there myself?" she repeated a few times on the phone. And Emily was another attraction, not just because she was Nick's daughter but also because of her age and her perspective on the race, what exactly her age group found interesting about it. "The same thing we find interesting," Nick said. "You never know," she answered. "If I ask enough questions, I'm sure to unearth a few new nuggets. And that's what the book's going to need—freshness."

That week Garrett had remained in New York, and he and Flo had begun organizing their separation by e-mail. Flo had met with her former realtor about selling the condo. She and Nick talked about finding their own place. On his walks home from work, he had begun browsing the pictures plastering the real estate storefronts along Charles Street. The photographs showed gleaming architectural spaces ranging from traditional to contemporary, and all of them pricey, out of his range—maybe not hers—but he enjoyed looking at the possibilities and imagining a home with her.

He was buying a coffee at Dunkin' Donuts when his mother phoned.

"Nick, we've had a bit of an emergency down here."

A rush of worry gripped him. "What happened?"

"It's your dad. He's on his way to Mass General. He has short-ness of breath and chest pain. An ambulance just took him. Ann's coming down from Maine, but neither of us can to get into Boston until after the marathon. We were hoping to stay with you."

"Of course. What happened?" he repeated.

"Well, as you know, he's been short of breath, tired out, and sleeping too much but refusing to go to the clinic. This morning, around four, he got up to go to the bathroom and was so dizzy he fell. The clinic took him in and decided he needed to go to Boston. They'll do all kinds of tests."

"I'll go over and meet the ambulance."

"Thank you, sweetheart. He's scared to death. When they fed him into the ambulance you could tell he was facing his own end. It broke my heart."

"Maybe it's just a warning."

"Let's hope. I'll see you tonight, and we'll stay in touch by phone."

This could be it, Nick thought as he put away his phone. His father might die today, or tomorrow. But since he was still alive, it was too hard for Nick to focus on how he felt about possibly losing his father. The layers and complexities of their relation-ship weren't the kind to ever be resolved, even if on his death-bed his father said, "Hey, Nick, I love you, I've always loved you." Such words were like concrete objects put down on a table in an attempt to fill a fathomless hole of bad emotions and lack of trust. Why did so many people wait for their deathbed to try to patch things up for the record? Nick wondered. He had ceased blam-ing and resenting his father for some time now, and just accepted their relationship—or most of the time. But he didn't think he felt love, and wondered if his father's death would show that he did. Or did love get mixed up with regret, pity, and a host of other nostalgic emotions?

His plans for the day, so keenly anticipated, had suddenly derailed. Now he would have to go to the hospital and see his father through the admission process and probably some tests. He might have to stay there all day. Somehow he had to fit in a break for the marathon and the women. He took out his phone to call Flo and Emily.

Flo picked up immediately. "Niiick!"

He quickly told her the news.

"Of course, your dad comes first. This is serious. Just keep me posted. I'm happy to meet for the second heap of runners—that sounds perfect. I'm still going to watch the winners. I want to see the Ethiopians and Kenyans battle it out for first place. I know I'll cry. Why are sports events so emotional? I've made a list of all the questions I want to ask spectators and families. I know I'm going to find the right angle today, or maybe afterward, when you, Emily, and I all sit around an Italian table and hash out ideas. Our mantra has to be, what do people want to read about this race?"

"You make the marathon more enticing than I remember it."

"That's because we're . . . *juntos*."

He smiled at her pleased use of *together* in Portuguese.

"*Amo-te*," he answered.

"I love you too," she replied.

When the ambulance arrived, Nick was waiting at the ER entrance. His father looked relieved to see him and held up his bony hand, which Nick took and squeezed. The old man was still handsome, with his straight features and taut skin that was a mesh of crosshatch lines. The blue eyes were just as sharp, wary, and contentious as always. But his complexion was ashen gray.

Hospital personnel whisked him through the admissions process, for he was already in the computer. As he was wheeled away to an examining cubicle, a smiling nurse bent over his gurney and joshed in the Boston way, "So you attempted the marathon, did you, Mr. Turner? What were you thinking of at your age? You should have asked your doctor first."

"He's the one who told me, Go for it, old man, running's good for your heart," Sheldon quipped back.

The nurse laughed. "We'll have you fixed up and out of here in no time. Maybe you can still get back in the race."

For the next few hours Sheldon went through a battery of tests, beginning with a chest x-ray, which showed no abnormalities. The d-dimer test that followed showed the presence of a blood clot somewhere in his body. Nick accompanied him to the various tests and they chatted benignly about the marathon, senior activities at Ballard Hill, and Nick's recent trip to Brazil. Sheldon enjoyed hearing about Chad's interrogation and offered a few speculations on what really must have happened. But as Nick himself had concluded, there were too many possibilities, and the truth would never be known unless Chad divulged it—and likely Chad knew only his own small part of the truth.

"Hang on to this job, Nick. Don't let what happened at Trowbridge happen this time around."

"Trowbridge went under. I wasn't responsible for that."

"Well, I only meant when you're getting up there in years it's pretty damn hard to find work."

"No joke. I plan to stay at Churchill as long as I can." Like a few more months, he added silently. But he didn't need to think about that looming anxiety now.

By noontime Sheldon's CT scan showed a pulmonary embolus, and the nurses settled him into the intensive care unit with an IV infusing an anticoagulant. Nothing more could be done at the moment. He needed to rest, give the medication time to do its work. Nick went outside to make phone calls, first to his mother, then to his marathon companions. It looked like their afternoon meeting for the second heap was going to work out.

Emily subwayed over and arrived at Sheldon's room looking fresh and pretty in black jeans and a leather jacket. Her dark wavy hair gleamed against her bright, intelligent face. She possessed an allure that made other people look twice and wish to meet her. Nick knew she had given thought to the outfit she would wear to meet Flo, and that Flo had done the same. He imagined Flo choosing jeans, a hooded sweatshirt, and sneakers to feel compatible with Emily's age group. She might be surprised when she found Emily dressed in her own sophisticated brand.

Emily gave Sheldon an affectionate hug, and he congratulated her on grad school. "But please don't try to change my diet when you become obsessed with all that food science. I've been through enough in my life. I'm going to eat how I like to eat."

"I'll try not to be a nuisance," she said, sitting on the edge of his bed and holding his ancient hand. "But I might find something interesting for you to read."

They chatted a few more minutes before Sheldon closed his eyes and admitted he was tired. "I think I'll sleep," he said. "Why don't you two go out and catch the end of the marathon?"

Good—green light, Nick thought with a smile.

"But thank you for coming, Emmy, I appreciate it. And you too, Nick," Sheldon said, his blue eyes piercing Nick's.

"Okay, we'll let you get some rest," Nick said. "We'll be back around dinnertime with Mom and Ann. We don't want to tire you out."

"Don't worry, I like having you here. I'll feel peppier after a nap."

Nick adjusted his father's pillows and helped him find a comfortable position that didn't interfere with the IV.

"Nighty-night," Sheldon said, eyes already sealed and dry lips forming a little smile.

Nick felt surprised at the tenderness that rose up in him when his father said those words—nighty-night, an echo from his earliest childhood, when his father used to kiss him goodnight. What year had that ended? When had his father taken a sharp turn and become belligerent?

Nick and Emily grabbed a late lunch in the cafeteria before heading out to meet Flo, who had not left the finish line since the winners came through around noontime. "I'm having a blast," she told Nick when he phoned. "I'm so sorry you missed all this—it's a natural high out here. I've met all kinds of people, including families of the runners and a few runners themselves. And get this—some nice guy from Maine bought me a lobster roll. Did you know that Maine used to be part of Massachusetts? That's why Mainers celebrate Patriots' Day too. His daughter's in the race, due to arrive any moment. He's going to put us in touch later for an interview. You should hear what her year of training's been like. Nick, it takes much more than passion, it takes something rare and completely obsessive inside the competitor. I want you to write the book—just think of it! I imagine a series of portraits that when combined as a whole capture the total marathon experience. A Churchill best seller, and you as author. Don't you see, it would solve our workplace problem!"

"Flo, that's brilliant. We'll do it together. You're an idea machine."

"I know, I do it without thinking. Where are you? I can't believe I'm about to meet Emily!"

"We're on Comm Ave., about to turn. Where are you?"

"More or less in front of Starbucks—I haven't budged since I got here, not that I have much choice, we're packed in like sardines. I'm wearing a broad-brimmed black hat with a fuchsia flower so you can find me."

"Great. See you in a few."

He clicked off and smiled at Emily. "She's near Starbucks, wearing a black hat with a pink flower."

They moved at a brisk pace down the green center of Commonwealth Ave., under the canopy of trees. They could see the sinewy runners in the distance making their turn at Hereford Street, but to join Flo they turned on Exeter. Nick felt the dynamism in the air, stirred up by the combination of the race, the runners, the finish line, and the vibes of a great city. Best of all, Flo and Emily were about to meet. When had he ever been happier?

Suddenly a loud boom went off, like a cannon firing, and the startling noise confused everyone on the street. Was the boom part of the race? Faces looked around for answers just as a second boom went off, followed by the sounds of mayhem—screams, alarms, sirens, and the odor of smoke.

"An explosion," Nick said, taking Emily's hand. He looked at her pale and stunned face—just the way he himself felt. "Oh my god, something's wrong, go home."

"Dad!"

He had already turned and spun off in the direction of the emergency. His head was pounding with thoughts of Flo—she was there, she might be injured, dead. He yelled over his shoulder, "Go home!" while the bedlam in the street spread, people not knowing which way to turn. He ran frantically toward Boylston Street, aware that Emily was following. He had caught the expression on her face just as he hurtled away. Every ounce of her was trained on him and the danger that lay ahead. There was no way she was going to let him plunge into that scene of possible carnage alone.

As he rounded the corner onto Boylston Street, a horrific sight confronted him through billowing smoke cluttered with debris and human flesh. Bloodied, blackened runners and spectators, victims with holes in their legs, or no legs, cried out for help. People with anguished faces ran in all directions, hoping to escape the danger. All was chaos, a living nightmare in filthy gases, and yet intense rescue work was already under way, with police, security officials, doctors, ambulances, and fire trucks taking charge. So many of those present, including the injured, automatically pitched in to help the fallen, the desperately bleeding, even though they knew another bomb could go off at any moment. The human instinct to aid the helpless was a powerful response to the terrifying crisis. While Nick helped an ambulance medic move a child onto a stretcher, his eyes ransacked the gray dust for a black hat and fuchsia flower. But it was hopeless. And so was his anxiety over Emily. Too much had to be done instantly to save the lives scattered on the street and sidewalk. Without even thinking, he found himself using his belt to tie a tourniquet around a young man's gaping leg, which was pumping out his life's blood. He knew he was crying as he worked, as much inside his heart as from his eyes. How could such villainy descend on a peaceful, happy holiday? On the Boston Marathon? How could all these innocent people become flesh-torn victims while they waited with joyful faces for their loved ones to pass through the waving, cheering channel to the finish line? How did all this happen? Why?

* * *

Later that night, with his family in his apartment numb and glued to the TV for any news about the bombing's perpetrators, Nick sent another text to Flo, just in case the sharp ping caught her attention. Her phone was still taking messages—he had left several—but the phone could be in the gutter on Boylston Street. And her house was dark. He was distraught, not knowing her fate, especially as his mind kept replaying the smoky, bloody, unreal scene he had witnessed. How could it be real?

Emily sat on the couch sandwiched between her grandmother and aunt in her own state of shock, for she too had helped the injured in the incomprehensible battlefield of severed flesh and screaming humans. The hospitals were filled with the victims, and so far three people were dead, including a little boy. The public wanted to know if this was a terrorist act or the work of a homegrown madman. Nobody could yet process what had happened that day—how a great tradition of such positive and inspirational magnitude had ended in evil devastation. But didn't such bombings happen every day in Baghdad, Kabul, Gaza, Syria, and Africa? Nick asked himself as he paced in agitation from room to room in his small apartment. Why was it he could read headlines about such atrocities every day in the paper and turn to the next page but feel himself in a reeling, shattered, surreal world when the senseless violence touched his own country, his own city?

"You okay, Em?" he asked, coming up to the couch.

"I'm ... like you," she said.

"Can I turn off the TV now? The news is just repeating. Why don't we all go to bed?"

Ann put her arm around Emily and smiled bravely. "Sleep will help. There'll be news tomorrow—something. This town's going to find out what happened fast."

"It could take weeks—that's what's killing me," Nick said.

"No, clues will come in. This is the age of cameras, digital trails." Ann got up and helped Emily up.

"You need rest, both of you, you're in shock, deep shock."

Eventually they all got settled in their beds, the women in the bedroom with the big bed and an air mattress, and Nick on the couch. He doubted that any of them would sleep. He lay on his pillow staring straight out at the room, at chair legs, but saw nothing, just his own tormented thoughts. The limbo was killing him, the double limbo—images of the bombing replaying nonstop in his mind and without any explanations from the ongoing investigation, and then Flo's disappearance. If she was safe at home, she would have called. *Please make her be safe*, he prayed to himself, and then thought how belief and faith came naturally to humans in times of utter despair. In the morning he could try to get information from the various hospitals, but he wasn't even a relative. He had Garrett's number stored in his phone—did he dare call him? Could he find her parents in New York? Could Sam or Tom pull strings for information? Tomorrow he would find her, dead or alive.

He dozed off, a tight band around his head from the overload inside. His phone pinged piercingly at midnight and showed Flo's name, causing his heart to leap so joyfully that its beats throbbed in his throat, shortening his breath. He opened the message and read several times over: *I'm alive, in shock, I think forever. Windows blew out—legs got glass. Nothing bad. Too many tests, even a CT. Garrett's here. It's so hard. xo Flo.*

Garrett.

He replied that he would go see her first thing in the morning. Where?

Brigham. But wait for my call. I'm deleting all texts.

He resettled on his pillow, holding the phone to his chest as if it were the Flo he had found safe at last. But his relief was mixed with inconsolable misgivings. Garrett. Garrett was with her. He should be there, not Garrett. Why had she summoned Garrett and not him? And their texting at this crucial moment bothered him—why hadn't she called, voice to voice? Why hadn't he called her right back to hear her voice? A real conversation would have taken place, instead of texting's shorthand. It bothered him that in just a smattering of years texting had replaced voice-to-voice communication and he himself had fallen into the new behavior. It was habit now. And texting was only an embryonic stage of human communication to come, but he wouldn't be around for that voiceless, touchless age.

The next day, after listening to the news, which repeated the same stories as the night before, the household scattered. Emily went home, assuring her elders she'd be all right and would check in later, maybe return for dinner. Valerie and Ann set off for the hospital to visit Sheldon, Nick declining his mother's soft plea to join them. She now knew about Flo and accepted his preference to wait for her call. But all morning the phone sat silent, despite Nick's periodic voicemails and texts. He phoned the Brigham and was told that no calls were to be put through to Mrs. Healy's room. She isn't Mrs. Healy, he wanted to shout. She's Ms. Wright. He hated Garrett in his frustration, Garrett who had access to Flo.

Eventually, unable to take the silence any longer, Nick drove to the hospital, got her ward and room number from the lobby desk, and headed up. Looking like he knew where he was going so that no one would stop him, he found her room. The door was ajar. He knocked lightly and when Flo said dully, "Come in," he entered. She was propped up in the hospital bed, brown hair lank and in need of washing and her face drained of its usual rosy radiance. She looked corpselike and didn't even smile when she saw him. She was despondent. Garrett got up from the chair by her bed, face turning livid. It was a bad moment and bound to become worse, Nick knew in an instant. But nothing could compel him to leave. He was finally seeing Flo, seeing her alive and laying his anxiety of the past horrible day to rest. But finding her in such bad shape brought a new wave of worry. Vaguely she said, "Oh, Nick," while Garrett blasted him: "What the fuck? No visitors allowed, especially you, asshole."

"Don't, Garrett. What does it matter?" Flo's voice was not her voice; it was flat and emotionless.

"Please leave. Is that better, Flossie?"

Flossie. Nick's feet glued even tighter to the ground hearing Garrett's pet name for Flo. If he left, how would he ever reach her again? This was his only chance, and something was really wrong here; all of his senses could feel the weight in the air.

"Go on, skedaddle!" Garrett shooed with his hand. "You've done enough damage, douche bag."

"Nick, it's bad," Flo said. "I have cancer. It's spread . . . from my ovaries." Her hands touched her pelvis with distaste. "Please, Garrett—he deserves to know what's going on."

"Deserves to? Are you out of your mind?"

"Yes, I am, but not about Nick. How many times do I have to tell you, I seduced him, not the other way around. I made the mess. He's not to blame."

"Bullshit. He's a fucking lech. I want him out of here or I'll call security."

"Nick, I have too much to process right now. I'll call you when I'm home again."

"Flo . . ." Nick's head shook incredulously. How could he just walk out with all this news overwhelming him? He needed to be with her, hear what had happened, all so fast, and share her grief. Share his. Was it really possible that she had ovarian cancer? How? What was her prognosis? He needed time to believe this was even happening. Wasn't the marathon enough? And he needed to be alone with her. Why was that angry beast at her bedside, poisoning the room, making things worse for her?

Flo's voice came to him, jaded, bitter. "I guess I'm paying for all my youthful follies. But why me? Everyone else is just as bad. Why my life?"

Nick looked from Flo to Garrett and back again. He would just have to pretend that Garrett was invisible. He stepped over to her bed, put his hand on the covers, and spoke just to her in a quiet voice. "My dear, we need to talk. Will you please call me tonight when you're alone?"

"She won't be alone, fucker. I'm staying here," Garrett's loud, harsh voice cut in.

"Stop all this name-calling!" Flo screamed, covering her ears and silencing Garrett. Her brown eyes rolled up to Nick. "I'm so sorry. I'm . . . Nick, I can't even think right now! Will everyone please leave me alone?"

"I'm trying to make that happen," Garrett said in a forced calm tone.

Flo took a deep breath and stared hard at Nick. "I won't beat around the bush. Garrett and I have to go through this thing together. I realize I need him. He's been so kind, so forgiving. I can't let him down again."

What? Nick's head spun with the latest blow. How could he take it all in—the marathon, the cancer, the choice of Garrett over him? He was speechless and in pain, his mind dashed to an uncomprehending state.

Then he saw her drawn face and dead eyes staring at him. He realized at once that his own feelings mattered little compared to hers. It was her life that had been suddenly, unfairly shortchanged, and she had a right to decide how she would play out her last days.

"I understand," he said automatically, even if he didn't, not yet. He looked at their ravaged faces; they looked like youngsters caught in a terrible nightmare together. There was something invisibly clinging between them that made them a welded pair. He was on the outside of that bond, their past.

He backed off, dazed that everything could turn off so instantly, as if a mere switch had been thrown. Hadn't she experienced the ineffable, unfathomable richness of their love? Was such love possible only with age and experience? It still filled him completely, went beyond him, and the minute he got to his car he would break down in a million pieces and not know how to put himself together again.

By Thursday, only three days after the bombing, two immigrant brothers of Chechen descent had been identified as the suspects and a manhunt began. The news hammered in after that, once again gripping the city in fear and bewilderment. In their frantic attempt to escape in a stolen car, the older brother died in a fiery shootout that also left a policeman dead. The younger brother, only nineteen, fled the scene, initiating a city lockdown. All of Boston waited tensely indoors while heavily armed police and special SWAT teams combed a swath of Watertown, where Dzhokhar Tsarnaev had abandoned the car and run for his life.

Nick and everyone else watched their TVs, stupefied that their lives were part of the week's horrific events. They wrestled with an initial empathy for the terrified boy, for obviously his radical brother had brainwashed him. At the same time, the kid had to be held responsible for the atrocities he had committed, like anyone else who perpetrated such appalling acts against humanity. In those tense moments of waiting for Dzhokhar to be found, it seemed inevitable that another violent shootout was imminent. And how would it end? Surely in the kid's death.

The next day a Watertown resident reported suspicious movement in his boat, parked in the backyard. The countdown to arrest or death began. Miraculously, no one died during the drawn-out confrontation. Dzhokhar eventually surrendered and was taken to the hospital for treatment of his wounds. The high drama was over, but not the aftermath of the marathon tragedy. Victims of the bombs faced long convalescences; many had lost a leg, some two legs. Four people had died. Dozens lost limbs, and hundreds had been injured. But the city could quiet down now and turn to its mourning. It could begin to process the week's turbulence without fear and also with a sense of closure.

Throughout the days of the bombing terror, Nick also hung in limbo about Flo. She had lost her future, and not once in all those hours since he learned the news had they talked. He knew her own needs came first, but until they talked he would be in a state of agonizing captivity. Finally she phoned him, on the weekend. Her voice was matter-of-fact as she told him what had happened. When the hospital admitted her to treat the glass in her legs, their routine tests showed anemia. The young resident who took her history felt concerned about her chronic indigestion and bloating when coupled with the anemia. She quickly underwent further tests and ultimately a CT scan. "The death sentence," she said. "It showed a mass with peritoneal seeding. Whatever that is."

Metastasis, Nick answered to himself, his ears filled with her dry, flat voice and his mind's eye seeing the bitter corners of her lips.

"It's incurable," she went on. "All in a day, Nick, the bombing, in front of my eyes, my legs cut and bleeding, then cancer. I'm a weird casualty of the marathon. I'll never adjust to all that's happened, never, even if I had time."

"I won't either," he said automatically. "Ever. When can I see you?"

"It's not the same anymore."

"I know it's not, but I love you, I care."

"We're moving back to New York."

He had expected it, but her statement of it was a blow. Their families were in New York; it made sense. But Nick had imagined himself seeing Flo and being her faithful support until he couldn't see her anymore. "When are you leaving?"

"Soon. I have to start treatments at Sloan if I want a few more months. It flabbergasts me that people can get cancer, quit their job, and move away all in a matter of a few weeks. Talk about being impermanent. Except that's obviously the best philosophy if you're really going to die. I'm impermanent."

"Let's meet in the Garden." He felt his desperation. But she was inured to it.

"I can't. To see you, I need to be somewhere in my head. Give me at least a week."

A week to put solid armor on, he thought, a new item for her wardrobe—iron chain from head to toe. He should insist that she see him now, while she was still vulnerable, while there was still hope he might keep her with him until her last breath.

"I'm grateful that you care so much," she added, a trace of the old music in her voice.

"Care? Flo, it's much more than care."

"I know it is, and that's what's too painful. I don't want you to see me when I'm all bones and ugly. Don't you get it?"

"I'd never see you that way. If that's all—"

"I can't bear the thought of seeing myself, let alone you!"

They talked heatedly in circles a few more minutes—their first argument—before she said she had to go. He knew it was just an excuse, a white lie. He could walk over to her house and try to convince her in person, but he already knew the futility of such an effort. She was obdurate in her decision; it was best to respect it. Feeling embittered, he said goodbye and put away his phone.

The next morning he kept his date to meet Emily for breakfast, though he had no desire to talk to anyone. It was a gray day that matched how he felt, but the air was light and cool with spring's breezes. The sailors would be out already, and all the bikers and joggers. Usually Nick was with them, walking briskly along the esplanade, his spirits elevated by the river and sky, but not this Sunday, no. He was gloom and doom and didn't even care if it showed.

He was the first to arrive at Café Jolie, the only coffee shop on Charles Street with outdoor seating. He bought a coffee with a shot of espresso and went outside. His metal chair grated over the brick patio as he pulled it out. He dropped into it and stared at nothing.

"Dad."

Emily stood above him, smiling. She looked so fresh and pretty, and he immediately felt his own slovenliness. He hadn't shaved since Thursday and wore the same jeans he had lived in all week when not at work. His T-shirt had holes. He wondered if depressed people unconsciously chose clothes to match their moods.

She sat down and touched his arm. "You look like shit, Dad. What happened? Is Granddad all right?"

"He's fine."

"That's good. I was afraid he might be back in the hospital."

"No. Flo has cancer. Ovarian. Six months to live."

"What?" Emily gasped. "How's that possible?"

"How's it ever possible?"

Tears filled her eyes. The sight of them made his own eyes fill up.

"Do you want to walk instead of sitting here?"

She nodded and their chairs scraped over the bricks again. Nick dropped his coffee cup in the trashcan and they turned down the side street toward the river. It was the only place to go. The white sails gliding over the water's rippled surface seemed to match the seagulls' carefree arcing in the mottled sky overhead. The natural scene offered solace, but at the same time its peace and beauty were the sharpest reminder of the eternal cycle of birth and death. They sat on the long dock across from MIT and watched the river. Emily put her arm around Nick's back and rested her cheek on his shoulder. He touched his head to hers in thanks. Yes, for many things he was grateful.

The day before Flo's permanent departure for New York, she and Nick met in the Garden. Ten long days had passed since their phone conversation. During that time Flo had made clandestine nighttime visits to the office to organize her unfinished projects, leaving Post-it notes on their folders. He saw these in the morning: most were left on his chair. Her personal items vanished. Her office became a hollow, sterile space, her spirit untraceable. When she e-mailed him on Friday to set up their rendezvous, she also attached a proposal and outline for her marathon book. Nick read it—a winner. And she was urging him to follow through on it. "Write it, Nick," her e-mail said. "I set it up for you."

Nick waited for her on the fairy-book bridge that mimicked the iron peaks of the Brooklyn Bridge. He was cleaned up again, working hard and keeping busy. For days he had been preparing himself for this goodbye, knowing that Flo would eventually see him in person.

The Garden offered them a divine spring day, with light warmth and delicate breezes that caressed the skin. Blossoms scented the air even when invisible to the eye. Families and lovers strolled along the peaceful paths looking relaxed. Nick recalled his visions of doing the same with Flo, as a family. But that had been a different time and place in his life: the past. How quickly humans transitioned to new situations, changing into new people as they did so. He was not the elated, lovestruck Nick of two weeks before—he had gone through grief since then. But he saw, as Flo came up the path to the bridge where he waited, that she had made every effort to be the Flo he had known so briefly at Churchill. She moved with the spring air, embodying it. The rows of sculpted yews heralded her arrival. Smiling, he drank her in, the radiant princess she always longed to be, with her pure smile and swinging brown hair, freshly washed and dried. She wore a patterned summer dress that swished out from the waist, the bodice fitting as if hand-sewn to her lines. A rose cardigan picked up the floral pink in her dress and accented her cheeks. Gold filigree earrings glittered in the sun and made tiny patterns on her jaw. Nick walked toward her, every bit of him surging with love. How was it possible that this glowing, beautiful person would vanish in a matter of months, turning almost to physical ash just before?

"Hi, Nick, how are you?" she said and offered a hug, the hug of a friend.

They moved off the bridge to the sylvan path, all the bushy trees fluttering their new leaves the way birds shook off water in their baths. "I'm dying to hear what's happening in the office," she said.

"The usual, and lots of concern for you. Everyone misses you. No one can believe the news."

"I got so many cards and e-mails. Everyone's been so kind. Flowers from the trio. I can't help it if I don't want to see anyone, fake all those conversations."

He nodded, easily imagining such forced conversations in the hall. No, she had been right to keep away and tidy up her affairs after hours.

"But what else? Tell me what's happening with *Island*. And did the food book finally go to the printer? What about Egypt—is Sam moving on that?"

"Yes, he and Margie have been talking to journalists. And *Food*'s proofs are in. *Island*'s selling steadily. Your favorite, Blaze Denis, has been calling, or I should say bleating, for attention."

"What a fraud. I guess he really believes all the hype he's made up about himself."

"Enough to convince himself and many others."

"How're you handling him?"

"Al is. He told him we're willing to consider his book as soon as he gets around to writing it."

"I doubt he ever will."

"Vladimir likes the translator's sample, so we're moving forward with *Diamonds*."

"What do you think?"

He nodded approval. "It's going to be a Flo Wright book."

"Hey, I like that. If I had stayed, we could have created a Flo

Wright imprint."

"I'll suggest it to the heads."

"Ha!" she laughed. "An imprint like a tombstone. And the marathon book? Did you read my outline?"

"I loved it. I'm bringing it to the acquisitions meeting next week. And Flo, I had an idea. Why don't you do the interviews? Use a tape recorder. You know the material, you created it. Sketching out an intro to the interviews would take you no more than an hour. The office could handle all the transcriptions, editing, and photography—whatever you need. We'd hand it back to you for your final polish. It would truly be a Flo Wright book."

She stopped walking. "Posthumous no doubt. But I like your idea. Though it ruins the idea I had for you."

"This is what I want."

She looked long at him to be sure he meant it. Then he saw her mind start to fire up in its old mode, setting off familiar lights in her brown eyes. His heart quickened.

"Ten interviews," she said like a chief editor. "A two-thousand-word intro marveling at marathons from the Greek to the present day, including their tragedies, and the remarkable people who compete in them. Those people are what make the story. Finally I finish up with a passionate tribute to Boston and the 2013 race—no one caved to the villains." She took a breath, calculated the components. "I could do a draft in two or three months. Better than sitting around moping." She turned to smile at him. "You're my savior, as always." She squeezed his hand. "Would you please tell Al on Monday that he can send me a draft contract? That is, if acquisitions approves the project."

"They won't be able to resist," he said, smiling back.

They strolled companionably again, her arm fed through his, as if the marathon book once more joined them professionally and spiritually—the quality, the chemistry, was just as it had been the first day they met. Nick realized it was the right moment to offer her his poems. He slid his backpack off his shoulder. "I brought something for you."

She turned eager eyes on him. "Your poems?"

He nodded.

"Thank god, because if you hadn't brought it up, I was going to ask, and how crass is that?"

"Not crass." He unzipped the bag and drew out the small printed volume, the front cover showing a Georgia O'Keeffe flower, the muted blue-purple petals intricate and sensual, the way he thought of Flo.

"To my favorite blossom," he said as he handed her the book.

"My god! It's beautiful!" she said. "*Drawn After You*. What a fabulous title."

"Stolen from Shakespeare."

"Even better. I'm connected to the bard for all time." She opened the cover and let out a pleased "Ah" as she read the dedication: To Florence. "You used my real name—I'm so glad." She hugged him with genuine gratitude. "Thank you, Nick. This is the best gift of my life—or you are. *Obrigado*."

He had things he had to say, in person, to her face, her eyes. "I'm going to miss you."

"Yeah, it sucks," she said in her bitter way. "I only made it to my fortieth birthday."

How many times during the past two weeks had he sat on his couch thinking the same thing? Why had he already lived eighteen more years than she, with many more likely to follow? Why was she being cut off at forty?

He stepped against her, his arms wrapping around her, his

body trembling with emotion. She hugged back, their warmth once more penetrating, and yet at the same time distance had come between them, the distance of circumstances. They let go, naturally linked hands, and followed the path as it wound around to the west entrance, presided over by a bronze George Washington mounted on a horse. They promised to stay in touch by e-mail and the phone. The marathon book would ensure this. "I want to give it a try," she said. "The marathon marks my life in multiple ways. It's fitting that I do the book." She paused for a minute, as if thinking of the labor that lay ahead; could she hold out long enough to finish, to see it to print? She looked abstractedly at Nick. "I know the minute they start their treatments it's going to be straight downhill. A race against the clock. Why does that happen?"

"I don't know," he said helplessly. Why did anything on the planet happen? Had anyone ever made sense of life? No, and they never would. Life would always be a quest, alternating as it did between ineffable beauty and unbearable sadness.

He couldn't assimilate that these were his last moments with the living, breathing, talking Flo. She was still alive. But he would never see her again. He lifted her hand to his lips, the soft skin, bones, and veins and the creativity they harbored, the Flo inside. Their eyes met over the delicate fingers, engraving the moment, the other person, the love. It was all ephemeral, from birth to death to love. For the last time their eyes shared the same thought without the need for words.